DEC 17 2015

Annja held out her sword in one hand.

Holding her phone in the other hand, as if its glow were a shield, she stared at that strange, incomplete face as he raised his hands to shield his eyes from the bright glare. At least, she thought it was a he….

There was so much of the thing in front of her that she couldn't see around it, but she knew it was there by the blast of its foul breath, a waft of stale sweat.

Then it staggered forward, striking out at Annja, its great clubbing fists slashing at the light, the creature seemingly ignorant of the threat her sword presented. She pushed the blade as hard as she could, feeling it slide through its heavy coat and into the flesh beneath.

A vibration ran the length of her blade all the way into her fingertips.

There was no pain in its childlike sketch of a face, no change in the thing's expression despite her sword plunging through its body.

Annja pulled the hilt to free the sword, but as she did the thing swung a fist at her. The impact of the blow sent her sprawling.

Before she hit thck.

Titles in this series:

ROGUE Angel

Alex Archer

THE MORTALITY PRINCIPLE

A GOLD EAGLE BOOK FROM

WORLDWIDE®

TORONTO • NEW YORK • LONDON
AMSTERDAM • PARIS • SYDNEY • HAMBURG
STOCKHOLM • ATHENS • TOKYO • MILAN
MADRID • WARSAW • BUDAPEST • AUCKLAND

If you purchased this book without a cover you should be aware
that this book is stolen property. It was reported as "unsold and
destroyed" to the publisher, and neither the author nor the
publisher has received any payment for this "stripped book."

Recycling programs
for this product may
not exist in your area.

First edition September 2015

ISBN-13: 978-0-373-62176-7

The Mortality Principle

Special thanks and acknowledgment to
Steven Savile for his contribution to this work.

Copyright © 2015 by Worldwide Library

All rights reserved. Except for use in any review, the
reproduction or utilization of this work in whole or in part
in any form by any electronic, mechanical or other means,
now known or hereafter invented, including xerography,
photocopying and recording, or in any information storage
or retrieval system, is forbidden without the written permission
of the publisher, Worldwide Library, 225 Duncan Mill Road,
Don Mills, Ontario M3B 3K9, Canada.

This is a work of fiction. Names, characters, places and incidents are
either the product of the author's imagination or are used fictitiously,
and any resemblance to actual persons, living or dead, business
establishments, events or locales is entirely coincidental.

® and TM are trademarks of Harlequin Enterprises Limited.
Trademarks indicated with ® are registered in the United States
Patent and Trademark Office, the Canadian Intellectual Property Office
and in other countries.

Printed in U.S.A.

The LEGEND

...THE ENGLISH COMMANDER TOOK
JOAN'S SWORD AND RAISED IT HIGH.

The broadsword, plain and unadorned,
gleamed in the firelight. He put the tip against
the ground and his foot at the center of the blade.
The broadsword shattered, fragments falling
into the mud. The crowd surged forward,
peasant and soldier, and snatched the shards
from the trampled mud. The commander tossed
the hilt deep into the crowd.
Smoke almost obscured Joan, but she continued
praying till the end, until finally the flames climbed
her body and she sagged against the restraints.

Joan of Arc died that fateful day in France,
but her legend and sword are reborn...

1

The peace was broken by the clatter of a trash can being overturned, which was followed by a burst of laughter.

Annja Creed glanced out of the window into the road below. Illuminated by the streetlights, a gaggle of young men jostled one another. She couldn't tell if the shoving was playful or if there was a simmering undercurrent of real violence to it. One thing was for sure, the young men were more than a little the worse for wear from the night's drinking. Her first thought was that it was the same in cities and towns the world over, but that wasn't true. This kind of rowdiness, playful or not, wouldn't happen in a Muslim state, or in places where poverty placed survival above pleasure.

She wasn't even sure it would have happened here in Prague thirty years ago. The world had changed just like the regime, and after the first flush of greedy capitalism, Prague settled down to become one of *those* cities. It promised excitement and just enough culture to satisfy the tourists, whether they came to cast off some imagined loss of freedom that marriage was about to bring, or simply to soak up another way of living.

For Annja it was simply a case of another city and another hotel room. They all began to bleed together in her mind these days. She couldn't remember the last time she had slept in her own bed. No, that was a lie; she could remember the last time she'd crawled into it, but she hadn't actually slept. It had been the night of the big network meeting. Doug Morrell had called her into the office with an ominous message of "Big changes are on the horizon. We need you here, pronto."

She'd crossed town to the office, carded her way through security and ridden the express elevator up to the boardroom on the top floor of the skyscraper, every step of the way imagining a worst-case scenario that was just a little bit worse than the last one she'd just imagined.

She opened the boardroom door to see the army of assembled faces looking up at her, Doug halfway down the line. He looked like someone had stolen his toys from his stroller. "Miss Creed, good of you to join us. First, let me just say what a huge admirer I am," one of the nameless suits said, indicating the only empty chair at the table. Annja took her seat, waiting for someone to explain what was going on. "We were just in the middle of discussing corporate restructuring," the suit went on. "We've got some exciting plans for the network."

Annja's mind raced, trying to play catch-up. She really didn't understand what was happening. Restructuring? Exciting plans?

"Obviously *Chasing History's Monsters* is a bit of a niche program," another suit spoke up. His thick-knuckled hand was wrapped around a network mug, warming himself. "It's got a loyal audience, but over the past eighteen months it's struggled to bring in new viewers, which means it's struggled to bring in more advertising revenue and basically isn't paying its way."

"In short," the first suit picked up, "we're not here to

educate the world, we're here to entertain it, and if we're not entertaining it, we're not doing our job properly."

The man stared daggers at Doug when he delivered this last line. Annja sensed a serious undercurrent of dislike between the two. It wasn't simmering so much as threatening to boil over. Somehow Doug managed to keep his mouth shut while the suits took potshots at the program he produced and, by inference, at him.

"We've got a duty to the shareholders," another voice chimed in. This one was female. Annja turned to look at the woman, realizing that with the exception of Doug, Annja didn't have a single ally in the room.

The first suit took that as his cue to drive home the obvious. "Meaning we can't keep on throwing good money after bad. *Chasing History's Monsters* is expensive for what it is. We could just as easily screen episodes we've got in the can in the same time slot, given there are almost one hundred now, or alternate them with stuff we can buy in from other networks that come with an established audience."

"Are you canceling the show?" Annja asked, sensing where this was going.

"Not yet," the suit said, dangling the threat of cancellation like the Sword of Damocles over her head. "But I guess you could say we're putting you on notice. Things have to change."

"Okay, so why am I here? What do you expect me to do?"

"We want you to justify the money the network is investing in you, Miss Creed," the fourth and final suit said, speaking up for the first time.

He was the youngest of the four, Annja observed, no doubt fresh out of some Ivy League school with a point to prove—that point being to tear down everything that had been created and rebuild it from scratch, reinventing the proverbial wheel.

"We want you to prove to us you're worth the long-term investment," he went on, "meaning we want you to go out there and interact, hit the social networks, build up followers on Twitter, post compelling little Vine video hints about what's coming up to lure people in, use hashtags to get people involved in your investigations, turn the viewers into your army of citizen archaeologists. Make them feel like they are part of the show."

"How's that supposed to work?"

"Well, one idea we've had is live broadcasts," the woman said, leaning forward. "So they can tweet you with what they want to see happen when it comes to the hunt. Say you're going after the Amber Room and there are three possible sites you've identified. They can vote which one you check out. Or maybe they can Tweet questions at you during live interviews, that kind of thing."

"Do you have any idea just how *bad* an idea that is?" Annja said, shaking her head. She couldn't quite believe what she was hearing.

"It doesn't really matter what you think, Miss Creed. You either find a way to make this work, or you don't. But if you don't we'll be forced to look at the alternatives. Tonight's meeting was merely a courtesy. We wanted you to understand the orders weren't coming from Mr. Morrell. He's fought your corner passionately, but some things are bigger than a mere producer. They come down from on high. In this case, all the way from the top. From the owners themselves. As I said, I'm a huge admirer of yours, Miss Creed. For your sake, I can only hope you've got a truly gripping segment lined up."

That had been a week ago. Now she was in Prague, unable to sleep, trying to work out how on earth she was going to make these changes work. Part of her wanted to ignore them and just turn in a segment like the hundred other segments she'd turned in, but she knew something like that would just rebound on Doug. It would have been different if it had only been her job on the line, but she wasn't about to put his in jeopardy, not after hearing how he'd gone to bat for her against the suits. For all that they argued, she knew he was on her side deep down. It was just that sometimes those subterranean depths were somewhere near the earth's core. She needed to map out a few prerecorded minutes, little minisegments to set up a bigger mystery that could go out live.

And that thought terrified her: a live feed going out to the world, warts and all, with so many variables she couldn't possibly hope to control. It wasn't just about veering off script, either. The suits wanted to set the lunatics loose to run the asylum. Somehow she needed to engineer it so they wound up making the choices she needed them to make, a bit like a magician onstage. It was all about direction and misdirection. Make the masses think you were giving them what *they* wanted, when really you were giving them what *you* wanted. Her head ached just thinking about it.

Annja's laptop stood on the desk that doubled as a dressing table. The cursor flashed on a blank screen, taunting her. She'd read all the research she had brought with her a dozen times in the past week, and she'd spent days just wandering around the city, getting a feel for the place. The amount of information on the internet about the city was overwhelming. Even when she tried to narrow the search parameters, the amount of data she had to wade through was daunting. She kept finding references to the city being Hitler's favorite, and how he'd preserved a lot of the Old Town because he wanted to keep it for himself. Every time she saw the same statement it was prefaced with the words *little known fact* despite that putting the words *Hitler* and *Prague* in Google returned several thousand identical little-known facts. For Annja, though, it was all about one thing, one story that had endured so much so it was part of the fabric of the city itself: the golem.

She'd sketched out brief notes covering myth behind the creation of the creature made of clay and given life by Rabbi Loew, but most of them were nineteenth century legends that claimed the Maharal—Loew—created the golem to defend Prague from anti-Semitic attacks back in the sixteenth century. Of course, now it was virtually impossible to tell how much truth was hidden within those sensationalized tales. As with most European legends, it didn't take long to isolate the common elements. There were enough of them for her to be sure that they originated from the same source, no matter how fantastical they eventually became.

Of course, Annja was reasonably sure that what she was chasing this time was nothing more than a feat of deception that had fooled enough people when they needed to be fooled. Illusion was the simplest way to give birth to a legend. It wasn't so different from the Hans Christian Andersen story of the emperor's new clothes. You had this miraculous defender of the city only seen by some precious few, but then more and more accounts of sightings started to emerge, not because people had seen the golem but because no one wanted to be the odd one out.

However, given the additional pressure from on high,

the piece on the golem was feeling like fluff, just a filler bit for the show, not an entire segment, and most certainly not enough to make it the focus of a live show. And being live, they wouldn't be able to pad it with lots of shots of the city. Even if they could have, that would have made the episode about the city not the golem—hardly something that would satisfy the ad-revenue-hungry network executives.

Eventually she gave up staring at the screen and crawled into the uncomfortable bed, knowing she needed to grab some sleep if she was going to be good for anything in the morning. Coping with jet lag wasn't the biggest problem, but even days after the event, being cooped up in a plane always left her feeling restless.

Her running shoes were still in the bottom of her case.

She was tempted to get up, get ready and go out for a run. She never felt more alive than when she was running, and these were new streets to pound. The problem was she wouldn't be able to sleep after that. But maybe that was better than lying in the bed, restless?

Another noise from the street drew her attention.

It wasn't the sound of the group of young men this time, nor was it a single drunk trying to find his way back home.

She recognized the sounds of violence for what they were. She heard a body fall and was at the window looking out into the near-darkness, unable to make out any sign of movement below. Annja threw the window open. There was nothing to hear but the distance rumble of traffic. No, she realized, under it she could barely make out the slap of a single pair of heavy footsteps moving away.

Whatever the argument had been, it was over quickly.

The question was how serious was it on a scale of licking wounds to bleeding out in a gutter?

In the week she'd been in Prague, she hadn't had a reason to think of it as a violent city. Sure, its past was rooted firmly in revolution, but she didn't think of any European city as being any worse than parts of New York or Chicago. That didn't mean that violence didn't exist here, just that tourists were kept away from it. Maybe it was the lack of gunfire, which seemed to provide a huge part of the New York night chorus, or the endless cycle of sirens that painted a sensory image of what a violent city ought to be like.

She waited at the window, listening, but heard neither so assumed the scrap had been fists not firearms.

The bedside clock flashed a few minutes shy of 3:00 a.m. Sleep still seemed a long way off. Annja turned on the radio, keeping the volume so low the half-whispered voice of the late-night DJ was so quiet it was impossible to tell what language he was speaking between the ripple of easy listening.

It was enough to lull her to sleep.

Annja woke to the sound of movement in the corridor outside her room.

The radio still provided its thin layer of background noise, but against the sounds of the waking hotel it was little more than a sibilant hiss. Her dreams had been filled with violence and fear. She knew logically there was nothing she could have done about the fighting in the street—it had been over before she was even aware of it—but that didn't stop her subconscious mind from tormenting her with a guilt-tripped sleep.

She had no appetite for breakfast.

Annja showered, standing in the steaming hot spray long enough to turn her body a dark shade of pink, then wrapped a towel around herself and made a particularly foul cup of coffee from the selection of instant blends on offer. The heat alone was enough to make her feel more alive.

It was barely seven-thirty. If anything was going to revive her, it was the crisp morning air, which would only be clean and crisp for maybe another thirty minutes or so before the city filled with traffic.

Five minutes later she was stretching on the pavement, her hair pulled back in a still-damp ponytail.

She started to run, moving lightly on her feet, weaving a path through the narrow alleyways around the hotel, up beyond the corner that would have taken her over the Charles Bridge toward the palace on the hill, toward Wenceslas Square. Her muscles were tight, but as the blood started to flow they loosened up. Her breathing came in little wispy puffs of steam that corkscrewed up in front of her face.

In the distance Annja heard the sound of a siren approaching.

Without realizing it she was running toward the source of the previous night's fight. Within the few minutes she'd been out, the streets had already begun to show increasing signs of life with café owners setting up the tables outside their windows. A newspaper vendor on the street corner beside the subway entrance was doing a brisk trade as people passed by in a rush to get to work. It was the kind of thing she saw in every street in every city. Every time she skirted that hubbub of life it reminded her how lucky she was not to be caught up in it. She couldn't imagine drifting through life. Annja harbored no illusions just how lucky she was to live the life she did. That was just another reason why this live-broadcast Twitter-chasing plan made her so uncomfortable. She had secrets, just like everyone else. The idea of turning the world into citizen archae-ologists and sending them out to chase monsters had the power to turn her life upside down.

She slowed as she reached the far end of the street. People had begun to gather, blocking the way.

One man stepped away from the group.

He pulled out his cell phone.

She was too far away to hear what the man said as he spoke into his phone, but his body language spoke volumes. He was calling the police.

At the sound of the approaching siren a few people peeled away from the crowd. They disappeared into the side streets and wider spaces beyond, happy not to be involved once the police arrived.

Annja stepped into a gap that had been created as a middle-aged woman stepped away. The woman's rigid expression gave plenty warning of what she was about to see. A shiver raced up Annja's spine as she peered through the cluster of bodies: a man in a blue suit crouched over someone lying on the ground in an alleyway that ran between two buildings. Annja saw the dark, damp patch staining the cobbles at his feet as she worked her way closer. The man was fighting for a life that wasn't there to be saved. He stood and shook his head to no one in particular. There was nothing he could do. Nothing anyone could do. As he moved away to the fresher air of the street, Annja saw the body properly.

The victim had been dead for some time.

Four and a half hours, Annja thought, looking at the ragged clothes the body wore, and at the stains that had turned them the same dark color as the ground around the corpse.

Judging by the state of his clothes, there was every

chance this usually quiet alleyway was where the dead man made his bed for the night. Could his death be the consequence of a fight over something as tragic as the meager shelter that the alleyway offered? If it was, then it was a poor way to end a life that had surely seen more than its fair share of troubles. Annja rubbed a hand through her damp hair. The body that lay in the narrow space was no longer a man; now it was evidence to be picked over in the mortuary.

It didn't need a pathologist to read the crime scene. This wasn't death by natural causes. There was nothing accidental about it. She'd been right the previous night; there *had* been violence in the air. She couldn't have stopped it. She couldn't even let herself think that way. The world wasn't her responsibility. She couldn't police every street and save every victim.

When the police car came to a halt only a few feet away from the crowd, the press of bodies miraculously thinned, gawkers suddenly remembering they had somewhere else to be. The man in the suit spoke to a policeman, no doubt explaining that he had found the dead man. Annja couldn't understand the few words she caught. One policeman made a note in his small black book, presumably of the man's name and address while the other worked his way through the remaining gawkers to the corpse. A few seconds later, after the briefest of glances at the dead vagrant, he began to usher everyone back.

The forlorn siren song of an approaching ambulance was wholly out of place and much too late, unless it was bringing a priest. By the look of the dead man, every last ounce of hope had been torn from him, shredded, before he had finally slumped to the ground and spilled what little was left of his bodily fluids out across the cobbles.

Annja was still wrapped up in her thoughts when she realized that the policeman was talking to her. She shook her head.

"Sorry," she said. "I don't speak Czech."

"Ah, did you see anything?" he asked, switching to English easily, though his voice carried a heavy accent. There was no way anyone would mistake him for a native speaker. Annja shook her head, so he moved on to the next person, no doubt sure this was a crime that didn't warrant investigating given who the victim was.

"I might have heard something, though," Annja said to his back. "Last night."

He made no effort to disguise his world-weary sigh as he turned back to her. His pen was still poised over his pad. "What did you hear?"

Annja chose her words carefully. She didn't want to risk any misunderstanding. "I heard a fight," she began.

"A fight?"

She nodded. "Two men," she said, though even as the words left her lips she couldn't actually be sure that it was the truth. She'd heard so little, even with the window open. In truth, she had no reason to believe the dead man had anything to do with the struggle she had heard in the night.

"Can you describe them?" the policeman asked. "Anything at all?"

Annja held out her hands, shaking her head slightly. "I'm sorry, no. I only heard them. I can't even be sure what I heard. It just sounded like fighting, but it was over very quickly, then I heard footsteps running away.

It could have been anything, really. I just thought you should know."

"When was this?"

"A little before three."

"And where were you when you heard this altercation?"

She pointed in the direction of her hotel room, and her window, which didn't really overlook the street by more than a few degrees, the laws of physics explaining why she hadn't been able to see anything. The expression on his face changed. She couldn't read him. He looked tired, and the stubble on his chin suggested a long night on duty was about to turn into an even longer day on duty. He made a note of her name and the room number, and offered cursory thanks as he moved on to the next face in the crowd, repeating his questions.

A man tried to enter the alleyway, but the policeman stopped him. The newcomer wouldn't be deterred. He was determined to cut through the narrow passageway, and no dead body was going to stop him. The officer prodded him in the chest with a stubby finger. He might as well have hit the man with a Taser gun; the effect was just about the same. Annja turned toward the hotel and walked away as the disgruntled man started threatening to have the policeman's badge. At least, that was what she chose to imagine his rant entailed. He could have been asking for alternative directions or if the good officer fancied a nice game of global thermonuclear war, for all she knew.

2

Annja still had no appetite.

She made her way into the dining room for breakfast, though she wasn't sure she could face much more than a cup of strong black coffee. The stronger, the better, given it was going to have to mask the taste of death that had been cloying at the back of her throat since she stood in the alleyway.

"Can I get you anything else?" the waitress asked as she topped up her cup with a third refill in half an hour.

"I'm good, thanks," Annja replied, picking up the cup without even thinking about it. She was no stranger to death, which wasn't something she would have ever thought she'd find herself thinking a few years ago, but things had changed since Roux and Garin had walked into her life. What should have been the most horrific thing imaginable had almost become a fact of life, and of course there were those harrowing times when it had been her doing, a matter of kill or be killed.

But this was different.

She couldn't shift the guilt. She *could* have done something. She'd heard it happening, had known instinctively something was wrong, but hadn't gone down to check it out. She'd simply lain there telling herself there was nothing she could do. And even now, knowing that she was right—at least academically—emotionally she couldn't banish the self-loathing that came with not even trying.

Someone had torn that vagrant open.

"Is something wrong?" the waitress whispered, her voice so quiet that none of the other diners would be able to hear what she said.

"Nothing that another cup of coffee won't put right if I know you," a familiar voice said, the man joining her at the table.

Annja didn't need to look up to know who her visitor was.

"Garin," she said. "I'm not even going to ask how you found me."

"Shall I get another cup?" the waitress asked, smiling at Garin.

"That would be great." Garin Braden tilted his head and offered a killer smile. "And I think maybe eggs Benedict."

"Of course."

At times it almost felt like he was stalking her. Wherever she was, he had the unnerving ability to find her without calling first.

"I really need to change my cell phone number," she said.

"Wouldn't help, I've had you tagged." Garin grinned, and she wasn't entirely sure he was joking.

"What do you want?"

"Why so hostile?"

"I'm not, I'm just exhausted," Annja said, which was partially true.

Garin nodded. "To be honest, I was just bored, and I

hate being bored. I thought about taking a trip, but you know how it is. The thrill of white-water rafting and wing suits and bungee jumping and all that just pales into insignificance against everything else we do, so I thought, 'I know, I'll go see Annja. She's normally up to her neck in *something.*' And here I am. I took the liberty of checking into the room next to yours. No adjoining door, alas."

"I don't have time to amuse you, Garin. I'm working."

"Actually, you're having a cup of coffee."

It had been a long time since Annja had worried about hurting his feelings; as far as she could tell he had no feelings to hurt. It didn't stop him pulling a face as if she had mortally wounded him.

"I'd hate to have come all this way and not be able to at least share breakfast with my favorite television star."

"Stop it, Garin. I'm not in the mood."

"In the mood for what?"

"You."

"Harsh, woman. Harsh."

"The world doesn't revolve around you. Hard to believe, I know, but someone's got to tell you the truth."

"And that, my dear, is why I love you most."

"Shut up."

Garin grinned.

"Anyway, I'm not sure I can sit around wasting more time today. I've already lost an hour this morning thanks to the police."

"Oh, see, now I knew you'd be up to your neck in something interesting. The police? Do tell." Garin leaned forward, elbows on the tabletop, all smiles and full of interest.

She knew that he was only sucking her in, a spider smiling at a vain fly, but she couldn't help herself. It wasn't that she was fooled by his easy charm; that only worked for so long. She needed to talk. If she didn't, the guilt would only fester. She knew that. She knew herself. The sooner she gave voice to her thoughts, the sooner she would be able to leave it behind. It wouldn't be the first time Garin had played Father Confessor to her. "There was a murder," she said.

"Next time we sit down for breakfast I suggest you starting with that. 'Hello, Garin, there was a murder.' That's so much more interesting than 'What do you want?' Did you see it?"

"No, but I am ninety-nine percent sure I *heard* it. I just didn't realize that's what it was at the time. I went out for a run this morning, and found people gathered around the body. I gave a statement to a policeman, but I'm pretty sure he was just humoring me by then. After all, it was just some homeless guy," she said bitterly. "It's not like the cops will lose sleep over it."

"Oh, so cynical for one so young," Garin said, with no hint of laughter even though his smile was still firmly in place, predatory now. "Sadly I think you're right. The system doesn't care about the poor bastards who slip between the cracks."

"I care," Annja said.

"I'm sure you do. So, what have you got?"

"Nothing, really. Time of death. That's it. At 3:00 a.m."

"I once heard that more people die at three in the morning than at any other time of day."

"Not really very helpful."

"No, but interesting. So, an argument over shelter? Or a bottle?"

She didn't have time to answer him. The waitress returned and placed a cup in front of Garin, filling it with rich black coffee. Annja pushed the cream in his direction, but he waved it away. "Watching my figure," he said.

The waitress laughed, no doubt another willing victim of Garin's charms should he decide to stick around. And judging by his appreciative expression as he watched her retreat toward the kitchen, he'd decided to do just that.

"You know what else is interesting? I read about a dead vagrant in this morning's newspaper."

"Not a chance. There's no way it was in the morning paper. They only found the body an hour ago."

"I didn't say *your* dead vagrant."

"There have been others?"

"Oh, Annja," Garin said patronizingly. "You really ought to take more of an interest in the here and now and pay a little less attention to what happened centuries ago. Dusty old books have nothing on television or the internet, you know. Not when it comes to living in the real world."

"Don't be a jerk. Just tell me what you know."

"You take all the fun out of life, Annja Creed, but you know that, don't you?"

"Share or shut up."

Garin smiled, clearly enjoying the moment and determined to make the most of it.

That stupid grin was really beginning to grate on Annja's nerves, but she wasn't about to let him know that, so she smiled right back, sweetly.

"Okay," he said at last, raising his hands in surrender. He'd had his fun. "There have been three deaths in as many weeks. Four now. One every week for a month. All of them have been street people. If the papers are right, the police are clueless. No one seems to know if this is a case of the city's homeless fighting among themselves or if they're looking for a lunatic who's taken it upon himself to try to clean up the streets."

"Clean up the streets? Surely no one in their right mind could think that they could kill every homeless person?"

"I did say lunatic, didn't I?"

Annja shook her head. "There must be thousands of people living on the streets. It's a capital city."

"To clean up the streets you don't need to kill all of them. You just have to make the ones left behind so afraid they gather up their few possessions and head out of town."

"But they've got nowhere to go. They're not on the streets for fun."

Garin shrugged. "Right, but then they're someone else's problem."

Annja knew he was right. "My enemy's enemy is my friend, sort of thing," Annja agreed. "And you think that's what's happening here?"

"I have no idea. Maybe. Hell, I'm sure Jack the Ripper thought that he was doing something positive about the number of prostitutes in London."

Annja was doubtful. There were plenty of sick people in the world who would do something like this for kicks. She said as much. She wasn't sure which was worse—someone killing out of some crazy idea that they were doing good or a calculating killer doing it for the simple pleasure of killing.

"Maybe the police are right," Garin offered. "Maybe

GIBSONS AND DISTRIG
PUBLIC LIBRARY

it really is just a case of the homeless fighting among themselves."

His eggs arrived while she was thinking about the possibility.

One thing was sure—she didn't feel any better about the fact that she hadn't intervened, even if it had only been to call the police when she heard the scuffle. The time between the act and the discovery of the act only made it more difficult for justice to catch up with the killer.

She needed to get out of there.

Her head wasn't in the right place. There was no way she was going to come up with something clever to say in front of the camera, at least not today. She made a call while Garin was eating and gave Lars, her cameraman, the day off. He wanted to know if she was okay. She assured him she was.

"So you're going to have some free time, after all," Garin said, wiping his lips as she ended the call. He'd made short work of polishing off his breakfast and was already signaling for a top-up to his coffee. He flashed the waitress that smile again, earning one right back.

"I've got things to do," Annja said, dropping her napkin on the table. "I'm sure you've got enough here to entertain yourself." She looked meaningfully toward the waitress, who in turn was pretending to look busy.

"I'm sure I can keep myself entertained for a few hours. After all, we're in a hotel. Lots of bedrooms."

"Just spare me the gory details."

3

Annja was itching to get out and about, to do something, see something, anything that would take her mind off the nagging guilt.

She picked up the research on the golem, skimming it without finding any inspiration in the dry text.

She needed an angle.

That was what made stories work.

A human element. Something…different. Fresh. Something that would make the whole thing a little more interesting. If she couldn't do that, maybe there was a second story from Prague she could stitch together to make something that might work.

The rack at the back of the desk held a well-thumbed collection of tourist brochures with dull photographs of landmarks and sites to visit in and around the city. Some of those brochures probably dated back to the Charter 77 revolution. A few of the landmarks were too obvious. They offered the shots of buildings that appeared in every holiday brochure and website about the city. They offered little of real interest to her. She didn't want to simply retread the footsteps of well-known history, especially with the added pressure on this segment from the suits. To be perfectly honest, it was bad enough that the golem was so ingrained in the psyche of the city that she couldn't find anything to say that hadn't already been said. It was the kind of myth that pushed all the other folk tales to one side. There was only room for one fantastic beast here. But surely that in itself should have helped her? It made the less well-known legends more appealing, didn't it?

Maybe.

If she could find one worth telling.

And with that thought it was as if something had clicked inside her head.

She had found something to search for even if she had no idea what it was.

This might be the golem's city, but there had to be a more fascinating story beneath it, something better, in a city as old as Prague. She'd come across an epigram in her notes: *Your problem, city, is that you have no soul.* She couldn't recall where she'd come across it, but she liked it.

Annja pondered the notion of going out to Sedlec, in the Kutná Hora suburb, to check out the ossuary. There was a building with a story to tell—a church dating back eight hundred years, with upward of seventy thousand corpses exhumed, their bones used to decorate the chapels. Chandeliers of bones, garlands of skulls, an altar consisting of every single bone from the human body, monstrances fashioned from childlike skeletons and the Schwarzenberg coat of arms, also executed in bone. It was like nowhere else on Earth. That a half-blind monk had done the exhumation five hundred years ago was the stuff of macabre fairy tale, rather like the bone sculptures of the carpenter František Rint, who was behind the decor. Could she somehow marry that in with the stories of the golem? A made man against a backdrop of a quite literally man-made chapel? It would provide an incredible visual for the live broadcast, she realized. It was a possibility.

She stuffed a handful of the leaflets into her bag and headed out with a little more of a spring in her step than when she'd come back into the room.

Even without consulting the street map she'd picked up from reception, she knew that there were any number of places she could start looking for her story that didn't involve heading out to the ossuary. The most obvious was the city's Old Town.

A convenient signpost only a few yards from her hotel pointed her in the right direction. The streets were considerably more alive if not teeming with tourists. Give it another hour, though, and that would be an entirely different matter. She walked on, looking at the endless matryoshka dolls on display in the shop windows around her.

The traffic had started to build up toward the morning rush hour, but the way the city was constructed, most of it never entered the more pedestrianized center. Some of the wider boulevards with expensive designer-brand stores were lined with lush trees and lusher price tags while the narrower streets were snarled up with people trying to take shortcuts. That was another legacy of cities first built before the invention of the internal combustion engines; some survived by keeping the traffic out of town as much as possible while others allowed developers to gradually change the landscape. Prague, it seemed, wanted to be the best of both worlds, but just might be the worst.

She turned onto Karlova Street and kept walking.

A delivery bicycle hopped onto the curb to pass a stationery van delivering parcels. Annja had to step out of the way, ducking into the deep doorway of a building. There was no point in yelling at the cyclist's back; he was already half a street away. No one was hurt, nothing was broken. An impatient car—a big black shiny SUV—behind the van sounded its horn. The van driver showed no sign of moving for the time being. He climbed out of the cab and gave a wave that, while it was meant to say *Bear with me, I'll only be a moment*, came across more like *Screw you, I was here first*.

Annja realized he was heading straight toward her, package in hand.

She stepped aside to let him get to the door, catching sight of the confused expression on the man's face, and guessed he'd thought she'd come down to take the delivery from him.

"Sorry," she said as she let him ring the bell.

He just nodded, obviously uncomfortable with the foreign language.

It was an unassuming little archway that promised the internet, a hair salon and a tobacco shop farther inside. There was a face carved into the keystone above the arch. As she stood on the sidewalk, she read the sign on the door. Kepler Museum.

She'd heard of Kepler, of course. He'd been a key figure in the seventeenth century scientific revolution, with his breakthroughs in the understanding of planetary motion providing the groundwork for Isaac Newton's gravitational theory.

She was still trying to trawl her memory for anything she could remember about Kepler when the door opened. A middle-aged woman appeared on the doorstep to take the parcel. She signed his clipboard, then looked up at Annja, obviously unsure what she was doing loitering in the museum's doorway.

She was still looking at her when the man slammed the door on his cab and gunned the engine, much to the relief of the waiting line of vehicles that snaked down the length of Karlova Street.

"Hello," Annja said.

"Ah, hello," the woman replied. "I'm sorry, but we do not open for another hour."

She took a step out from under the archway to look up and down the street, rather like some wartime spy looking for a tail. Annja couldn't help but smile to herself at the image. Maybe being in Eastern Europe was beginning to rub off on her way of thinking.

The traffic began to move again, following the van down Karlova Street toward the wider roads that waited beyond.

There was no one else on foot.

"You're welcome to come inside, if you don't mind the old house being a little on the chilly side. We seldom get visitors so keen they're standing outside waiting for us to open."

"Thank you," Annja said, offering a smile, happy to play the excited tourist rather than correct the woman's assumption. The entirety of her plan today was to follow the whims of the universe. If this was where the wind blew her, to this door in this part of town, then this was where she needed to be. How she got here, by accident or design, didn't matter.

She followed the woman inside.

The air was a good ten degrees colder on her skin than it had been outside.

The woman disappeared through a doorway along the corridor, the old wood-and-glass paneled door swinging closed for a moment before she opened it again. She wedged a rubber stop under it to prevent it from swinging closed again.

"Please," the woman said, beckoning Annja into her small office where papers and files covered every inch of the two desks. "Would you like coffee? I find that I can't do anything until I've had at least my second cup of coffee in the morning. That is, unless you'd be happier taking a look around yourself?"

"Actually, it's been one of those days already, so I could use a decent cup of coffee. And then, if you're willing, I'd love it if you showed me around," Annja said.

"Then coffee and the grand tour it is."

The woman busied herself with an expensive coffee machine.

Annja picked up one of the brochures from the pile that lay on the top of the filing cabinet. It was newer than the ones she'd seen in her hotel room, but offered much the same information. It was hard to imagine that the glossy paper produced all that many additional visitors. But then not all tourists were as jaded and world-weary as she'd been feeling recently.

Looking at the brochure didn't inspire any great sense of adventure, though, and surely that was how you sold history? You made it come alive and feel real. This one offered little other than the fact that Kepler had worked in the city between 1600 and 1612, and was written in five different languages—though not well, it seemed, in any of them—beneath a reproduction of the portrait that was set in the keystone above the arch outside. There were a few pictures of the exhibits, as well. The flipside provided a small street map with an arrow pointing to the museum's location, which, given that she was already standing in the middle of it, was fairly redundant. That said, Annja wasn't sure she would have been able to find the small museum on the basis of the map alone, even though her hotel was only a few streets away.

"It doesn't give a lot away, does it?" the woman said with a beaming smile on her face. She handed Annja a mug that bore the same portrait. She wondered idly how the astronomer would have felt to know his face had become a brand. "But then, we wouldn't want too many people banging down the door in search of some Holy Grail or other. We like it just as it is."

If it was good enough for the woman, it was good enough for Kepler himself, and that meant it was good enough for Annja.

"So, tell me, what brought you to our doorway? Do you have a special interest in Kepler? Or is it going to rain?"

Annja smiled at that.

"Perhaps I should explain," she began. She fished out a business card from her bag. She handed it over. The woman looked as if she was being offered confirmation that they were receiving a surprise visit from the tax man, but eventually her expression lightened.

"Annja Creed," she said. *"Chasing History's Monsters."*

It never ceased to amaze Annja when she came across people outside the mainland United States who'd heard of the show.

"I'm afraid I've never seen the program," the woman

said, piercing that particular bubble apologetically. "But my sister lives in New York and her son loves it. He talks about it every time I speak to him. You've made quite an impression on him, but then, he is a teenager." Her grin was knowing.

"Do you think I could get you to sign something to send to him? He would be absolutely thrilled."

"Of course," Annja replied.

The woman looked around for a piece of paper, then decided it might be more fun if Annja signed one of the museum's brochures. She was more than happy to oblige. It wasn't exactly a hardship to send her best wishes to the budding archaeologist, and it gained the woman's gratitude. She had no idea if there was a story here, but if anyone was likely to be able to help her find it, it was the curator.

"So are you thinking about doing a program about Kepler?" Her brow furrowed for a moment, seeming to realize something. "I would never have thought anyone would consider him a monster."

"Unless you know some deep, dark secrets," Annja said. "I'm in Prague to make a segment about Rabbi Loew and the golem, but I'll be honest, I'm not exactly finding it inspiring."

"Ah, yes, the golem. Now there was a proper monster," she said. "In the oldest sense of the word. So what are you looking for?"

"Inspiration," Annja said, painting as broad a canvas with the single word as she possibly could. "The city *has* to have more than one story to tell. If not here, then somewhere nearby. I am just following my nose. If I can't find anything, then I'm not really sure what

I'm going to do just yet. Maybe back to the golem if I can find a fresh perspective."

"Well, that's a relief," the woman said. "It would probably be more than my job's worth to help you if you wanted to turn Kepler into a monster. After all, the whole purpose of the museum is to celebrate his life and work."

"Fear not, you bought me with coffee." Annja raised her cup as though toasting the astronomer, and took another gulp. "The show's never been about tarnishing someone's reputation, living or dead."

"I'm glad to hear it," the woman said, the concern that had begun to build up on her face melting away.

Which of course only served to make Annja wonder if that meant Kepler had a secret worth hiding. But that was just the way her mind worked.

"So, inspiration…"

"Indeed," said Annja. "Inspiration."

"Finish your coffee and I'll give you the grand tour."

Annja took another sip, surprised that the woman had already finished hers, and then offered the mug back with half of the black treacle still in the bottom.

"That's the best part," the woman said, taking it and putting it next to her own like paperweights atop the bundle of papers. "Let's make a start, then, shall we?"

Annja followed her around, listening to one explanation after another. The woman was a wealth of information when it came to the twelve years Kepler had spent in the city. Annja didn't hear anyone else enter the building during the hour they walked between display cases, moving from room to room. She wondered how many visitors the museum received every day. It was getting on toward lunchtime, or at least brunch, so the tourists were no doubt still enjoying a leisurely stroll around the town, waiting for the hour to chime and the figures of the astronomical clock to do their macabre dance come midday. Perhaps more would come by in the afternoon. Or had people stopped caring about men like Johannes Kepler and all that they had done to further humankind's understanding of the world?

She listened attentively, and it was obvious that much of the talk was stuff the woman had learned by rote and recited many times each week. It covered most of Kepler's scientific achievements and the contributions that his studies had made to the science of astronomy. It was interesting, but it wasn't show material. She'd already begun to forget some of the opening facts and she hadn't even walked out the door.

She concentrated on what the woman had to say about his involvement with the city itself, but there was very little of that in her prepared speech.

As they approached the end of the tour, Annja knew as much as anyone could possibly ever want to know about the astronomer, but there'd been nothing to send a shiver up her spine. Nothing that told her she was listening to a story that would be worth chasing.

"A few of the places connected to Kepler are still standing," the woman said. "Obviously you're standing in one of them, but there are a few others worth taking a look at, if you are interested."

Annja said she was. "Where would you recommend?"

"You might like to take a trip out to Benátky nad Jizerou if you're taking a tour of the area. It's a small town, half an hour away. It was where Tycho Brahe was building his observatory when he invited Kepler to join him. I've no idea how much they have there, but the town and the castle are worth visiting."

Annja had heard the woman mention Brahe several times as they walked through the exhibits. Like Kepler, Brahe had been an important figure in the study of the planets at the time. Although his name hadn't left such a lasting global legacy, he had clearly been an instrumental figure in the foundation of Prague as a center for scientific thought.

"I might just do that," Annja said. "Thanks."

They headed toward the door, making small talk as they took the wooden stairs back down to the street level. It had been an interesting way to pass an hour or so, but it hadn't solved Annja's problem, and as far as she could see there was nothing pointing her in the direction of the next story.

"It's been lovely to meet you," the woman said as they reached the door. She made a show of looking up and down the street and shaking her head. "I'm starting to think that you might be our only visitor today."

"Things are that bad?"

"Worse," she said.

"How come?"

Annja's first thought was that the place wasn't making itself visible enough. After all, it was hidden away, and failing to appeal to the young. But then Prague was more commonly thought of as a party city where visitors could leave behind the consequences of their actions, not the kind of place you came to soak in the legacy of almost-forgotten scientists. That being the case, no amount of glossy brochures or clever marketing gimmicks would help.

She'd jumped to the wrong conclusion.

"It's the murders," the woman said. "You can hardly blame people for keeping away, I suppose. Who wants to go wandering around when people are getting murdered right outside their front doors? So, we struggle, and if the police don't find the killer soon, it will be too late for some of us."

"Is it really that bad?" Annja asked.

She'd been in Prague nearly a week and had been so wrapped up in her own problems she hadn't even noticed. That was what Garin meant about living in the real world for a while.

She avoided mentioning just how close she might have come to the killer, hoping that the woman would fill in some of the details Garin had hinted at over breakfast.

"Oh, yes. There have been several of them. Poor homeless people found dead in alleyways and parking lots. Some huddled in doorways, their blankets still drawn up under their chins as if they were just sleeping." The way the woman talked about it, it sounded like there were far more than four dead bodies that had been accounted for.

"Are the victims always homeless?"

The woman nodded. "Yes. Every one of them. There's nothing to say that ordinary people like you or me are at risk, but it has put people off coming into the city. The hotels are half-full where usually they'd be booked up at this time of year. It's worrying."

"I've been here a week and I didn't even know about the murders until this morning," Annja admitted. "Not that it would have made much difference if I had known. My bosses wouldn't have let me duck out of this trip. The way things are back home, I think they'd probably like it if I came face-to-face with the killer. Better for the ratings than another show about the golem."

"I've never understood why everyone is obsessed with that story," the woman said. "It's just a fairy tale. One of the newspapers keeps trying to link the killings with that old story, too. They're willing to do anything to sensationalize the whole thing." She shook her head sadly. "If you ask me, they'd be better off getting people to help find the killer or putting their efforts into making sure those poor souls had some kind of shelter for the night."

Which, Annja knew, was not merely true; it was obvious. If a killer was targeting the homeless, the very best thing the city could do to protect its people was to see that they had somewhere to sleep that was safe. But it was also obvious, from a narrative point of view, for the journalists to build up a story that linked real life events to the myth. Myths had power—power to thrill, power to chill. Telling the story would not only increase the sense of fear gripping the city, but it would sell newspapers. And, judging by the suits back home, that was the only thing that mattered to some people.

She gave her thanks to her guide, accepting a couple of brochures that the woman offered her, and highlighted the village that she had suggested Annja visit. Annja slipped them in her bag and pulled out a twenty-euro note. The woman tried to wave it away, but Annja insisted on leaving it as a donation. If things were as bad as they seemed to be, there was no way that the woman could afford to refuse any money coming her way. Despite protesting, the woman put it into the donations jar beside the door.

Annja stepped out into the street.

She felt the warmth on her face that had been missing inside the building.

She might not have found anything new relating to her story, but she might just have stumbled onto the obvious angle for the story she had. People's macabre fascination with murder sold newspapers. And if it was good enough to sell newspapers, then it ought to be good enough for the network's suits. But would it be good enough to save *Chasing History's Monsters*?

Only time would tell.

4

A quick visit to the newsstand confirmed which newspaper had been carrying the stories that connected the vagrant murders with Rabbi Loew's golem.

Even though the words were incomprehensible, the front page of one of the papers in the newsstand's racks carried Loew's name and an etching in place of a photograph that detailed the golem's nighttime wandering through these streets. Unable to read it, she decided she needed a different course of action. Thinking on her feet, Annja noted the name of the reporter whose byline appeared underneath the headline: Jan Turek.

A call to the newspaper resulted in her being passed from person to person until someone was found who spoke a language they had in common comfortably enough to answer a few questions. Then she discovered that Turek wasn't on the staff at all, but was a freelancer, and the staff member was unwilling to pass on any contact details for him without knowing more about her and her credentials. She provided Doug Morrell's contact information and told the staffer he could check in with him. She hoped that being on staff with a cable television corporation in the US would be enough to persuade them to put her in touch with Turek. She gave the staffer her number at the hotel and returned there to wait for Doug to confirm she was who she said she was.

When the phone rang she snatched it up and answered.

It wasn't Jan Turek.

It was the staffer, who confirmed that Doug Morrell had vouched for her, though he hadn't appreciated being woken up at six in the morning. Annja couldn't help herself, she laughed at that, having completely forgotten about the time difference when she'd given the staffer Doug's cell number. The woman promised to take a message and pass it on to Turek, but couldn't promise when he'd get back to her.

"He's not exactly the most reliable soul," she explained. "Which is why he's not on the staff here. But I'll call him now and leave your message. He's more of a night bird," the woman said, which Annja immediately corrected to *night owl* in her mind. "I think he sleeps for most of the day, so don't expect a call back from him for a while."

"But he's definitely the man I need to speak to about the stories you've been running about the killings?"

"Oh, yes. Can I ask, are you looking to buy the story from Jan?"

"It's possible," Annja said. She knew how papers worked. The reporter would have a lot of material that hadn't made it into the finished copy. Was there anything in there that would be of interest to her? Maybe.

"I'll make sure I tell him that. He's more likely to give you a call if there's a chance of money changing hands. You know how these freelancers are. If you don't hear from him, you might want to check out some of the places where people sleep outside. He's been talking to a lot of the homeless people late at night. I think he's even slept on the streets himself a couple of nights this week in the hope that he might catch the killer himself. The police warned him off that, though, so hopefully he listened to them. To be honest, I don't like the idea of him out there. It's not safe."

"Thanks," Annja said.

If the man didn't call her back, she was going to have to go looking for him, but she would have somewhere to start, which was more than she'd had an hour ago. How many Jan Tureks could there be in the city?

She was more than capable of looking after herself no matter who she found herself up against. But it was still seven or eight hours until it would start to get dark, and another six or seven until it was the right time to go hunting the killer, which made as much sense as hunting for the journalist who was writing about him.

That meant she was at a loose end.

She had time to kill.

She had exhausted the research she had brought with her three times over, but now she had another angle to chase. She decided to check the internet to see if there were better reports about the killings that had made it into the international press. Worst case, she could run Turek's reports—assuming they were online— through a translation app and at least get some sort of idea what theories he was putting forward. It wouldn't hurt to know just how much fear he was causing with his pieces, either. That was where the comments sections came in.

She headed back to the hotel, assuming Garin would still be occupying himself for a while yet.

From outside, the hotel was an unassuming building.

It had been a Dominican monastery back in the golem's day. Now it offered her space for quiet contemplation. Both the businessmen and the tourists had long since left, leaving the foyer empty. Annja walked toward the desk, which was between her and the single flight of stairs that led to the first floor where her room was. The receptionist looked up and smiled, returning to her work when Annja turned toward the stairs.

A middle-aged couple talking rapidly in German emerged from the stairway and walked straight to the reception desk without giving her a second glance.

Annja climbed the stairs two at a time, eager to get to work now that she had something to focus on.

She passed Garin's room, hearing voices behind the door. No doubt he was charming the waitress with talk of his jet airplane and a trip to Paris for champagne and strawberries that evening. That was his usual technique when it came to sweeping women off their feet: leave them dizzy with the heady rush of a life barely even imagined. If not Paris, maybe it would be pizza in Rome or Venetian ice cream, gazing out over the Lido. How many times in the past few years had Garin tried to impress her the same way? More than enough was the answer, though in truth he'd never impressed her more than that very first time they'd come face-to-face as she hunted the Beast of Gévaudan. He'd saved her life that day. To Annja's way of thinking that was more impressive than traveling half the world to dine at some fancy five-star restaurant, but as she'd quickly come to learn she was pretty much one of a kind.

She smiled to herself as she moved on to her own room.

5

Two hours sped by with Annja reading the various reports. It wasn't easy, the language barrier present even online, but she managed to track down more and more articles on the internet—though, painfully, as the translation site had a habit of turning the original Czech articles into gibberish.

She could have taken them to a translation service, but that would take time and cost money and probably only serve to annoy her paymasters. Or she could have asked around for a person who was fluent in English—fluent enough to give her a real idea of just how emotive the language in the articles was.

Of course, she had an ace up her proverbial sleeve. Roux. The man knew so much and had seen so much more. Even if he didn't have the answers, he would know someone who did. And in this case, he had no agenda, no wish to gain anything from her requests for help. That was the primary difference between the old man and Garin. Garin was like the song: he was his first, his last, his everything. He *always* put the interests of Garin Braden ahead of the interests of others. It wasn't just about being selfish, it was about being himself. You didn't live six hundred years of decadence without picking up some bad habits along the way. It was only inevitable that centuries of getting neck-deep in fecal matter and somehow emerging smelling of roses gave you a warped perspective on life. Roux was different. She didn't know why—on a fundamental level—that should be so. But it was. The only thing she'd noticed, and it was through years of quiet observation as opposed to direct confrontation, was that Roux welcomed the idea that he might not live forever whereas Garin dreaded it.

The old man might come across as cantankerous at the best of times, but he was the rock she could rely on while all else around her floundered. And he wouldn't ask for anything else in return, even if he wasn't completely enthusiastic about getting involved. That was another sign that age was catching up with him. She'd noticed it time and again since what had felt like Garin's ultimate betrayal beneath the Pass of the Moor's Sigh. He'd taken that hard. It wasn't just that Garin had shown his true colors; it was that maybe, just maybe, Roux had finally accepted that he couldn't change his former apprentice's nature.

She played with the phone for a moment. Roux was the touchstone that linked both of the lives she lived. He was a constant in an ever-changing world.

She punched in his number and waited for the phone to ring.

"To what do I owe this pleasure, my dear?" the old man said. There was no hint of surprise in Roux's voice.

"How are you doing?"

"Much the same as I am always doing," the old man replied. "As wonderful as it is to hear from you, I take it this isn't a social call? What can I do for you?"

"How good is your Czech?"

"Written or spoken?"

"Written," she said, unsurprised that he'd made the distinction rather than dismiss her question straight-away.

"Fair," he said. "As long as it's not too technical. What are we talking about?"

"A few tabloid articles. I'm sending you the links now."

"I didn't say that I *was* going to help you," Roux chided lightly. "Sometimes you take things for granted."

"You also didn't say you weren't going to help me," she said, wishing that he would be a little more obvious when he was feeling prickly. Some sort of code word would save a lot of misunderstanding. "Let's try again. Will you help me? Pretty please, O great and powerful Roux?"

There was an audible sigh that he exaggerated for her benefit, which guaranteed he'd read the articles for her.

"All right. Send the links. I'll call you back once I've had the chance to digest them. I assume we aren't look-ing at *War and Peace* here? I have a busy day ahead of me."

"There shouldn't be too much," Annja said. "I'm only interested in the pieces that refer to the golem."

"The golem?"

"Yeah, you know, Rabbi Loew... The Golem of Prague..."

"I'm not a simpleton, Annja, I know exactly what you're talking about. I just don't understand what your interest in it might be. After all, it's a fairy tale." He paused for a moment. There was an anguished tone lurking beneath his voice when he continued. "I've always thought that you considered what you do to be a proper job. Something worthwhile. Not frivolity. Was I wrong?"

Annja didn't think she'd ever heard him use those kinds of words to describe what she did. "There's a story here. It's something that viewers might be interested in, yes, but it's more than that. If I didn't know better, I'd think you were deliberately being antagonistic. This isn't like you. So I'm just going to ignore it. I refuse to rise to the bait."

"Not antagonistic, merely surprised." She heard the tap of keys as Roux followed up the links to the webpages she had sent him. "There's quite a bit here," he said after another minute or so. "I'll call you in half an hour." He hung up without waiting for her response.

It wasn't the first time he had done that to her, and odds were it wouldn't be the last. With half an hour to kill, she carried on scrolling through everything she could find about the recent spate of killings in the city while she watched the seconds crawl by. Once upon a time losing herself like Alice down the rabbit hole of the internet could have swallowed thirty minutes in the blink of an eye. All she had to do was follow a link, then another that branched off from the first toward something vaguely interesting, and then another, and suddenly half the day was gone. It wasn't like that now. Now every second dragged and every link offered frustration.

Even so, fifteen minutes had been wasted by the time her phone rang.

Roux's name flashed on the screen.

"That was quick," she said, after snatching it up.

"Some things don't take long to read," the old man

said. His voice had changed in the few minutes since he'd hung up on her. She knew him well enough to know that meant something was wrong.

"Talk to me. What do you think?"

He waited a moment, as though weighing up what, precisely, to say to her. Finally he said, "I think you might be getting caught up in something you don't understand." It was blunt and to the point. And it meant there was no way she was walking away from this now. Because, as well as she knew him, the old man knew her, too. He knew exactly what to say to plant the seed that would grow into obsession.

"I know what you're doing," she said. "You're not the kid-gloves kind of guy. Spill."

She could hear the smile in his voice. "I was merely observing that this might not be as simple as it seems."

"And you know what it's like when you dangle imminent danger in front of me," Annja said. "I can't resist."

"I know, but that doesn't mean I wouldn't rather your television show had taken you somewhere else, just this once."

"So, what do they say?"

"Ostensibly they cover a spate of murders in the Czech capital, and the journalist who wrote these articles—Jan Turek—has found a way of linking them to the legend of the golem. But this, I suspect, you already know."

"I do. It's why I sent you them."

"Almost everything in Prague can be linked to the legend in some way, Annja. It is a city filled with hidden dangers. Most of the time they stay hidden, but every now and then one of them finds its way out into the daylight."

"What does it say, Roux? I'm a big girl. I can look after myself."

"Just that Turek believes some ancient evil has stirred. I want you to promise me you won't do anything stupid, Annja."

"I can't promise that," she said, trying her best to sound light and breezy rather than like some petulant teenager. "Anyway, it's not like I'm on my own."

"I don't think that cameraman of yours is likely to be much help."

"I'm not talking about Lars. Garin turned up this morning."

"Garin? What on earth is he doing there?" Roux asked. Annja noted the change in his voice. It was more than just the mention of Garin's name. Maybe, she surmised, it was even part of the reason why he was here in Prague.

"Did he say why he wanted to see you?" Roux asked, following an identical train of thought.

"No. He made out that he was bored. And to be brutally honest, he seemed intent on relieving that boredom with the waitress who served us breakfast." She expected some kind of response from Roux, some barbed comment about the younger man's proclivities, some damning indictment of his lifestyle. None came.

Instead, he said, "If we're going to do this, we're going to do it properly. I'm coming. Don't go out after sunset. I'll be there in a few hours."

"Roux?" Something really had him spooked. "You don't have to."

"I do. Believe me. There are things about that city you don't understand. Ancient forces. Evil. I am not leaving you alone there."

"Okay, Roux, now you're scaring me."

"Good. It's good to be scared."

"Should I warn Garin?"

"He went there with his eyes open. He almost certainly knows what these murders mean. He isn't a fool, and to use one of your own rather eloquent turns of phrase, he's big enough and ugly enough to take care of himself. I have a few things to take care of, but I'll be with you before sunrise. In the meantime, do not go out after dark. Promise me."

"I promise," Annja said, knowing it was a promise she was absolutely going to break, but promising it, anyway.

He hung up on her again. Twice within the hour, now that was almost a record.

What had gotten him so spooked? Ancient evil, dark forces. He wasn't prone to talk like that. So what was so bad it would bring him running? And why no concern for Garin's well-being? There was something she wasn't being told and she didn't like that. She didn't like it at all. While she was the first to admit that she had a habit of getting into scrapes, she had something none of her enemies had: Joan of Arc's sword. She didn't need a bodyguard. All she had to do was to reach out into the otherwhere and close her hand around the reassuring familiarity of the hilt and it was there.

The sword had been reforged after so many years shattered, Roux having scoured the four corners of the Earth to find the shards of metal. That was how this had all begun so many years ago. It wasn't a blacksmith who had healed the wounded blade—and yes, she'd come to think of the sword as something very much alive— she had done it, with nothing more than her bare hands.

Garin had been there, as had Roux. They'd all been in this together from that moment on, despite some hiccups along the way.

Roux hadn't exactly told her not to talk to Garin, only that he could look after himself. There was no way that she was going to stay cooped up in the hotel room. She thought about checking in with Garin, see if he wanted to do a patrol of the streets, try to shake something loose, but decided to call Lars, her cameraman, to warn him that he wouldn't be getting a lot of sleep later.

"We're going monster hunting," she said when he answered.

"Now?"

"After sundown."

Lars Mortensen sounded like his head was still somewhere up in Stockholm, his home base. When she'd settled on Prague for the segment, she'd reached out to a few of the cameramen she'd worked with in the region. Lars, who had been with her during their coverage of the Beowulf dig in Skalunda Barrow a couple of years back, jumped at the chance to work with her again. He'd told her he'd meet her under the astronomical clock in twenty-four hours, and like the punctual guy he was, he'd been waiting there for her twenty-three hours and fifty-nine minutes later.

"When you say monsters, you mean?"

"We've got a segment to tape."

"Excellent. I've been getting antsy kicking my heels here all day."

She laughed at that. "I don't know if you've been watching the news, but there's a killer on the loose in the city and we didn't even know about it."

The penny dropped. "Are you out of your mind? There's a lunatic out there and you *want* us to go looking for him? I thought we were here to shoot a segment about the golem."

"We are. But it's not quite that simple," she said. "There's a journalist who seems to think that there's a link to the golem."

"You mean like it's the golem doing the killing kind of link? Or some kind of homage?"

"I don't know. I want to talk to him, but that means finding him, and the best link I've got is that he's living on the street right now. He's been covering the story since it began, living among the people who are the most vulnerable."

"You mean he's sleeping outside when there's a killer who's preying on the homeless? That's one crazy mofo."

"He's certainly dedicated to the truth," Annja said.

"And you want us to go out into his hunting ground? Are you planning on painting a target on our backs, as well?"

"Nothing so risky. I just want to poke about a bit."

"I remember the last time you just wanted to poke about, Annja. Just promise me no burning churches this time."

"We'll be fine," Annja said, trying to reassure him even though she remembered all too vividly what had happened the last time they'd gone out on a shoot together. How could she forget? She really hated fire.

She didn't *have* to take him out on this little recce, but given what she had in mind for the live show, grabbing some footage of the homeless on the streets of Prague might just be useful filler, assuming the program came together the way she wanted it to. It certainly wouldn't hurt.

"I'll hold you to that. Just tell me what time you want me and I'll be there."

"I always want you," Annja said, deliberately flirting with the Swede. They enjoyed a good bit of lighthearted banter. It helped to take her mind off what they were about to do, and that was not a bad thing. "There's no point in heading out before dark, and this place doesn't feel like it slows down even then. All the shops around the Charles Bridge are still open, selling their tourist crap, so we're looking at a late night. Probably after eleven. Turek, the journalist, is almost certainly going to be tucked up in bed until then, but if I hear from him earlier I'll let you know."

"He knows you're trying to get hold of him?"

"I left a message with the newspaper that's been running his stories, and they promised to reach out to him. Who knows?"

"Well, if that's the case I may just continue my sightseeing tour. First stop, I think, the House of the Black Madonna, the cubist café. Might even catch a movie after that. Someone mentioned an English theater in town."

"Knock yourself out."

6

The rest of the day passed slowly.

The hotel lobby filled and emptied, filled and emptied, all walks of life seeming to drift through the atrium and yet it maintained its sense of calm. She could imagine the monks all those years ago shuffling through the same chambers, heads bowed in quiet contemplation. There was a conference in town, medical supplies by the sounds of the jargon being bandied about by the participants as they tried to one-up one another with jokes and punch lines that made no sense to Annja.

By early evening she was finally starting to feel hungry. She thought about calling room service, but the menu was fairly unappetizing and she had an entire city at her disposal. She'd heard about a place down by the river where the intellectuals and artists used to gather that had become a hive of secret activity during the revolution and now was renown for cheap good-quality eats in an authentic environment. It was proper precapitalism Prague, and it was only a five-minute walk away along one of the wider boulevards. Nothing was going to happen at five-thirty, she told herself, and ventured out in search of food.

Shop windows with words she couldn't read emblazoned across them shone invitingly at one end of the street and were boarded up at the other. She saw young women walking in groups, laughing, and young men behind them, studious with book bags slung over their shoulders and earnest expressions behind their black plastic-framed glasses. She heard snatches of conversation in English about Kafka and a church around the corner that they were sure was featured in one of his stories. Those strands of intellectualism were cut across by more mundane chatter, including the fact that some website had gone down. What she didn't hear was anyone talking about the murders.

The restaurant itself was the last building on the street, with huge plate-glass windows looking out over the Vltava. Inside, soft lighting from huge chandeliers gave the impression of opulence that was contradicted almost immediately by the tables beneath them, which looked like they would have been at home in a greasy spoon in the Bowery.

She sat at a table by the window, with a great view of the castle on the hill, and watched as one by one the stars came out. She asked the waiter what he'd recommend, something local, authentic Czech cuisine. He came back with a sampler filled with all sorts of peculiarities. She had no idea what she was putting into her mouth. Some of it was delicious, some of it wasn't.

The meal killed another hour, the leisurely coffee after it another thirty minutes. Annja was good when it came to keeping her own company. She didn't need to hide herself in a book, either. She was just content to simply *be*. To sit, gazing out of the window at the world as it passed by. To think.

And tonight she was thinking about Roux and Garin.

There was obviously something going on between the pair of them again. They were like a couple of teenage girls sometimes. She wanted to bang their heads together. But Roux was right: Garin's simply turning up this morning was uncharacteristic even if he tried to pass it off as boredom. Very little Garin Braden did was without some underlying cause, and that cause only ever benefited Garin Braden. That was just the way of the world. It was hard to be angry with him for it. It was who he was. You might as well be angry with the wasp for stinging you or the milk for expiring. To quote the motivational poster: shit happens.

By the time Annja headed back to the hotel, the sun was a thing of the past, and the sky was verging on black. Cities were a different animal at night. Streets that had felt safe even just an hour earlier had a hostile undercurrent once the moon ruled the sky.

Annja made it back to her room for nine. Garin was nowhere in sight. It was still early to go out looking for the journalist, but she called Lars, anyway. "Fifteen minutes?" she said.

Getting back out there seemed to be more useful than sitting there tapping her foot. She didn't know how life on the street worked. Turek might already be trying to lay claim to a sheltered spot for the night.

"Thought you'd bailed on me," Lars replied. "I've been watching the news for the past three hours, but there's been no mention of the killings."

Annja wasn't surprised. She said as much to Lars.

They arranged to meet down in the atrium.

Annja didn't take much with her. All she needed was the street map where she'd marked a few possible locations and landmarks of interest. It hadn't been difficult to identify the kinds of places where the homeless gathered, where soup kitchens were set up to feed them and where the hostel beds could be found to keep a few of them warm at night. But she wasn't interested in those places. There was safety in numbers. She knew she should focus on isolated places where someone would be alone and therefore more vulnerable.

She headed to the lobby.

Her cameraman had managed to beat her to the punch and was leaning against the wall, his camera still packed in its flight case at his feet. He was chatting with the doorman just inside the glass doors. They slid open as she approached him.

"Ready?" Annja asked as she felt the cool air on her face. The temperature had dropped a good five degrees since she'd come back from the restaurant. It was only going to get colder out there as the night wore on.

The streets were filled with late-night tourists following the curves of old cobbled streets around to the famous bridge to get their photographs taken and gaze up at the castle under the bright spotlights. The distant sound of traffic was barely audible over the music piping out of the row of tourist-trap restaurants with their tables spilling out into the streets. That was where the lucky ones would be congregating—those who could afford to go out for a good time knowing that they would have a warm bed to go home to when they'd finished having fun for the night. Plenty of them would be there until the early hours, but they would have taxis to take them to their homes or hotels. They weren't the ones at risk.

"The guy on the door told me that there are a few

places around here where people try to make a bed for the night," Lars said.

She fell into step beside the big Swede. He was every bit the archetype of his people—big, blond and burly. "We were just talking about the murder that happened last night. He said that it wasn't far from here. Want to go check it out?"

"I saw the body."

"You did what? And you didn't think to mention it? Way to bury the lead."

"Consider it exhumed." She quickened her pace. There was no point in hanging around so close to the main roads and the hotels this early in the evening. They needed to find the darker corners, away from the eyes of the kind of people who would be uncomfortable if they saw the genuine poverty of the city they'd come to visit.

"I've already marked on the map a few places we might want to check out," she said as Lars hustled to keep up with her. They moved with a purpose. No one else did. That meant she had to twist and weave between milling people, looking for breaks in the press of bodies to step into. Part of the reason for the haste was to avoid questions. It was harder for Lars to pepper her with them if he was chasing to keep up with her. Part, though, was that she was eager to find the journalist. He was the only one who seemed to know anything about what was happening on the streets. That, of course, had prickled her suspicions, too. It wouldn't have been the only time a killer had played the press for his own agenda. But she didn't think Turek was the killer. Not that she had anything to base that assumption on, not even his picture.

"Let's start with some background shots of the conditions these people are forced to live in."

"This really doesn't feel like *Chasing History's Monsters*," Lars said.

He was right, of course. There was a fine line between history repeating itself and exploitation, and she wasn't sure which side of that line she was walking right now.

"We don't need much, just a few shots to give the story some genuine impact."

She hesitated for a second when she reached the alleyway where she'd seen the body that morning. There were strands of police tape tied to downspouts on either side of the mouth, but the tape had been snapped and hung loose against the wall. The black stain on the ground wasn't going to stop anyone from using the alleyway as a shortcut to wherever he or she needed to be.

"This is where it happened?" Lars asked, looking at the dark patch at his feet.

Annja found herself nodding. She focused on the gloom between the buildings. The streetlights penetrated only a short way before the alleyway was swallowed in darkness. She could understand why the homeless man had picked it for his shelter.

She heard the sound of something shuffling in the darkness and her heart skipped a beat.

"Hello?" she called to whoever was hiding inside the alleyway. It wasn't like she thought they'd stumbled on the killer, no matter what pop psychologists said about returning to the scene of the crime. "Hello?" she called again, feeling a tingle up her spine.

Instinctively Annja caught herself flexing her fingers, ready to reach into the otherwhere to call on her sword. She glanced around, looking at Lars, who was peering over her shoulder, camera trained on the darkness. *Well*, she thought, *if we get killed by some psychopath, at least he'll get the shot.* It wasn't the most comforting of thoughts.

Annja took a step closer to the darkness, her breath catching in her throat as she strained to hear whatever it was that was hiding back there.

The shuffling stopped.

Annja didn't move.

Didn't breathe.

But she could hear breathing.

Inhale.

Exhale.

Inhale.

Exhale.

Each one grew louder with every tentative step that she took into the darkness.

The space was suddenly flooded with light as the lamp in the camera behind her burst into bright life. The only darkness that remained was cut out inside her shadow.

The blinding light was greeted by a scuttle of panicked movement and then, a fraction of a second later, whoever it was hiding in the darkness charged straight at her in a whirl of panic.

The source of the movement was much closer than she'd expected.

A body swathed in streaming rags of shadow barreled into her, slamming Annja back against the wall.

The air was driven from her lungs by the impact. Even as she gasped for breath, she grabbed out with one hand, her fingers snatching at the material of her attacker's sleeve. Annja hung on until the owner of the coat lost his footing, and she used her weight and his momentum to help him stumble and fall.

The man stared up at her. Blinded by the light of the camera he threw his hands in front of his face. Annja looked down at him. He was babbling, pleading. She couldn't understand a word he was saying, but the meaning was obvious: *please don't hurt me.* She released her grip. This wasn't the killer. This was one of his potential victims.

Annja held her hands up in apology, trying to help him to his feet as she said, "Sorry. Sorry. My mistake."

The man didn't take her proffered hand. He scrambled away, the soles of his feet pushing him along on the ground as he grabbed for his precious few possessions, which had spilled out of his pockets as he charged her in fear. She felt nothing but pity for the man, unable to imagine what it would be like to walk a mile in his shoes.

The world was cruel, that much was undeniable. She'd seen more than enough of that cruelty to last a lifetime, but she was lucky. She also got to see the amazing stuff, too, the stuff that made life worth living.

Did he? she wondered, and then hated herself for so immediately patronizing the man without knowing a thing about his life or what had driven him to this desperate end.

"Please," Annja said, reaching into her pocket and pulling out a neatly followed twenty-euro note. The look of fear and panic in his eyes was replaced with one of surprise, then avarice, as he reached out and took the money from her. He spirited it away in a heartbeat like the greatest magician to walk the streets of Prague, then scrambled to his feet without a word of thanks and backed away from her, nodding over and over as he pushed his way past Lars, who had stopped taping the events.

The man hurried along the street, clutching a plastic bag that she assumed was stuffed with his tattered sleeping bag.

"I'm thinking we need a better plan," Lars said, deadpan.

Annja didn't argue.

As plans went, it had been pretty thin, anyway.

"Maybe we should just head back to the hotel and wait to see if your man gives you a call?"

"Are you chickening out on me, Lars?" she asked.

"Just checking."

"We need to get this right. I haven't told you what's going on back at the network, but basically, if I screw this up, no more *Chasing History's Monsters*. I really don't want to screw this up."

"We don't even have a story to screw up. Not really. We're just wandering the streets at night."

"Now you're making me sound a little bit too much like a hooker for my liking," Annja said, shaking her head. He was right, though. That's pretty much what they were doing. "What else can we do?"

The question was rhetorical.

Lars pointed his camera back into the gloom of the alleyway and shot some footage of the place where the body had been found. The spotlight from the camera gave the dark stain a macabre cast. Annja pointed out the strands of police tape, making sure that he got them in the shot, as well. She didn't want him to linger on the stain. She didn't want the viewers making the mental connection between it and the reality that they were looking at the last vestiges of the poor man's spilled blood. Showing the police tape would be enough. It would pull the heartstrings of their audience and show that this was real. She didn't even want the stain in the footage that went back to the network. She knew all too well what those ratings whores would use it for.

So often her contributions to the show had been about monsters from the past, just as the name of the program demanded, that had no relevance to today. This was the chance to do something different. She realized the shape of the show now; it was going to be a monster hunt, yes, but a live one. The trick would be linking the horrors of today with the horrors of the past, but that was what she was good at.

"Got enough?" she asked when he had covered just about every inch of the alley.

He nodded. "With plenty of space for you to add voice-over stuff. It's pretty dark, though." She didn't know whether he meant in terms of exposure or content.

The sentiment, if the not the words, were becoming something of a mantra for this segment.

Annja liked Lars because he was never afraid of a challenge, and his eye when it came to framing the establishing shots was second to none. He had a way of making everything come alive when it fell under his lens. He was a pro. Versatile. And like a Boy Scout he was always prepared. He could have his camera in position, shooting, in seconds, more often than not before she'd even realized the shot was worth capturing herself. It was almost like telepathy sometimes.

It didn't hurt that he was easy on the eye, either. "Let's get moving," Annja said. It felt like there were eyes everywhere, watching from the shadows, following them every step they took. That was another difference between the day and the night city: at night ordinary things turned creepy. Just thinking about it was enough to have a shiver chase up her spine as if someone had walked over her grave. She wasn't superstitious. She didn't believe in omens. But she trusted her instincts, and right now her instincts were telling her it was time to move.

Lars gave up his position two steps behind her to walk by Annja's side.

The rest of the streets near the hotel were quiet, which, of course, was exactly what she was looking for. Too many people meant there was no chance the killer would strike.

They walked for an hour, hearing the distant chimes of the astronomical clock tolling on the quarter hour.

It was easy to get paranoid about all the things they couldn't see.

Across the way she noticed crates and barrels being unloaded from a truck and carried in through the back door of one of the clubs. It struck her as odd that they'd take a delivery so late at night.

A naked woman walked down the street, followed by a man with a handheld video camera recording her. It was obviously some kind of exploitation flick destined to wind up on the internet. Annja was sickened. She was in half a mind to walk over there and have it out with the photographer. Lars sensed it, too, and very artfully steered her away from making a scene. "We've got a reason for being here," he told her. "And it's not to fix all the ills of the city. It's to catch a monster. Let's not tip our hand. We've got no idea who's watching us."

And as he said it, she knew he was right. Not that she shouldn't intervene—that felt absolutely right. No, he was right when he said someone was watching them. She'd known it since they left the alleyway.

"I'm going to remember his face," Annja said, fixing the man's features in her mind. "And if I see him again, he's going to regret it. That's a promise."

"I have absolutely no doubt you will. You're a frightening woman, Annja Creed. I wouldn't want to be on your bad side," Lars said.

They walked down one of the narrower streets, emerging near some sort of outdoor theater with marionettes being artfully manipulated by hidden puppet masters. There was quite a crowd gathered around. The city certainly offered a rich and varied nightlife, considering it was now past ten at night, and showed no signs of slowing down.

There were plenty of shadows for them to explore, though they didn't venture deeply into any of them. She was fairly sure that Turek wouldn't be settling down in one place this early, especially if he had managed to gain the trust of the vulnerable people on the streets. He would keep moving, talking to the disenfranchised around the inner city. Most would be young, she reasoned, drawn to the capital by the promise of a better life, of excitement. Some would be like the girl she'd just seen paraded naked through the street, too. Exploited. Others might have had a good life and lost it, or suffered a breakdown or simply not been able to cope and have turned their back on society, not wanting to be a part of it. There were as many possible stories out there in the night as there were people to tell them. Only one of them would help her get closer to the monster she hunted.

Did Turek have any idea where the killer might strike next? Was he working on a divinable pattern? Chaos versus order. Chance versus predestination. But there were ways to limit the randomness of that chance. There were ways to help exert order on a chaotic city. Annja checked her street map a few times to be sure that she was still heading in the general direction of one of the major landmarks she'd marked, a church that kept its doors open to offer hot soup, sandwiches and salvation all night.

How many times had people accepted a mug of soup in exchange for their mortal souls? The thought put a smile on her face and for the first time that night she found herself thinking of Garin and Roux and their unique longevity. She was pretty sure they hadn't bought it with soup.

They turned the final corner and saw the lights in the distance like a beacon to all who were looking for shelter.

Her cell phone rang.

Annja didn't recognize the number.

"Hello," she said, barely breaking her stride. "Who is this?"

"Is that Annja Creed?" the voice asked without answering her question.

"It is," she replied. "Is that Jan Turek?"

"I've been told that you wanted to talk to me."

"Yes. Yes. Absolutely. I'd like to pick your brains."

"And not to be too blunt about it, but is there money in it for me?"

"I can't make any promises."

"And you're the same Annja Creed who does the television show *Chasing History's Monsters*?"

"That's right."

"I've never seen it," he said. "But I did a search on the internet to find out who you were. Seems you're quite the celebrity."

"I wouldn't go that far," she replied.

"You're too modest," he said. "You get more hits on your name than our own prime minister does." She heard his laugh, but wasn't sure she was meant to laugh along. A man could laugh at his own country, but from an outsider it could come across at worst as mocking, at best condescending.

"Can we meet?" she asked. "Tonight?"

"Where are you?"

She stopped under a streetlamp and checked her map, giving him the name of the street and the church they were heading toward.

"I know it," he said. "I'll meet you there in ten minutes. Don't go inside. They won't know you, and you won't fit in. Strangers aren't welcome these nights. I'm sure you can understand why. There's a late-night café on the same street, a little farther along."

It wasn't hard to pick out the only shop front still illuminated.

"I see it," she said.

"I'll meet you there. Tell Maria that you're waiting for me. She'll take care of you."

"I've got my cameraman with me," she said, hoping that wouldn't put him off.

"Then I'll see you both in the café."

7

The café was like a Czech riff on the old Edward Hopper painting *Nighthawks*.

It had a central bar island and a huge brass espresso machine that dominated the back wall. Four diners were inside and a waitress wearing candy stripes. Annja opened the door. There were a dozen seats at the bar, another dozen tables. All four of the diners were at the bar. They seemed to know one another, and were comfortably chatting with the waitress as Annja walked through the door. The waitress—a middle-aged woman with tired eyes and a tired smile—walked toward them with a pair of menus in her hand.

"Anywhere you like, folks," the woman said, in English, immediately picking Annja and Lars out as tourists. She gestured toward the private tables.

"Are you Maria?"

"Yes," the woman responded cautiously.

"Great. Then we're in the right place. We're supposed to meet Jan Turek here in about ten minutes."

"Ah, that old rogue." All signs of concern disappeared in an instant. "Please," Maria said. "This way. Let me take your coats."

She ushered them to the booth near the window,

away from the people propping up the bar. A plastic checkered cloth covered the stains on the old table. Marie gave a questioning glance at Lars's flight case.

"Camera," Lars said, patting it.

"Camera, eh? I've got one of those on my phone. Fits in my pocket, too." The woman chuckled to herself. "Sometimes smaller is better." She winked at the big Swede, who just shook his head with a wry smile. Maria wove a path back to the bar without leaving the menus on the table. She returned a couple of minutes later with a bottle of red wine and three glasses.

"Jan's favorite," she said. "Your food will be ready by the time he gets here."

"But…" Annja started to say that they hadn't ordered, but the woman was already heading back to the kitchen. This, no doubt, was what Turek had meant when he said Maria would take care of them. It was going to be interesting to see what came out of the kitchen.

It took nine of the ten minutes for the reporter to appear in the doorway.

Turek might well have been the mythical golem himself. Easily three inches taller than Lars, and twice as wide, he looked like a mountain as he lumbered into the room. It took Annja a moment to realize a lot of his bulk was due to the several heavy layers of coats he'd wrapped himself in.

Turek raised a hand to Maria, who was back behind the bar again.

She smiled back. Annja knew that kind of smile. Turek was more than just a regular diner at the café. Maria nodded toward their booth, and the reporter wandered over, sliding into the seat beside Annja.

"Jan Turek," he said as he shook hands with both of

them. He offered Annja an easy smile that softened the hard edges of his angular face. He had the dark shadows of four-day stubble on his cheeks, and hollow eyes. His many coats were wrapped around a rather fragrant body. There was no doubt in her mind that Turek was living the part, every night out on the streets among the homeless. She admired him for that. Turek poured himself a glass of the red wine and raised it in the direction of the bar before taking a healthy swig. "Nectar of the gods," he declared. "Maria keeps a case in stock for me."

The wine was a touch harsh for Annja's palate, with a bite to the aftertaste that made it bitter going down. It was definitely an acquired taste, one that Turek had and Lars was happily in the process of getting by the looks of things.

"As nice as it is to share a glass with friends, we're not friends, are we? You want something from me, so how about we get down to business. What do you want to talk about? No, let me guess. The killings. That's all anyone wants to talk about."

"In a way, yes, but actually I'm more interested in your angle about the golem," Annja said, leaning back a little as Maria approached the table and placed a bowl of steaming soup in front of her.

"Kyselica," Jan said. "Fermented cabbage soup. It's Maria's specialty. You have to try it."

The woman returned with a plate of sourdough bread and put it down between them. "Enjoy," she said, placing one hand on the reporter's back and planting a kiss of the top of his head. He was definitely more than just a regular.

Annja pushed her spoon through the soup before lifting it to her lips to taste.

It was surprisingly good, and much better than it smelled.

Even though she'd had a good meal at the restaurant by the river, she took several mouthfuls before she spoke again. "It really is very good," she agreed, nodding and smiling. Annja glanced across at Lars, noting that he'd already finished his.

"So what do you want to know about the golem?" Turek asked.

"You said you'd researched me, so you know I do a cable TV show back in the US. I'm looking to do a story about the myth of the golem. The thing is, it's all been done to death so I was trying to find something new. That's when I came across your pieces in the paper. Sadly I don't read Czech, so I thought the best thing was to try to talk to you."

The man laughed. "So basically you're looking for a translator?"

"Not at all. I'm after the stuff you left out."

"What makes you think I've left anything out of my stories?"

"You're a freelancer. You need to spin the story out over as many articles as you can. There's no way you've put everything out there already. Maybe you're only left with supposition and wild theories, but you'll have something that supports those theories. I know it and you know it. There's no way you'd be making claims about the killer's links to the golem legend if you didn't have something else."

Annja waited while he thought about what she had said.

The pause alone was enough to convince her that she was right.

She was good at reading people.

She was also good at appealing to their vanity.

She'd deliberately intended to make him seem more special than he actually was. The reality of the situation was that Turek knew something, and she wanted to know what that something was. There was nothing to say it was important. It could just as easily have been some crackpot theory every bit as out of it as the idea that the killings could somehow be linked to the golem's legend in the first place.

Turek mopped up the last of his soup with a chunk of the sourdough and popped it into his mouth, then picked up his glass to wash it down. He leaned back in his chair and drew every ounce of drama out of the moment for effect, then he delivered his punch line: "The killer has been seen."

That was the last thing she'd expected him to say. "What? Seriously? Who saw him? Did you get a description?" The questions tumbled out of her mouth before she could stop herself.

"To answer the first question, the killer was seen by two homeless men. They saw him flee the scene of the third murder. To answer your second question, yes, but we'll come to that."

"Do the police know?"

"Of course, but tell me, what makes you think the police are ever likely to consider the word of a well-known pair of drunks as gospel? Especially when they don't *want* to believe what they are saying."

"But surely they have to follow it up?"

"That's the problem. They are adamant it wasn't a man…" He paused again, clearly still enjoying the chance to play to an audience.

"It couldn't have been a woman," Annja said. She'd seen the state of the body in the alleyway. There was no way a woman would have caused so much damage in the process of killing someone. It wasn't just a case of not being physically capable; it was part of the psychology, too. Women, it was said, preferred poisons to more intimate forms of killing.

"No," the journalist said with a laugh. "Not a woman."

"They think it's this golem, don't they?" Lars said, shaking his head. "Just how drunk were they?"

That would explain why the police weren't interested. The golem of Prague, one of its fabled defenders, suddenly a nocturnal killing machine? No. That didn't fit any of the myths, no matter what two drunken men imagined what they'd seen.

"According to their description of the killer, they saw something that didn't act like a man, didn't move like a man. It was larger than the average man. Well over six feet tall, broad shouldered and barrel chested."

"They could have been describing you," Annja said. "Or him." She nodded toward Lars. "There are plenty of big guys in a city this size."

"Yes, indeed there are, but how many of them can scramble up the side of a building?" Turek asked.

"Okay, now I'm seeing why the police decided they'd heard enough."

"Indeed," Turek said. "They claimed that the killer scaled the side of the house like a spider."

"Definitely drunk, then," Lars stated.

"Probably, but why did they say the same thing?"

"People talk," Annja replied. "They might have convinced each other that they saw the same thing."

"A shared delusion?"

Annja nodded.

"The only problem with that explanation is that they weren't together. They both make the same impossible claims about the killer's escape despite having been three streets apart at the time? One of them close to the old Jewish cemetery, the other over beyond the synagogue." His eyes narrowed as he leaned forward. "And these two do not agree on anything, believe me. They'd come to blows over an argument about what's black and what's white, never mind a bottle of vodka or something more serious. They can't stand the sight of each other. There's no way they'd have cooked up a story together."

"And his face? Did they get a look at it?"

"Oh, yes, and that's another thing that the police weren't happy about, despite the fact two independent witnesses said exactly that same thing."

"And what was that?"

"He didn't have one."

"What? A mask?"

"I said the same thing, but no. They are adamant it wasn't a mask. They said that there were dark patches where a mouth and eyes should have been, but no features to speak of, just flat planes, nothing any more defined than a child might draw."

"Or maybe as if it had been made out of clay," Lars offered helpfully.

Annja shot him a dark stare. A little mental telepathy and he'd have been able to read the two words on her mind right then, too: *not helping*.

The thought of it churned Annja's stomach.

How could anyone live with ragged holes for a face?

She could understand now, though, how it could be possible to make the mental leap between some form of deformity and the legend of the golem. Especially living in a place like this where the story was part of the very fabric of the city, engrained in the stone of the oldest buildings. So was that what they were looking for, someone born with some hideous disfigurement? It would be hard for anyone fitting the description to move about by daylight, too, but surely the person would have to eat and shop and live like anyone else, so someone somewhere ought to recognize him.

"And you said that he climbed the side of a building?" She deliberately didn't use the word *it* to describe the killer.

"I've even seen marks on the walls where one of them said that they saw it. Gouges. I've no idea of what made them, but fingers didn't make them. There's no way of even knowing if the marks have got something to do with the killer or if they're just… I don't know… weeping plaster?"

"But you believe the men, don't you?"

Turek nodded.

"I do. Maybe not all of it, but enough to know that they saw something extraordinary. Maybe not the golem, but something strange. Something that doesn't fit with the world as we know it. A giant with no face who can scale brick walls and is killing people who are sleeping on the streets. No matter how impossible their claims, I believe there's an element of truth to them."

Annja found it hard to disagree. She'd seen plenty of things during the past few years that didn't quite fit with the world as most people knew it. So, assuming the two homeless men had seen something, how much truth could there be in their accounts? A giant didn't have to be a giant, and ragged features didn't have to mean no face at all. Maybe the handholds had already been chipped into the wall—or several walls across the city—to make an escape easy. It wasn't inconceivable, was it? A killer could be that methodical, and could have planned in that level of detail to eliminate the element of chance in his escape.

She knew that she should leave it alone and let the police do their job. No matter how compelling Turek's joining of the dots might be, this wasn't a monster. She was less and less sure there was anything she could use in a segment for the show. And, more tellingly, why did Annja suddenly think it was her job to catch the killer herself? Because that's what was happening, wasn't it? She was taking on the role of protector for the city, rather like the mythical golem had been. Was that the story she was looking to tell? No. That wasn't her style. She didn't want to turn the camera on herself and transform Annja Creed, TV host, into Annja Creed, the freak show.

Something else gnawed at the back of her mind: Roux.

Something in Turek's article had tweaked Roux sharply enough to tear him away from his home comforts back at the estate and bring him here. And Garin had just decided to turn up in the same city at the same time? Roux had said it often enough: there was no such thing as coincidence, meaningful or otherwise. Something was wrong here. She knew that she wasn't going to be able to rest until she discovered exactly what it was. That was just the kind of woman she was.

"I've shown you mine. Isn't it time for you to show me yours?" Turek said.

"I don't have anything to share," she said. "At least,

not yet. I've been closer than I'd like to have been to one of his victims, but aside from hearing footsteps in the night, I've got nowhere in terms of tracking the killer."

The reporter's expression changed. He took a gulp of his wine, then topped up his glass. "If you come across anything, will you let me know?"

"Of course," she said. "I'd like to talk to the two men who say they saw the killer, but I assume I'll need a translator."

"I think a medium might have better luck," Turek said.

"I'm not following."

"You've already met one of them. He was found dead in an alleyway this morning. The other, well, I haven't been able to find him tonight. To be honest, I think he's running for his life. But even if I could find him, I can't promise he'll want to talk to you. Not after what happened last night."

The body she'd seeing lying in a pool of his own blood had been both victim and witness.

But first he had been a witness.

Was that why he had become a victim?

8

They spent a couple of hours trying to locate the second witness, but the man was nowhere to be found.

In those two hours Annja learned just how many cracks there were in the city for people to slip between, and just how many sheltered nooks there were for them to make their bed for the night. They disturbed many of them hiding from prying eyes—some bums, some old alcoholics, some frighteningly young and broken—but failed to find the man they were looking for.

Turek was recognized by several of the street people. They greeted him with the same hollow, haunted look as he spoke to them rapidly in Czech, only to shrug or shake their heads. Body language was universal. No one had seen the witness. More than one said they thought he'd left the city, gone back home because he'd convinced himself he would be the golem's next victim.

It wasn't hard to imagine what had to have been going on inside his head. First, he had seen that strange killer, then learned that the only other person to see it had been found dead that morning. In his place she would have run, too, put as much distance between herself and the imagined creature as quickly as possible, put her head down and hope for the best. Their chances of finding him faded like grains of sand slipping through her fingers. In the end, they accepted that and gave up looking. It was well into the early hours of the morning, and all Annja wanted to do was sleep.

All the while Lars had been shooting, getting a couple of hours' worth of material in the can.

"Get anything worthwhile?" she asked as he packed his camera back away in the flight case.

"More than enough," the cameraman said. "I'll put it together as a montage for you do to a voice-over."

"Now all we've got to do is find a way to actually link the story to the golem."

"Difficult given that one of our witnesses is dead and the other is in the wind."

"That's why they pay me the big bucks," Annja said. "Anyway, it's time to head back to the hotel. There's nothing more we can do tonight."

"I don't know about you, but I wouldn't mind a beer before hitting the sack," Lars said. Turek took little persuading.

Annja checked her watch. It was past three in the morning, but there were still plenty of clubs with their neon signs sizzling. "Not for me. I need my beauty sleep," she said, offering a smile. "I'll catch up with you guys tomorrow. No hangovers."

"We can't let you walk back to your hotel on your own. I'll call you a cab."

"No need," Annja said. "I'll be fine."

"In a strange city with a killer on the loose?" Turek shook his head. "Are you crazy? There's no way we can let you do that."

"Very chivalrous, but you're not actually *letting* me do anything," she said. "Besides, the one thing that's been pretty well established is that our killer isn't interested in tourists. He's hunting people who are sleeping on the street. Now look at me and tell me how I fit the profile."

"You don't," Lars agreed.

"Very observant. Now run along and have some fun." She felt like a mom sending her kids off to school.

"Just one?"

"Which will lead to two, then three. No, it's fine. But thanks."

She was long gone before they'd even reached the steps leading up to the black doors of the bar that Turek had chosen.

The streets were much quieter than when she had left the hotel earlier in the evening. There was no traffic along the main road for one thing. The moon was full and high in a sky that was devoid of clouds. Annja enjoyed the stillness of the cool air as she walked. The closer she came to the hotel, the quieter the streets became. There was no late-night revelry now, just the dim background noise of a city asleep.

Without even thinking about it, Annja had brought herself back to the alleyway where the witness had been murdered. The nearest streetlight wasn't working, which meant that an entire stretch of the street was illuminated only by moonlight. The shadows along the sides of the street were thick. There was no way of knowing what might be lurking in them. She hurried on, glancing left and right, into the nooks and crannies of the alleyways and narrow gaps between buildings.

Annja considered crossing to the other side of the road. It was purely psychological; the danger wouldn't have been any less whichever side of the street she

walked on, but on this side she knew a man had lost
his life and her footsteps were taking her closer to that
dark stain. She wasn't frightened. That wasn't it. If anything came out of the shadows, she was more than able
to deal with it. Peering deeper into the darkness, she
flexed her fingers. Without thinking about it, she began
to reach into the otherwhere, her fingers closing on the
familiar grip of Saint Joan's blade. Her blade.

Annja felt the sword start to gain weight and substance as she drew it into the here and now, pulling it
into existence.

Her breath caught in her throat, the silvery glow
of the materializing weapon casting a very peculiar
gleam across her features. She held it there, half in this
world, half not, for a moment before pushing it back to
its resting place.

She didn't need the weapon, but it was there, an ever-
present in her life, only an arm's length away. She savored the reassurance of it being so close, so easy to
summon into existence.

A faint gust of breeze caused the police tape to flut-
ter at the opening to the alleyway. The ripple of sound
startled her for a moment. But the air was still, she
thought. She hadn't felt it on her skin. What caused the
breeze? What made the police tape shift?

She peered into the darkness, her mind working
double-time to convince her gut instinct that it was
nothing more than her imagination playing tricks on her.

There was nothing in there.

She turned away and continued walking to her hotel,
her footsteps echoing on the cobblestones, telling herself that she was all alone, there was no one there, nothing to chase. The logical part of her brain knew that it

was nothing, a stray dog, maybe, or a cat. There was no way one of the city's homeless would have clambered into the dead man's bed so quickly, was there?

Her footsteps seemed louder somehow, and continued to grow louder the faster she walked. She could hear her heartbeat creating a strange syncopated rhythm.

Annja counted as she walked, refusing to look back.

Five, six, seven, breathe.

Do not jump at shadows.

Just get inside, go to bed, sleep. You're tired. It's been a long day. Too long. You're letting your imagination run away with you.

Then she heard the scream, and she knew she wasn't imagining anything.

Without a second of hesitation Annja turned and started to run toward the source of the sound. The screaming started again. It was a man.

Annja reached out into the otherwhere, knowing she was too late to save him because the screaming stopped.

9

Annja didn't break her stride as the great sword slipped out of the otherwhere, solid in her hand.

Her heart hammered, but it was through excitement not fear.

She always felt that thrill when the sword was in her hand. Giant. Powerful. Like a creature out of legend. A colossus.

She breathed in sharply, listening for the sound of movement, then plunged into the alleyway, her eyes struggling to adjust to the change of light. Three steps deeper into the darkness and everything around her exploded with sound and movement that seemed somehow to come from everywhere at once. She strained to see, to make out any darker shapes within the pitch-black alleyway, but it was impossible.

Another sudden flurry of movement.

Annja braced herself, ready for impact, expecting whoever had killed the man she'd just heard die come charging at her.

But still nothing.

Another two steps and her foot caught against something on the ground.

The corpse.

She didn't look down.

The next sound came from overhead.

A scrape of nails?

She glanced up, finally making out a darker smear within the darkness up there, picked out against the handful of stars twinkling beyond it. The shape clung motionless to the brickwork. Her first thought was that the witnesses had been right about one thing—the thing could climb up walls—so did that mean they were right about the rest?

She shook her head.

She couldn't climb after him with the sword in her hand, so she slipped it easily back into the ether and reached up, feeling around the bare brick for so much as a fingerhold—anything that would mean she could follow the killer up the side of the building. She positioned herself directly under the silhouette, feeling for gouges in the brickwork. Her fingertips found fresh holes in the masonry. They were big enough for her fingers to easily sink in beyond the distal phalange, providing the perfect holds for climbing. She moved quickly, hauling herself up off the ground.

The shape above her began to move, sensing her coming after it.

Brickwork crumbled, showering down into Annja's eyes as she climbed. No matter how quickly she moved, reaching from one handhold and fumbling for the next, the killer was faster, surer. She blinked the dust away and reached up again, her questing fingers finding the edge of a brick that offered enough purchase to lever herself up another few precious inches.

The walls were just too far apart to be able to brace herself against them both to work her way up as though climbing a chimney, but conversely it was too cramped to try to use the sword to dig into the mortar and make fresh holes where she needed them.

The handholds, she quickly realized, were uncomfortably spaced for her ascent, suggesting whoever had made them was considerably taller than her, or at least had a much longer reach.

That, too, supported the witnesses' descriptions of the giant brute.

Her shoes weren't really designed for free climbing.

There had to be a better way of getting onto the roof because she wasn't going to catch him this way.

The shadowy figure was already disappearing over the gables and onto the roof, out of sight.

She realized she wasn't going to be able to get up there quickly enough to see where the killer went. It just wasn't happening, no matter how athletic she was. She couldn't defy the laws of gravity.

She dropped back to the ground, her foot missing the body by mere inches. Annja knelt, checking for a pulse that wasn't there. There was absolutely nothing she could do for the killer's latest victim. There were no threads of life, no shreds of hope. She pushed back up to her feet, trying to judge the way the killer had run and carve out a path down below.

She ran out into the main street, scanning the rooftops for shadow or silhouette, anything that might betray movement.

Nothing.

It was difficult to get any kind of line of sight because so many of the old buildings were huddled close together. That also meant it would be easy for the killer to leap from one to the next if he was athletic. It wasn't just down to agility; someone of his size and shape might not be as fast as she was, but it was impossible to track him from the street.

She scanned the street quickly, looking for a fire escape or something that would offer roof access, but this wasn't New York where every building had iron stairs bolted onto the facade. These buildings were old, three hundred, four hundred, even five hundred years old in some cases. Fire-safety regulations were obviously different when they'd been constructed, and now it was all about preserving the beauty of the original design.

They still needed gutters, though, and not cheap plastic modern drainpipes, either—good old-fashioned cast-iron drainpipes.

Annja found one that looked sound, tested it, then took a few steps back. She lowered her head, took a single breath, then launched herself up the wall, making a grab for the drainpipe high above the second bracket fixing it to the brickwork.

It groaned for a moment, threatening to pull away from the wall, but it held.

Annja pulled herself up, hand over hand, the muscles in her arms straining with every scrabbled step, but she rose much faster than she could have done trying to follow the killer using the almost-invisible handholds in the wall. It took less than a minute for her to reach the rain gutter below the roof. How it overhung the street like the brim of a hat made it impossible for her to just haul herself up and over the top of it.

Concrete and plaster crumbled under her weight, spilling to the ground below like tears weeping into the silence of the night.

It wasn't going to hold much longer, she knew.

Annja braced her feet, gripping the pipe with one hand, and reached up for the iron rain gutter. The bracket holding it began to buckle under her weight. Committed now, she had no choice but to go all-in, and reached up with her other hand. She squatted, bouncing once, twice, three times, and launched herself into a handstand high above the city streets, hanging there upside down for half a second. She then pushed off with her hands and flipped into a somersault and came down on her feet, the red clay tiles cracking under the unexpected impact. She moved quickly away from the edge as the bracket gave way and the length of iron drainpipe fell thirty feet back to the ground.

Moonlight illuminated the rooftops. Annja scanned the horizon, looking for the killer. Her hotel was the only taller building in the vicinity. Silver light shimmered on the ridged tiles. Too late. She'd wasted too much time getting up there. The killer was gone. She turned in a full circle, desperately trying to make out any sign of movement, any uneven shape along the line of rooftops, but there was nothing.

She'd misjudged the killer again.

He was long gone.

She'd had him in her reach only for him to slip through her fingers.

She crouched low, frustration threatening to bubble over inside her. He couldn't have gone far. It was impossible. The night was even quieter up there. She could barely hear the strains of music from the bars and clubs, no more than a distant susurrus like the wind. She was listening for a very particular sound: footsteps, or more accurately, the grating of clay with weight being put on the tiles, then removed as the killer fled.

Nothing.

It was pointless to blindly walk over rooftops without some sort of clue as to which direction the killer had taken.

He could, she realized sickly, have escaped a few moments after climbing, disappearing through a fire door, or down the side of another building. There was absolutely nothing to say he'd run across the rooftops, and the longer she stood there scanning the rooftops, the surer she became that he hadn't.

She was about to give up and make her way back down when the scrape of a tile sliding from a roof and falling, followed by the almost delicate smash on the ground below, had her moving again quickly, as sure-footed as a cat across the cold tiled roof toward the source of the sound.

A shape rose from the skyline and started moving.

The killer was more than two hundred yards away. He'd managed to get much farther away than she'd expected. She had no idea how many buildings were between them or how many streets she'd have to traverse, but at least she knew which direction she needed to go.

Another tile crashed.

He was moving quickly, without any kind of care for his safety, or for stealth.

Annja started the chase.

She moved faster than the lumbering shadow, light on her feet, barely seeming to rest on top of the centuries-old tiles as she moved quickly across the rooftop.

The gap between them closed quickly.

Annja ghosted across the rooftop, but as her foot came down, inches from the edge an instant before she jumped, the tile slipped. The clay tile grated across the surface of the final tile, then spun away into darkness. Then she was in the air and it was shattering below her. She came down on the other side hard, falling forward. Her fingertips dragged across the tiles as she stumbled away from the edge.

A light came on in one of the windows. A second later the window was thrown open and a shout filled the air. The anger in it was universal, even if the words weren't. She could only assume the speaker was demanding to know what was going on.

The killer was still several rooftops away, moving with an almost-simian gait, knuckles seeming to drag across the tiles. He didn't slow for so much as a heartbeat, launching himself from one roof to another, and charging off again across the flat surface, putting more distance between them.

Watching him go, Annja realized that his bulk should have inflicted far more damage on the roof than it appeared to be doing. There was nothing graceful about his movement, but he kept on moving, not once looking back.

Annja launched herself in pursuit of the lumbering figure again, but the tiles offered little purchase and she felt herself slipping and sliding as she advanced. She crossed the middle of the roof, looking up to see the killer outlined by the moon. Her breath caught in her throat. He was huge. She recalled the illusion that Jan Turek's coats wove around him, but this was different. The killer wasn't padded with a dozen coats for warmth.

She misjudged the next leap, too focused on the man in front of her, putting her foot down awkwardly as she pushed off.

She felt herself falling, knowing she didn't have the

height or momentum to stick the landing on the other side, having horribly misjudged the width of the alleyway beneath her. It was a long way down. Too long. She arced her back, arms and legs pinwheeling to try to stretch a few more precious inches out of the leap.

It was all about nerve now.

Annja reached out for the rain gutter as she fell, knowing it was her only hope.

Rough metal dug into the palm of her hand as she tried to support her weight and reach up with her other hand. She kicked out with her feet, scrabbling desperately for purchase on the smooth wall as the rain gutter failed. The brackets groaned, the iron itself buckling slowly as the entire thing pulled away from the brickwork. The old mortar couldn't hold her weight.

There was a moment, the long, lonely silence between heartbeats, when it held and then the whole assembly began to fall away in slow motion.

Annja glanced around frantically, desperately hoping to find something she could use to slow her fall. Her gaze raced over the iron braces running through the center of the building to prevent the ancient walls from pulling themselves apart. No good. She looked across the line of the roof to other anchor points that were out of reach. No good. Then she glanced at the French balcony ten feet below her feet, desperately trying to work out any possible combination of gymnastics and contortions that might offer up a chance of grabbing hold of one of the elaborately filigreed bars before the ground came rushing up to meet her. She looked all the way down to the ground, where a pile of cardboard boxes lay invitingly, promising a soft landing that would be anything but. The image of her broken body lying amid the crumpled cardboard flashed across her mind. No good.

The metal pipe continued its relentless collapse, peeling farther and farther away from the safety of the wall.

Annja scrambled her feet against the concrete, desperately trying to change the angle of descent, when the pipe lurched beneath her, two anchor points pulling away at once. She had no choice but to go with it, pushing herself back toward the building she had launched herself from.

The change of angles brought new pressure points to bear on the iron. It couldn't hold, shearing away into dozens of fractured pieces.

Annja held her nerve, waiting for the last possible second to reach for the French balcony.

Her fingertips snagged the metal bar for a second, but as she tried to close her fist around it, an iron leaf stabbed deeply into her palm and pain exploded in her hand. She recoiled, and by then it was too late.

The world above her was filled with stars.

And then it wasn't.

10

Roux had been on edge as soon as he'd hung up on Annja.

The old man knew her too well. He knew that by saying don't go out she was going to go out. Annja wasn't the kind of woman you could tell what to do. He'd known she was going to dive head-on into the investigation the moment she'd called simply because there was something strange going on. It didn't matter that she didn't know what it was. That only ensured she'd chase down every possibility until she did know.

He wasn't worried about her well-being; she was more than capable of dealing with the threat gripping the city of Prague.

That was not the issue.

The issue was that he knew who the killer was.

Or rather, what.

And it was his job to take care of it, not hers.

Maybe once upon a time, like in the fairy tales, he could and should have taken care of it, but he'd screwed up and the opportunity passed. How many people had died because of his mistake? More than the handful of most recent victims, that was for sure. That wasn't even the tip of the iceberg. This time he was going to have to take care of it, no matter the cost to him, even if that cost was his life, which he suspected it would be. He'd always known there would come a time he'd have to face the reality.

Even the great Roux couldn't expect to live forever.

But maybe there was another explanation?

Just because he saw patterns within the killings and could connect dots no one else seemed to see didn't have to mean he was right. Garin being there, for instance. Was he involved? It was inconceivable that his appearance in Prague was a coincidence. The universe and Garin Braden didn't function that way. Garin had chosen this time to track Annja down for a reason. But what might that reason be?

The flight seemed to take forever despite being a short-haul trip, and it wasn't helped by the fact it had taken hours to tie up the few loose ends he thought would take minutes. In the air he'd put out a couple of calls of his own to people to see if they could shed any extra light on what was happening in Prague. There was nothing in those conversations to make him doubt his gut instinct. He looked down at the world through the window, the lights of the city looking like ley lines directing power all across the surface of the Earth. It was quite beautiful, but he didn't have the time for beauty. The miles weren't passing fast enough.

There would be another death tonight. He knew that. It was part of a pattern that went back centuries now. In daylight it would be impossible to track the killer. It moved only at night, using daylight hours to recuperate, falling into an almost-hibernation state. It was how the monster had always worked. And yes, that was the word he chose to use, not killer, not beast, not man. Monster.

The time passed agonizingly slowly.

There was nothing he could do but think as the plane made its way toward its destination, beginning its descent. He needed to devise a suitable plan, something that would deal with the problem once and for all. The problem was, the only thing he could think of that stood a chance of working was no more sophisticated than scouring the streets. London would have been better, some kind of city with the level of surveillance cameras that covered every rooftop and every angle, not Prague, which was almost backward when it came to that kind of security. He was going to have to rely on luck, and he hated relying on luck.

Unless, of course, Garin held an ace up his sleeve. He wouldn't put anything past the man.

Morning was already fast approaching as he saw the runway lights of the Prague airport inviting the plane to touch down.

By the time the aircraft had landed and Roux had dealt with the officious representatives of customs and border control and picked up a rental car, the sun would be rising. Once that happened he'd be helpless for twelve hours or so, the killer holed up in his den, safe from his vengeance.

Roux knew he was going to need to get his hands on every last shred of evidence the cops had gathered, assuming they'd gathered anything. Given the nature of the victims, he didn't harbor high hopes. He had tricked his way into more than one police station before, and the various degrees of disinterest to ineptitude never ceased to amaze him when it came to tracking down what seemed bizarre or unusual.

Why should this time be any different?

Who out there was remotely prepared for the possibility of someone like Roux himself even existing? Let alone anything beyond that? The real monsters of the world? Not a prayer.

11

"Well, good morning, beautiful," a voice said through the fog of her mind.

The light hurt as Annja opened her eyes.

She was lost.

This wasn't the alleyway.

And she hurt. Everywhere. She had aches in places she didn't know existed. She tried to move, but couldn't. Not at first. A searing stab of pain lanced up under her shoulder blade, causing her face to twist in agony. It took a second or two for the pain to subside. When it finally did, she asked, "Where am I?"

"Hospital," the voice said. "You're not dead, if that's what you're wondering. I'm not Saint Peter come to check you off my list, to see if you've been naughty or nice."

Garin.

He sat in the chair beside her with a brown paper bag resting in his lap. The brown skeletal stems were all that remained of the grapes as he popped the last one into his mouth.

"How…?" she started to ask, but then remembered the stars as she fell to the ground.

"To be honest, everyone here is hoping that you'll be

able to tell them. It seems that you were found sprawled on a pile of boxes in someone's backyard. I assume you haven't taken to sleeping on the street, but I will admit, I have absolutely no idea how you managed to get there, or how you managed to sustain your injuries. Looking at the state you're in—there are some really tasty bruises on your back for a start—I'd say you had a lucky escape."

She couldn't argue with that.

"So, I'm thinking you fell from the roof, and yet managed miraculously to not break a single bone. The docs seem to think that it's some kind of miracle. I just figure its par for the course with you." He offered a wry smile.

"How did you know I was here?" Annja asked. She knew better than to try to ease herself up in the bed.

"Do you really need to ask?" Garin made a telephone out of his thumb and little finger and held it up to his ear. "I'd like to pretend I tracked you down through cunning and brainpower, triangulating the signal, pinpointing it off various cell towers, then calling in a favor with the local law enforcement, but when you didn't come down for breakfast I tried your cell phone. The nurses did the rest. It's almost as if fate's playing a hand, isn't it? I arrive, you suddenly need me."

"I'm not sure I'd go so far as to blame fate. Stupidity, maybe, Czech plumbers, more like," she said, but the pain in her head left her feeling pitiful. She'd screwed up big-time, but she was still in one piece, and to be honest she was glad he was there.

"So, are you going to tell me what you were doing up on that roof?" Garin asked, looking disappointedly down at the empty bag of grapes. He shrugged, crushed the bag and tossed it into the trash can beside the bed. "I take it you haven't taken up parkour?"

Annja shook her head and regretted it an instant later.

She squeezed her eyes shut, trying to isolate the pain and push it away into some convenient nerveless quadrant of her body where she couldn't feel it. It didn't help in the slightest.

Her eyes were still closed when she sensed the presence of someone else standing at her bedside.

"Can you tell me where it hurts?" the voice asked. It was a woman's voice, soft and tender and speaking in English.

"Everywhere," Annja answered, not joking. She opened her eyes, needing one hand to shield them from the light.

"With good reason," the nurse said. "The human body isn't designed to bounce. It's a fundamental flaw in the design process, if you ask me."

"You speak English," Annja said.

"Nope, you're just suffering a really bad case of concussion," Garin said.

The woman laughed.

"Don't flirt with my doctor," Annja grumbled, earning another laugh from the woman.

"They called me off another ward when they realized you were a tourist. Then your rather charming friend appeared."

"He's not charming. He's a very bad man. You really don't want to fall for it, believe me," she replied, and that was the biggest understatement she could have offered.

"The handsome ones always are," the doctor said.

"Hey, I am here, you know, and contrary to popular opinion, I do have feelings."

The doctor offered Garin a lopsided grin, before she leaned in and whispered conspiratorially, "So, he's single?"

That earned a laugh from Annja.

"I'm serious. In this place, I don't get to meet too many complications that look like he does."

"Maybe I should leave?" Garin offered. "I'm beginning to feel like a side of beef in a butcher's window."

"That might be a good idea," the doctor said.

"I'll go and grab a coffee. I'll just be down the corridor if you need me."

"And if we don't, you'll still be just down the corridor, right?"

"Right," Garin said. "I'll be back later. Don't go anywhere without me."

The doctor waited until Garin was out of earshot before saying anything else.

"You've got yourself a looker there."

"Oh, I haven't got him at all, and I'm not sure I'd want him." Annja chuckled, correcting the doctor's assumption. "You don't want him, either, trust me. He's much more trouble than he's worth."

"Ah, but he's so pretty." The doctor grinned. "I could make an exception for that pretty face."

Annja laughed and wished that she hadn't. The doctor offered her a small plastic cup with a couple of painkillers inside, and then handed her a glass of water. "They should help. I don't want to give you anything stronger if we can avoid it."

"Thanks," Annja said as she threw the first of the pills back. The water on the back of her throat made her feel a little more alive. She offered the glass for a refill when she had drained it.

"Better?" the doctor asked when she'd taken the second pill. Annja put the empty glass on the nightstand.

"How long before I'm up and moving again?"

"You took quite a battering."

"But nothing broken? No internal injuries?"

"You're an incredibly lucky woman. You're going to feel pretty sore for a few days, but apart from a few cuts and some pretty impressive bruises, you don't appear to have done any lasting damage."

"So I can leave?"

"I'd rather you didn't, to be honest. But I've got to do my rounds. I'll be back in an hour or so. If you can get yourself out of bed and make it to the bathroom and back before I do, we can talk about it. No guarantees, though."

The doctor left her on her own, with Annja thinking that there were no guarantees in life, anyway. She was already starting to feel better, most likely because of the heightened metabolic rate and increased healing properties of her own flesh and blood ever since she'd bonded with Saint Joan's sword. She wasn't like other women. What would break them barely served to bend her, and where her spine should have been shattered, all she had to show for it was a blue-black stain at the base of her back. Gritting her teeth, Annja pushed against the blankets, and swung her legs around, knowing that if she couldn't get out of bed she wasn't getting out of this place.

There was no way she was staying in here a minute longer than she needed to.

Annja called to Garin, pitching her voice just loud enough for it to bring him back to the door. He poked his head inside. "You up for busting me out of here, big guy?"

"I thought you'd never ask," he said. "And you realize by doing so I'm blowing any chance of getting together with the lovely Sam."

"Sam?"

"Dr. Sammica." He nodded down the corridor.

"I guess it's not love, then."

"It very rarely is, Annja. It very rarely is."

She planted both feet on the floor and tried to stand. It didn't go well.

Garin caught her, and eased her back down onto the mattress. "Maybe we'll try the great escape in a few minutes, eh?"

"Maybe five," she agreed.

12

But five turned into ten, then turned into twenty.

By the time she finally made it out of the bed and onto two very unsteady feet, her cell phone was ringing. The noise earned her a withering look of disapproval from one of the nurses who happened to be passing her door, followed by a muttered instruction she could not understand.

Sometimes there were advantages in being a stranger in a strange land.

It was Roux.

"Where are you?" he asked without preamble.

"The hospital," she said.

That didn't faze him. He didn't ask what was wrong or what had happened. He simply asked, "Which one?"

"I'm not sure."

"Never mind. I'll find it," he said. "Don't go anywhere until I get there. This time I'm serious. Wait there."

She was about to reassure him that she wouldn't leave when the doctor returned trailing a gaggle of students like a line of ducklings. She read the notes that hung from the metal frame at the bottom of Annja's bed.

"Got to go," she said before she realized that Roux had already hung up.

She waited while the doctor talked rapidly, not in English this time, offering her students the opportunity to take a look at the notes. Annja saw the look of surprise cross a couple of faces as they discovered the cause of her injuries—or lack of injuries—and the double take as they checked her notes again trying to understand how it could possibly be the case.

The doctor smiled her way. "So, how you are feeling now?"

"Stiff and sore, and a headache that feels like a hangover without all the fun of the night before, but other than that, still in one piece," Annja said, earning another of those lopsided smiles from the doctor. Her examination was cursory at best. Annja was banking on the fact they'd want to discharge her to free up the bed for someone else.

"I'd really like to run another scan to make sure there's no internal bleeding, but if that's clear I can't see any reason to keep you in here any longer than necessary."

"Wind me up and point me in the right direction," Annja said.

"Don't worry, we'll have a nurse come by to bring you down to radiology in an hour, then if it looks fine, you're good to go."

ANNJA WAS ALREADY dressed and waiting for her prescription painkillers by the time Roux arrived. He looked harried.

She didn't expect to need the pills once she wrapped her hand around the sword's hilt again and got the blood flowing through her muscles.

"I thought I told you to stay in your hotel," he said.

"And you knew I wouldn't," she replied, not moving from the chair.

"Touché." The old man shook his head. "Hoisted on my own petard."

"Which sounds incredibly painful," Garin said from the doorway.

Roux looked Annja up and down, taking in the bruising. "But, like it or not, if you had done what I said, you wouldn't be in here now, would you?"

"You're not my father," she said.

"Or even her grandfather," Garin offered helpfully.

Yes, he had been her teacher, her trainer, her mentor, even her friend, who she could turn to when she was in trouble, as if they were family.

That ended the objections. The hurt in his eyes was plain to see. Annja regretted the biting comment, but she didn't apologize.

"So what happened?"

Annja filled them in on everything that had happened to her the night before, including Turek's assertions about the first body she'd found being a witness to a previous murder, and how she'd stumbled across another body in the same alleyway. She described the witness reports kept out of the papers, and why Turek believed the golem was hunting. Finally she explained how she'd gone in pursuit of the killer across the rooftops, matching some if not all of the eyewitness reports with her own eyes, but how at last the roof had betrayed her and she'd lost her footing.

"Thirty feet is a long way down," Roux observed.

"Hey, at least she found something nice and soft to break her fall," Garin said.

"If I'd have had a choice, I wouldn't have fallen at

all," Annja said. She spotted the doctor coming up behind Garin. She had a clear plastic bag in her hand. "Your meds," the doctor said as Garin moved aside. And to Garin, "My number." She handed him her card. Garin pocketed it with a grin.

"I'll make sure I give you a call."

"Can we get out of here now?" Roux asked.

"She's free to go."

"Excellent. Up you get, then."

Roux turned to Garin. "Any chance you could make yourself scarce? I was hoping to have a little time with Annja alone."

"I can take a hint," Garin said, showing no sign of taking offence at the old man's directness. He turned to the doctor. "So, what time are you due to take a break? A girl's gotta eat, after all."

Dr. Sammica inclined her head slightly, a gesture that was deliberately flirtatious as she bit down on her lower lip. "My shift doesn't finish for another three hours."

"Bend a few rules," Garin said, linking his arm with hers and steering her toward the door.

"Thanks, Garin," Annja said, raising the coffee cup in salute. "We'll catch up with you later."

"Sure," he said, giving her a wink, and then he was gone.

"That was a little rude, don't you think?" Annja asked once he was out of earshot.

"Not here," Roux said, then as an afterthought, "Hospital food is generally foul. I take it you haven't eaten?"

From somewhere down the corridor she heard the unmistakable sound of a cart heading in their direction, and pointed toward the door. "Sounds like room service."

"Then for heaven's sake, let's get out of here before they force you to eat it. Back to the hotel, I think. I'm going to need you to tell me *everything*. Don't leave a thing out, even stuff you think is inconsequential."

She nodded.

"And then I'm going to need you to tell me everything you've told Garin."

"I haven't told him anything, but I don't get it. Why are you trying so hard to keep him at arm's length?"

He picked up her jacket. "Like I said, not here."

13

Moving, even gingerly, helped Annja's aches and pains. Waking up in the hospital bed had shaken her up, but it was a thing of the past now. She wasn't about to lounge around and moan about the aches and pains even if she didn't exactly feel like slipping on her running shoes and hitting the streets. She was very much fit for the fight.

They walked through the restaurant. The breakfast service had been cleared away, and dinner was still hours away from being ready, but they managed to get someone to put together a tray for them in Annja's room when Roux explained, in fluent Czech, that she'd been in the hospital and needed a little TLC.

Room service arrived five minutes later, along with a bowl of fruit and a bouquet of flowers wishing Miss Creed a speedy recovery.

"How about now? Just us and these four walls. Is that secret enough for you to tell me what it is that's gotten under your skin?" Annja said. "Seriously, what is it with you and Garin and this place?"

Roux scratched at his beard, his hand covering his mouth. Always a sign of a liar, Annja thought, wondering what half-truth her friend was concocting for her benefit this time. "I… It's difficult to know where to begin exactly. Why don't you tell me what's been going on, then it'll be my turn."

"All right." In quick fashion, she relayed the various important facts that she'd managed to collect so far. "Now, what's your story? And start at the beginning."

"No story ever truly begins, Annja. There are dozens of points in the unwinding of history where we could look at something and say, 'Here, at this point in time, this is where it all started,' but even then there are links that we're not party to, things that influenced us getting to that point."

"Very poetic, Roux, but you know what I mean, just spit it out."

The old man drew a deep breath, then shrugged as though defeated. "Let me ask you a question. Do you trust Garin?"

"What?"

"After everything we've been through, after all the times we've seen him act out of self-interest, every betrayal of trust, do you *trust* Garin? It's a simple enough question, Annja. Yes or no?"

Annja paused. Not so long ago the answer would have been a straight no, no need to even think about it. Before that it would have been a resounding yes, again with no need to contemplate any other response. But now? Now things were not so clear-cut. "I trust Garin to always do what is in his best interests. But I also know that he has come through when I needed his help." Which was absolutely true. And more often than not their interests intersected. "How does that sound?"

"It sounds like a starting point."

"Okay, then, story time," Annja said, pouring them

both a cup of coffee so thick she thought she might be able to stand the spoon in it. She put the French press on the tray. The dregs of coffee grounds swam around the bottom.

Roux nodded. "The most obvious admission is that this is not the first time this killer has struck. Far from it. It has been hidden for a long time, yes, dormant like a virus, but there inside the body of the city, festering away. I thought that it had been defeated, trapped where it could never again harm people. I was wrong."

"You need to be very precise, Roux. Are you telling me you know who the killer is?" So many questions were tumbling through her mind. She fixed on the most obvious one. "You think Garin is involved, don't you?"

"Honestly, I am not sure what I think. But if I am right about the killer, your close encounter last night was not with a man. Or at least not a normal one. It is so much more than a man, but so much less than one, too. It will not fall victim to old age or illness. I don't believe it will ever naturally die, not in the way that we understand death. It does not need food or drink to sustain it, neither does it crave the company of others. It has been incarcerated for many, many years. Only two people knew the location of its prison. I am one of them."

"And Garin is the other," Annja finished for him, understanding, even if what he was saying was instinctively impossible, the man himself was an impossibility. If Roux said that the killer was inhuman, then who was she to argue, especially given what she had witnessed on the rooftop?

"He was with me, yes."

"Is it possible someone could have stumbled over

this thing by accident, setting it free without knowing what they were doing?"

Roux shook his head. "It has been imprisoned on and off since the eighteen hundreds, finally captured and kept as such from the last days of the Second World War."

"Could it have escaped on its own again?" She was thinking on her feet. Just because something had been safe and secure seventy years ago didn't mean that it would still be today.

"Even if Garin knows where it is, that doesn't mean he was the one who has released it. That's purely circumstantial. And worst case, even if he did, what's to say he did it on purpose?"

Roux fell silent, mulling over the possibilities. The benefit of the doubt lasted no more than three seconds, then he was shaking his head. "There's only one way to be sure we are facing what I think we are, and that's to go to its prison and see for myself."

"You're not going without me," Annja said.

"You need to rest."

"No, I don't. I need to find whatever I was chasing last night. Now, you know me, old man. You know that if you try to go without me all that will happen is that I'll follow you."

It was true, she would, and he knew it.

"Then rest. We can leave when you are stronger."

"So you can sneak off on your own while I'm asleep?"

"So, you don't trust me, either?"

"It's not about trust."

"No?"

"Let's just say that sometimes you think you know what's better for me than I do."

"Well, I have lived a lot longer," the old man observed.

"Age doesn't bring wisdom with it." Annja smiled. "Look at Garin."

"Humor me. At least sit long enough for me to tell you the story of our killer and how our paths first crossed. It is a long story. And, I think, one that will appeal to you."

"You still haven't told me *what* it is we're up against."

"All in good time. I can tell you that, if I am right, no one's life is in danger for the moment. It will be resting, recharging itself before it ventures forth again. It may not even be out on the streets of the city again tonight, or tomorrow, maybe not for a week."

"So we have time?"

"We do, but it will kill again. That is why I must stop it."

"We," Annja corrected him.

"Hmm," Roux said noncommittedly. "I am not sure you will be fit for a fight before night falls. When I go up against this thing, I will not be able to protect you at the same time. It is all or nothing."

"You won't have to protect me," Annja said.

There was no way that she was going to let the old man sideline her. An immortal killer? This was why Saint Joan had granted Annja her incredible inheritance. Hers was not to walk away. Never. She could feel the pull of the blade from the otherwhere. Its siren call sang through her blood, stronger than she could remember feeling it in years. Perhaps it was her weakness that gave it such strength, her need? Even though they weren't connected, Annja could feel it pulsing through her veins, and felt the irresistible urge to draw it, to grasp the hilt and stretch and swing over and over until her muscles remembered what they needed to do to truly live and the pain faded.

"Are you all right?" Roux asked, leaning forward intently. "You look…different."

"Just a twinge," she lied. "Tell me a story, Grandpa." Annja grinned, trying to shake off the siren song of the sword, but it just wouldn't be silenced. It rang out like the tolling of a bell inside her mind.

"It was a dark and stormy night…"

"No, seriously."

"It was."

14

That summer had been unseasonably cold.

June was full of storms. The houses in the village of Cologny seemed to huddle together for warmth, fighting the elements. One great house stood apart from the homes of the people who lived there all year-round, scraping a living however they could. Although much of the house felt cold and damp, the insidious chill having crept into the very fabric of the walls, the Villa Belle Rive had great logs snapping and crackling in the grates of the open fire as they burned, warming the group of people gathered in the room.

The party was garnering attention from the locals. Several ventured forth from the elegant houses around Lake Geneva in the hopes of catching a glimpse of the infamous Lord Byron. Scandal followed him wherever he went, and with good reason. He truly was a fellow who had learned to suck the marrow out of life, draining every ounce of pleasure from the world as he walked through it. Now that he was separated from his wife amid rumors of an affair with his half sister, life in England had become intolerable. How much truth there was in the rumors Roux had no idea, but the appeal of acting as a servant to the household had proved too fascinating an opportunity to refuse. There were people who lived so large even someone like Roux was drawn like a moth to their bright flame. Byron was one of those compelling souls. Garin had been keen to move on, but a woman stole his heart as was ever the case with the feckless boy. In this instance it was the cook Byron had employed.

Roux and Garin had found themselves in Russia when Napoleon had marched on Moscow in 1812. Roux had watched the flames rise from the great city threatening to purge it from the face of the Earth as the retreating Russians set fire to every building, rather than let it fall into the hands of the ruthless French. It had taken them three years to make their way across Europe until they finally reached the first peaks of Switzerland. By then all Roux wanted to do was to find somewhere to settle for a while, to be done with wandering.

The house had presented itself.

At first the party had consisted of just two men: Byron and his physician, John Polidori. Roux had found them both to be odious little men of little worth. They were joined partway through the summer by the poet Shelley and his young bride-to-be, Mary. They had brought with her Mary's stepsister, Claire, who pursued Byron with as much fervor as the doctor, though for very different reasons. Or perhaps not so different, after all… There was a history between them, and Roux enjoyed watching the machinations as they fought for the poet's affection like it was worth winning.

No one seemed to notice Roux as he moved around in the background. He was only a servant, after all, barely worth their attention.

Roux rather enjoyed the anonymity and did his best to preserve it.

In the hours when they languished, half in sleep usually, he had even risked reading one of their diaries, thumbing quickly through the pages to be sure that neither he, Garin nor the cook were ever mentioned. It was as if the young men and women enjoying their decadent summer by the lake were running the household without any assistance. All they seemed to be concerned about was ensuring there was a never-ending supply of wine and brandy, not where it actually came from or how it got to the house. Such trifles were irrelevant to their way of thinking.

The rain came almost every day, robbing them of the summer they had expected.

Despite the size of the great house, it quickly became stiflingly claustrophobic. More than once the poet lamented that the very walls were closing in on them with every passing hour. He postured and preened, a goblet never far from his hand. He reclined on the arms of the great upholstery, holding forth on this virtue or that sin, positing the impossibility of immortality and the inevitability of the end. Always that, always obsessed with the end. That there was nothing beyond the now. The five of them bickered, deliberately launching barbs that would sting and prick and linger. On the third night one of them came up with a notion that should keep them amused.

"We should each create our own ghost story," Byron said. "A story that will chill the very bones of our audience. And when we are finished we must read our creations to the others."

"We shall need an arbiter, shall we not? Someone

to decide which is the best and most chilling?" Polidori noted.

"We shall let Roux decide," Mary proclaimed.

"It's a competition?" Claire clapped. "But who is Roux?"

Roux said nothing. Three days and only one of them even knew his name.

He waited for the young Mary to point him out.

She was aware of the working of the household—the only one of her group who did. Roux suspected that she even knew about Garin and the cook stealing every moment they could to spend alone in one of the unoccupied rooms. Roux inclined his head slightly, and smiled in acknowledgment.

"As you wish," he said.

"In that case," Byron grinned ruefully and said, "we are all agreed. Now, I believe your first duty—and most vital task—as judge of this great literary competition is to supply us with wine."

The declaration was enough to bring a cheer from Polidori and a round of applause that echoed to the high ceilings of the room. To be brutally honest, Roux wanted no part of their great ideas, but he was more than happy to play along with them while it suited him. He fetched enough wine from the cellar to see them through the night, then left them to their amusements.

The night was falling and with it the rage of the storm increased.

Maybe they would work on their stories, Roux thought, or perhaps more likely they would drink and talk until the morning or unconsciousness, whichever came first.

There was no sign that the rain was likely to abate.

Roux kept to himself.

As well as wine, there was enough bread, cheese and fruit to keep them satisfied should hunger cravings stir. If they wanted more, they could wake Garin and the cook. There was nothing left to keep Roux from his bed, and so he retired to his room and settled down for the night.

His candle burned slowly as he read one of the books that adorned the shelves in the chamber. Eventually he grew tired, set the volume down and listened for a short while to the sound of the rain hammering against the windows. The ill-fitting glass rattled in the frame, allowing a draft to waft the curtains gently back and forth, creating the illusion of someone standing behind them.

Despite the tricks of his mind, Roux soon drifted into a deep sleep that was shattered by the sound of a scream.

He dressed quickly and raced down the winding staircase to find them all standing around the window in the room where he had left them. Each one stared out into the darkness. Lightning flashed. He saw what had frightened one of the women. It was a face. The face of a man that was somehow not a man. It was a tragic and yet brutal visage staring in at them.

"What deviltry is this?" Byron demanded, as if he expected someone else in the room to offer up the answer his rational mind was searching for. Polidori tried to speak, but was no more capable of giving a solution than any of the others.

Another lightning flash slashed across the deep night, but this time the image was gone.

"No doubt it was merely your ugly reflection in the glass," Shelley suggested with a wry smile.

"Nonsense," Mary replied, intent on peering out into the night. "I saw someone out there. We have to see if he's all right."

"I saw him as well, a monstrous thing he was. Surely not a man at all. You cannot let that monster in here," Claire said. "For the love of all things holy, make sure that all the doors and windows are bolted. He was a thing of hell itself." She clutched on to Byron's arm, but he showed no sign of wanting to comfort her.

"If you will permit it, I will go and check," Roux said to Byron. "If it is some poor wretch from the village lost in this storm, I will make sure that he gets home safely."

"And if it is not?" Claire asked.

"Then I will deal with him appropriately, miss. On that you have my word."

"Good man," Byron said, a sardonic smile on his lips as he assayed a bow in Roux's direction.

There was obvious relief among the gathering, save for Mary herself, who seemed more fascinated than fearful at whatever she had seen out there. As ever with the rich, they felt the undercurrent of need, but none of them wanted to be the one to see it done. Roux taking control meant that they could once more lounge back in their seats, lifting their glasses, and simply forget that there might ever have been a man on the other side of the window. Something was being done, and all was right with the world once more.

Before venturing outside Roux retrieved his sword and his greatcoat.

While he had no idea of what he had seen through the window, he knew that it was not his reflection. He was also certain that it was not some lost villager. A poor soul with such a monstrous visage would be well known in the vicinity even if he hid himself away, fearful of being cast out as a demon, or tortured like some devil. People had ever thus been cruel and fearful of difference and things they did not understand.

Roux could not shake the feeling that he had seen something unearthly.

"Garin," he shouted, banging on the door of the cook's bedroom, earning grunts and grumbles from his young protégé. He had been of two minds about summoning the man, but if it was going to come to blows out there, Garin's sword would be invaluable. Besides, two sets of eyes hunting the intruder were always going to be better than one.

When Garin emerged he was already half-dressed, sword in one hand and the rest of his clothes in the other.

"What's the ruckus?" Garin demanded, far from happy to have been dragged from his pit.

"You did not hear the scream?" Roux asked.

"This place is full of screams, old man, especially in there." He hooked a thumb back over his shoulder toward the bed where the cook was wantonly sprawled out. "Am I supposed to react to all of them?"

"On with your trews and boots, man. We need to be out there before the thing escapes."

"Thing? I don't like that choice of word."

"An intruder."

"Inside the house?"

"The grounds. One of the women saw him through the window."

"The cause of the scream?"

"Indeed."

"Surely it's just some poor wretch lost in the storm?"

"That was my first thought," Roux said. "But then I saw him."

Garin grinned ferociously. "You always save the best part until last, old man. What are we waiting for?" Garin asked with his hand on the door, ready to head out into the raging elements looking every bit as fearsome as the storm itself.

"You don't want a coat?"

"Who wears a coat for fighting?" Garin pulled the door open, filling the hallway with the squall of wind and rain. Roux buttoned up his own coat, ready to follow the younger man out into the night, fist wrapped around the hilt of his sword.

On nights like these he could easily believe once more in heaven and hell even if his own passage into either had been long denied him.

They plunged into the storm, battered and bullied by the elements.

Lightning flashed, lighting up the sky. The willows cast shadows that crept stealthily down to the water's edge. The silver fork was reflected in the ripples of the storm-tossed lake, chasing across the surface toward the shore. The rowboat bobbed and pulled at its moorings, trying to break free as it filled with rain.

Roux shielded his eyes against the deluge, scanning the lawn as another fork of lightning split the sky, seventeen tines spearing toward the earth.

"This really isn't the weather to be waving a giant lightning conductor around," Garin shouted above a crash of thunder that shook the firmament. His eyes were manic. Garin was more alive than he had been in months. He was enjoying himself. He raised his sword to the sky as though daring some unseen god to strike him down. The lightning when it came was answered by a shrieking tear of wood as it ripped into one of the trees no more than two hundred yards from where they stood. The thrill of electricity from the strike tore the sword from his hand and sent Roux staggering backward. The impact, even at that distance, was akin to a punishing fist.

Garin's laughter rolled with the thunder that followed.

Gasping, Roux straightened and looked back toward the house.

The orange light of the fire blazing inside silhouetted one of the women, Mary, as she stood lonely vigil at the window.

There was no sign of the creature.

15

"Hold on a second, let me get this straight, Roux. You're telling me you and Garin were there when Mary Shelley wrote *Frankenstein*?"

"Polidori wrote his story, *The Vampyre*, too," the old man agreed.

"That's insane. I keep forgetting…"

"That I'm older than the hills?"

Annja offered a wry smile. "You can't leave it like that. What about the face at the window? You found out what it was, didn't you? That's how it links to what's happening here." Her mind raced to its own conclusions, not waiting for Roux to finish his incredible tale.

"Not that night, but it was the beginning for me, how I was drawn into what is now legend. We spent the next couple of hours out there in the storm, looking desperately for the intruder, but there was no sign of him anywhere around the house or in any of the outbuildings. Soaked to the skin, we had returned, but rather than appeased, the women would not rest. Fear had wormed its way into them. So, to do our best to calm them we searched the house from top to bottom to make sure that the intruder had not found its way inside while we hunted it out there. Claire was convinced that they were all going to be murdered in their beds." Roux smiled almost fondly at the memory, which struck Annja as odd, until he finished the thought. "After we came back inside Garin just flopped down amid them, so easy and natural, so absolutely one of them, they welcomed him into their number without ever realizing it was happening. He's got quite a way with people when he sets his mind to it."

"It's a gift," Annja agreed, thinking of the waitress and now the doctor and how it had taken less than five minutes in his presence to succumb to his charms. If he could bottle whatever it was about him that made Garin quintessentially Garin, he'd be an even richer man.

She knew the story of that summer in the Villa Diodati and how that group of people had challenged one another to come up with ghost stories; everyone had heard it in some form or other even if they didn't realize it. But in all the time she'd known him Roux had never mentioned that he was there. It was incredible to think he'd been there at the birth of Dr. Frankenstein's monster, one of the first truly famous monsters that has endured so many years later. But that was Roux all over. He had been to so many places, seen so many things, lived so many lifetimes, that he couldn't possibly have told her even a quarter of the things he'd seen and done. "How does it connect?"

"All in good time, dear heart. I didn't see or hear anything about the thing for some days after. It made a great impression on young Mary, though. That much was obvious. She used it as inspiration for her story. The rain kept coming, thunderclouds so dark they succeeded in transforming day to night. No one left the house. Those who worked on their stories looked up from their pages, constantly scribbling.

"The day stretched into night and out the other side. Nothing seemed to change. On the third day the rain stopped; sunlight breaking through the thick cloud layer and spearing down in bright beams that seemed to scatter a wealth of gold across the lawn. At last we ventured out of the house. It was only then that we learned of the killings."

16

It was the first time they had seen the sun for days.

The ground was sodden underfoot. Pools of rainwater gathered on the lawn. The lake had burst its banks, spreading out across the muddy slopes where the earth simply couldn't soak up the downpour fast enough. The soil sucked at his boots with every step. The sky was full of thick banks of cloud, but every now and then they parted just long enough to allow the sun to come streaming through. Its heat caught them unawares.

Roux was glad to be out in the open.

He strode around the curve of the lake, luxuriating in the fresh air as it cleared the cobwebs from his mind. It made a refreshing change to be haunted by the echo of his own footsteps as he paced the corridors of the Villa Diodati.

The village was a good thirty minutes' brisk walk away.

Garin walked arm in arm with the cook, moving even slower than the gaggle of giggling guests from the villa led by Byron, who was once more acting as if he were lord of the manor. Roux resisted the urge to hold back and play subservient, and lengthened his stride.

He reached the village several minutes before the others.

That meant that he was the first to hear the news that there had been two murders in the past three days, covered by the storms, and that the bodies had only just been discovered now that the awful weather had abated.

"Who were they? The victims?" Roux asked the shopkeeper, who was more than happy to share the shocking news with anyone who passed the front of his premises.

"Strangers," he said meaningfully. "Seems the poor souls were seeking out shelter but found more than they bargained for there near the woods."

Strangers murdered in and around the same woods that separated the Villa Diodati from the village? "We saw a stranger up at the villa a couple of nights ago," Roux said, adding to the gossip at the shopkeeper's disposal. "Is there any way I could see the bodies?"

"Why ever would you want to do something so macabre?"

"Ah, merely to ease my own guilt should it turn out he proves to be one of them. You understand, I am sure—it would be most awful to contemplate that someone lost their life because I turned him away."

If the shopkeeper doubted his explanation, he didn't voice those doubts. "Of course. I understand completely. The curse of being a good man." He nodded. "They have been laid out in the church and will remain there until they can receive a good Christian burial. There did not seem to be anywhere more appropriate."

The rest of the party was still way down the street.

Roux nodded, expecting the man to make the other obvious connection: that if their nocturnal visitor was not among their number, then surely Roux had encountered their killer.

The shopkeeper was clearly torn. By accompanying Roux to the church, he might learn even more twists to the story that so fascinated him, or perhaps he would earn some coin from the purses of the wealthy strangers walking toward his premises if he stayed. In the end greed won out. "The church will be open now. I'm sure the priest will be looking over the bodies. Tell him you have spoken to me and—" he leaned forward conspiratorially "—be sure to return to let me know how you get on, won't you?"

"I will," Roux said, though he had no intention of doing so. The gossip would find its own method of multiplying without his help. Soon enough it would fill the entire village.

He crossed the quiet square to the doors of the church, which were open to welcome the congregation, and entered. The priest knelt in front of the altar, offering a prayer for the two corpses that were stretched out on boards before him. The arm of one of the dead hung free, almost touching the floor. The priest did not move from his prayer at the sound of Roux's approach, though Roux made no effort to hide his footsteps. When he was almost beside him, Roux cleared his throat. The priest finished the final imprecations to the Lord, his Master, and rose, brushing down his robes as he turned to face his visitor.

"Can I help you?" the priest asked.

Roux offered him the same story he had given the shopkeeper. Skeptical, the priest reluctantly agreed to allow him a look beneath the shrouds. With the utmost respect, Roux peeled back the layer of cloth that separated the living from the dead. He looked down at the corpses, studying their features. There was no doubt in his mind. There was no way that either of these men could have been the near-featureless hulk he had seen through the window. Armed with that knowledge, he knew the reality was that he had almost certainly seen their killer.

The two bodies belonged to men who had been sleeping in the open air for quite some time. Their clothes were torn and tattered and caked with thick mud. They had almost certainly been looking for shelter when their killer found them. Could he have saved either man? Had the fact that the featureless brute had evaded their swords damned these two hapless souls? Perhaps. That was the best answer he could offer. Now it was between him and his God. He lowered his head and offered a prayer for the damned.

The priest echoed his "Amen."

Roux used the silence to think.

The woman, Claire Clairmont, had been right to be afraid. How close had they come to being murdered in their beds? They were dealing with something so far beyond the known and the holy, something on the very verge of aberration, that it could never know redemption. Someone needed to find this ghastly killer and put an end to its reign of terror before it could truly begin, and that someone was Roux.

He was the Lord's sword in this just as he was in all things.

17

Annja woke with a start to find that her room was in darkness.

She had been covered by the throw from the bed.

She had been listening to Roux recount his story, but had fallen asleep during its telling. The painkillers had to have been stronger than she'd expected. She struggled to focus for a moment, realizing she had lost much of the day. It was night outside.

"Roux," she called, throwing the bedspread aside, and attempted to stand. She felt the dull stiffness in her bones, having slept in such an unnatural position. Her muscles ached every bit as they had when she'd left the hospital.

There was no reply.

The bathroom door stood open, and the room beyond reduced to a single white contour, the curve of the bathtub's side; the rest of it lay shrouded in darkness.

Annja was alone.

Despite Roux's promises, she had no more idea of what the killer was than when she had chased it across the rooftops.

Her cell phone lay on the coffee table in front of her.

A quick glance showed that it had been switched to

silent and that there were missed calls from both Garin and Lars, her cameraman.

Only Lars had left a message. "Hi," Lars's voice said sheepishly. "Hope you aren't angry with me, boss. Turek drank me into the ground. I have only just surfaced and I've got no idea what day it is, never mind time. Give me a call if you need me to do anything. I'm really sorry about this."

She could hardly complain. It wasn't as if he was the only one who'd slept the day away.

Annja's mouth felt dry and her tongue a little too large for it.

There was no point in calling him back yet. It wasn't as if they could get more daytime footage, and they'd gotten more than their fill of night shots the previous day. She wasn't even angry with him for going to the bar rather than returning to the hotel with her. That had been as much her call as his, but if he'd headed back with her, then maybe they would've gotten some footage of the killer, which would have been priceless.

Roux, she was sure, was already out searching the streets.

He knew this killer and had for a very long time.

She wondered for a moment if he had slipped her something when he'd brought her the water to wash down her painkillers. He'd wanted to go after the killer himself, and her unconsciousness certainly made that possible. But that wasn't him, was it? That was more Garin...

So where did she start?

She needed to get out, really stretch, work her muscles, or she wouldn't get her body back into shape. Really, what she wanted to do was reach into the otherwhere and draw the sword back into the here and now, pushing herself through a punishing workout with it in her grasp. But she needed more space than the hotel room offered for something like that—and that added its own complications. Where could she go that a woman brandishing a sword wouldn't attract attention?

She was easing herself into her jacket, wincing as she moved her shoulder, when her phone rang.

It wasn't Roux or Garin. It was the journalist, Jan Turek.

She snatched the phone and answered.

"Jan," she said. "I hear you had a good night."

"Something like that," he replied noncommittally. "I'm just calling to see if you've heard the news."

"Assume I haven't," Annja said. "What news?"

"There's been another killing."

"Last night?" she asked, the memory of the body in the alleyway flooding back as if her mind had pushed it away, but like the tide it was impossible to fend off forever. And then there was the memory of falling.

"No. I mean *now*. Like right now. Within the hour. I got a tip. I'm heading over there to check out the scene."

"Where?" she asked, grabbing a piece of the hotel notepaper and scrambling for a pen to write down the directions to the crime scene. It wasn't inside the city.

"He's on the move," she said, more to herself than Turek. The thought had leaped into her mind, but she knew instinctively she was right.

"You think?" the journalist asked, though obviously the thought had occurred to him, too. "Maybe he was afraid that things are getting a little too hot for him inside the Old Town. Too many people looking for him here."

"No. No one even knows what he looks like. He's got no reason to leave what's proved to be a very rich hunting ground," she disagreed.

Not true, she contradicted herself, *he's got every reason to leave if he knows we are closing in on him.*

"I'll see you there." Annja hung up on him, aches and pains of her fall forgotten.

Five minutes later she had punched the details into her rental car's navigation system and was pulling out of the hotel parking lot in search of another one of the lonely dead.

18

It felt good to be behind the wheel.

The traffic moved steadily as she picked up the flow moving out of the city. The headlights transformed Prague yet again. It was no longer the tourist trap or the site of some bachelor's last stand. Under the headlights it was a city out of time. A relic. A monument. It was like the castle up on the hill, on display. Something to be marveled at.

The moment the road widened, Annja floored the accelerator and watched the needle climb on the speedometer.

There was something about speed that brought her to life. She didn't want to think what that said about her personality.

She took the bends faster than she needed to, ignoring the blaring of horns as she wove in and out of traffic, determined to reach Turek as quickly as she possibly could.

She flashed past road signs without taking any notice of them, relying on the screen on the dashboard and its orders to take the next left in two hundred meters to direct her through the labyrinth of the city and beyond, as the numbered distance to her destination slowly fell.

When she saw the blue flashing lights ahead of her, she knew she had reached her destination.

Turek was already there.

"What have we got?" she asked when she saw the reporter walking toward her.

"The police aren't letting anyone near the body, but the word is that we're looking at another vagrant. This one was trying to get out of the city."

"Any idea if he's connected to our witnesses?"

Turek shrugged. "Not without seeing him."

"And we're sure it's the same killer?"

"As sure as we can be," a voice behind her said. Annja turned to see the same police officer she had spoken to at the crime scene the previous morning striding toward them.

"Miss Creed, isn't it?" He pulled her name from somewhere in the recesses of his memory. "I'm beginning to think your being here is more than a coincidence."

"I couldn't keep away," she said.

"This is not a tourist attraction," he said reproachfully. "I think now would be a very good time for you to explain why I find you at the site of a second murder in as many days."

"She's with me," Turek said. "I've been following the case for the press."

"Oh, yes, I know all about your conspiracy theories, Turek." The policeman shook his head like he couldn't quite believe anyone was stupid enough to fall for the journalist's nonsense about the golem coming back.

"I've only been reporting what the street people have been saying. I don't tell them what to think."

"Because that would be immoral, wouldn't it? I'm not sure whether I should laugh at these newfound ethics of yours, Turek."

"You're sure that it was the same killer?" Annja said, putting herself between the two men. She didn't want this to turn into a fight they couldn't possibly win. They needed to have the police on their side, or at least not have them against them. Deliberately antagonizing the law was about as stupid as it got.

The officer turned to face her. "The injuries are consistent with the previous victims. That's as much as I'm going to tell you, Miss Creed, until I understand the part you are playing here."

"I almost caught it, whatever it was," Annja said, and regretted it as soon as she had said it. She wanted to find the killer, but she wouldn't be able to do that if she was in an interrogation room batting away endless questions about her involvement in the investigation.

"I think you need to tell me a little more about that," the policeman said.

She'd caught Turek's attention, too.

"Last night," she said, "after I left Jan and my cameraman, I was walking back to the hotel when I heard something. It took me a moment to realize the noise was coming from above me. Someone was up on the rooftops."

"Not from your window this time? That's twice you've come close to our killer. I suppose you know that there was another murder last night."

She nodded that she did.

"I'm surprised we didn't see you there actually. I'm not sure I want to know the answer to this, but are you able to give us a description this time?"

Annja nodded again. "Big. Well over six feet tall. Thick-set, barrel-chested but light on his feet. He didn't walk—*loped* is a better word for the way he moved. And he was fast. Sure on his feet as he ran across the roof."

"Did you get a look at his face?"

"Not really," she said.

She was sure that she had caught a glimpse of his

face, of features that looked as if they weren't quite finished, like a child's drawing rather than a face itself. But how could she tell him that? Or, more correctly, how could she expect him to believe her if she told him that? It didn't matter if her description echoed those of the two homeless witnesses…in fact, that would almost certainly convince him that she was screwing with him. So no, she wouldn't offer a description of the killer's face.

The policeman made a few quick pencil strokes in his notebook that didn't resemble the words she'd said, nodding as he did so. He didn't ask any more questions. Annja waited patiently for him to say something, but he didn't. He just turned and started to walk away. Nothing she'd told him came as a surprise, of course.

The policeman stopped and turned after he had only taken half a dozen steps.

He tilted his head slightly to the right and said, "I hope you're not keeping anything from me."

"Nothing," Annja said, holding up her hands. "I've told you everything I saw."

"Too bad. Well, there's nothing here for you to see. If I'm honest about it, I would be very grateful if I didn't see you at another crime scene." It was a dismissal.

Turek started to mumble something about the freedom of the press, but Annja silenced him.

There was no reason for them to stay there.

The killer was long gone.

Finding him meant working out where he'd go, and that was more important than wasting time trying to get a look at the corpse. One dead body at the killer's hands would look very much like another. They wouldn't learn anything from it even if the police allowed them to get close enough for an examination.

Annja was sure the killer was traveling on foot.

An hour ago he had been here. Even if he could move fast, he could be no more than a couple of miles away and tiring.

"Where does this road lead to?" she asked Turek when the policeman was out of earshot.

The journalist shrugged and reeled off a list of towns that meant nothing to her. "After that you reach the border with Poland."

Poland?

Would the killer try to leave the country?

Did he even think in terms of geographic borders?

She stared down the road, but there was no movement save the wind through the treetops.

The Villa Diodati was on the shore of Lake Geneva, hundreds of miles away across the breadth of Germany. The killer, assuming he was Roux's killer, was a long way from home, but Poland was in the wrong direction to suggest that was where he was heading.

If he managed to escape them here, there was no telling where or when he might resurface to begin killing again.

She couldn't allow that to happen.

Annja already blamed herself for the homeless men who had died since she had first heard that scream from her window. This was at her door. The man on the road up ahead was dead because she had failed to stop the killer when she had the chance. His blood was on her hands. Whatever guilt Roux felt for failing to stop the killer all those years ago was nothing compared to the swelling grief and rage Annja felt at her own culpability now. The baton had passed between them. Now it was up to her to stop the killer.

Whatever it was.

19

Roux had been prowling the streets for an hour before he caught the whisper of gossip: another body had been found.

At first he'd dismissed it, thinking the street people were still learning about the death that had landed Annja in the hospital, but he quickly realized he was wrong when they started talking about a location on the outskirts of the city.

He had almost gone in search of the dead, but stopped himself. The trail of bodies wasn't about to go cold, but Garin was most certainly up to something and that was what he should be following. He was absolutely sure of it. Roux had almost lost Garin a couple of times, as there was no seeming pattern to his movements as he tracked from main plaza to narrow alley from narrow alley to tourist trap to seedy side street and back again, checking the twists and folds of the Old Town in search of the killer.

These were the places the killer knew.

Roux knew that because they were the same places that he and Garin had trod long ago, too.

Eventually something about the elaborate pattern

changed—and it changed so quickly Roux was almost cornered and caught as Garin doubled back on himself.

He ducked into a deeply recessed doorway, under the shelter of gargoyles, and hoped that scant cover would be enough.

He watched and waited, listening to the soft footfalls as they faded, until he was absolutely sure Garin had kept walking and it was safe to emerge from his hiding place.

Luckily for him, Garin had been concentrating on his cell phone as he had walked, oblivious to anything else going on around him. His stare had been obsessive. He didn't look up from the screen once. It took Roux a minute to realize what was going on: Garin was using the phone's GPS to track someone. Or some*thing*.

He watched from fifty yards behind as Garin entered the hotel's underground parking lot, glad that he had moved his own vehicle, parking it on the street.

The game was changing, but how, exactly, and why? There was every chance the sudden change of plans was due to a woman, but Roux had a sneaking suspicion that wasn't the case—and it wasn't just because he trusted Garin about as far as he could throw him, either. Garin was up to something. His intent focus on the phone pretty much guaranteed it.

Roux barely managed to slip behind the wheel of his rented four-by-four, only moments before Garin roared out of the parking lot in a flame-red Ferrari. There was no way Roux was going to be able to keep up with the Ferrari as it peeled away from the standing start, laying a thick strip of rubber on the blacktop. He instinctively lowered his head as Garin thundered by, but he shouldn't have worried; Garin had eyes only for the road in front of him.

Roux watched the taillights flare and gunned his own car into life, setting off after Garin. It took everything the four-by-four's engine had to keep up with Garin's labyrinthine chase through the canyons of the city.

As he drove out of the city, Roux turned on the radio.

Once he had been fluent, but the years hadn't been kind to the old man in that regard. The language had mutated and now he was reduced to speaking a smattering of Czech rather than claiming any sort of fluency. He understood enough, though, to follow the report that there had been another killing. Talk now was of a serial killer stalking the city's homeless.

Roux didn't like what he was thinking, but that didn't mean he could stop himself from thinking it: Garin was fleeing the city. That he was here and not on the outskirts where the latest murder had occurred,might prove his innocence in one regard, making Roux his alibi, but his actions now surely damned him in so many others. There was a connection here, whatever it might be, and Roux was determined to get to the truth before the night was over. The city stank of betrayal. Again. How many times would he fall for Garin's repentance and contrition? How many times would he allow himself to think, right up until that crippling moment of realization, that things could ever be the way they once were between him and Garin? Fool me once, Roux thought, shaking his head. He didn't need to finish the rest of the aphorism.

The only small mercy was that Annja would not be there to witness the confrontation.

Garin drove aggressively, pushing the sports car into

gaps that didn't appear to be there. Its engine roar was like a dragon's claiming the night for its own. It was all Roux could do to keep him in sight as Garin overtook another slow-moving vehicle.

Four seconds later Roux was behind it, trying to find a route through with his wider four-by-four. He counted the seconds, willing the driver in front to pull over to let him through, but without the flashing light of an ambulance or cop car, that wasn't happening. Frustrated, Roux rode hard on the vehicle's fender, tailgating it. Some bland late-night lonely-hearts music came on the radio. He reached down and killed it, then took a gamble, changed up and mounted the sidewalk, forcing the car in front to pull out into the center of the road as he bullied his way through. A couple of pedestrians scattered, terrified as the madman drove on the sidewalk for fifty yards before dropping back onto the road proper. Horns blared in protest. Roux ignored them, eyes fixed on the road ahead.

Garin was way off in the distance.

He had to hope Garin was still fixated on the road and hadn't seen his stupid maneuver in the rearview mirror.

He didn't seem to have seen him.

Roux followed him, keeping his distance, until they were well out of the city.

Garin gave no indication that he knew he was being followed.

That was the one benefit of a rental car—anonymity, even if Roux had a penchant for big bulky four-by-fours with off-road capabilities. One set of headlights at night was much like any other set of headlights at night. Now it was so dark that even he was riding Garin's tail hard, and there was no way he'd be able to see the face of the driver in the car behind him.

On the road ahead the blue flashing lights of a police car bit into the night.

Roux understood their destination now. They were heading out to the site of the latest murder.

But Garin showed no sign of slowing.

Maybe he was wrong about the lights. It seemed unlikely, but Prague was a big city. That murder wouldn't be the only crime committed tonight. But as long as he followed Garin he'd get to the truth eventually, even if it was only a confirmation of what he already knew: that thing was killing again.

The Ferrari accelerated once they were clear of the police cordon and started to pull away with serious intent, Garin opening up the engine, its roar filling the night. It didn't sound like a dragon at all, Roux realized. It sounded like a banshee's wail.

His headlights picked out a road sign. Roux saw a name he hadn't thought about in a long time. It conjured a memory that he had worked so hard to bury.

20

Roux had found the tracks within an hour of seeing the bodies laid out in the church.

The incessant rain had left the ground sodden and slippery.

He crouched over the oversize prints of a shoeless foot in the mud. They were filled with rainwater.

"As ever with you it comes to either/or, doesn't it, old man? This time it's love or adventure. It's not much of a choice, is it?" Garin asked, no anger in his voice, just a kind of resigned amusement. Roux already knew his answer from the tone of his voice. It wasn't love. Garin didn't have any conception of what love actually was. His definition focused purely on the physical side of things and kept the spiritual as far from the relationship as possible. The cook—Roux didn't even recall her name, so transitory were these kinds of relationships for his young squire—had done well to capture his attention and hold it for this long, but the first flush of passion was already gone and the novelty of waking up beside her was wearing thin.

Their mistake was delaying their departure. They should have left the village immediately, not returned to the villa to gather their belongings, and for Garin to disappear for ten minutes while Roux hunted high and low for him. He knew exactly what Garin was doing in those ten minutes, too. Kissing the cook farewell across every inch of her buttermilk skin. She'd forget him soon enough, unless, of course, he'd left a seed in her that would grow. They needed to move on, be gone and forgotten.

So they followed the tracks around the lake, thankful that the storms had made their task so much simpler. More than once they were treated with suspicion. News of the killings had spread like wildfire, outpacing them. Boatmen out on the water shared the story until it became the only talking point. Stranger was shunned and sent on their way without ceremony.

Their biggest problem, though, was that as the weather continued to improve, the tracks began to fade.

For days they followed those footprints as they set firm in the ground. But they never seemed to gain even an hour on the killer, arriving in villages two days after another spate of killings had taken place. Always two days behind the murderer. They needed horses if they were going to stand any chance of closing in on him. It was Garin's task to locate a pair and liberate them, knowing that the men would be long gone before their crime was discovered. They rode as if the devil himself was at their back, driving their heels into the flanks of their horses, hanging on with hands tangled in their mounts' manes for want of a bridle and tack. It was a wild ride like none Roux had known before, a race and a chase, filled with an exhilaration that made his heart pound. They were the hunters, their quarry a merciless killer who had racked up more than twenty corpses to his name in the month since he had stared in through the villa's window.

But somehow they lost him.

Despite everything, the trail grew cold.

They were forced to move from village to village, hoping to hear news of another killing, knowing how sick that hope made them, but without it they would never find the right path again. Someone had to die. They sought out any hint of death, relishing each report as they gleaned what little information they could before setting off on their journey again, no closer to catching up with the killer than they had been that first night as lightning tore the sky asunder. So close and yet so far away.

They had to rest from time to time, their mounts able to take them only so far in a single day before exhaustion claimed them. To push them harder risked running the horses into the ground. Yet the killer never seemed to tire. His endurance was inhuman. He could outrun the horses, pushing himself faster and farther.

"There must be a way to anticipate his destination," Garin said one night as they warmed themselves over a makeshift fire pit. "We've traveled this world a dozen times. There isn't an inch of ground we haven't covered. If we knew, then we could find a shorter route, travel smarter not faster. We could take a coach, travel through the night instead of sleeping. Change the horses every few hours through the daylight ride."

Roux knew that it made sense.

They would need to change horses regularly. Though that was not impossible, there was nothing to say their fresh mounts would be Thoroughbreds capable of matching the punishing pace the chase demanded. They had plenty of coin between them to purchase passage and to have bought the horses ten times over and then some. Work was something Roux chose to do, rarely something that he needed to do. He said it kept him honest. That was the beauty of having lived so long. Their wealth, secreted at different establishments throughout the nations under different names, may have been accumulated as the spoils of war but that didn't make it any less valuable. Some of the treasures he had hoarded would be worth a great deal in years to come—fortunes beyond imagining—and he was determined to enjoy that money when he was ready. But for now, adventure and excitement held more value than any currency or trove of gold.

He lived by challenges.

He lived for a different kind of worth.

His single purpose was to find the shards of Saint Joan's shattered blade and reunite them so that the curse may be lifted. He had no hankering to live forever. He was tired. He had been tired for years. That was why he hunted this killer. Perhaps it might bring about an end for Roux and his apprentice.

21

A name on a road sign rang a bell somewhere deep inside her mind.

A mile or so ahead there was a fork in the road, and to the left a place called Benátky. She'd heard that name not so long ago, but couldn't remember quite where or in relation to what. It was unlike Annja to not be able to place something to do with a story. Maybe there was something important there, some piece of history in relation to her segment and what was supposed to be the live show going out in a couple of days.

The killer could not be that far ahead of them if he was heading for the border, she reasoned, so deciding to take the brief detour she saw no reason to delay Turek.

She made the call.

"I'll meet you there," she promised.

"Got a better offer?" Turek asked.

They had decided to take both cars, but he was only a matter of twenty yards ahead of her.

"Something I need to take care of," she said. She didn't elaborate because she didn't really know what she could say to explain the hunch.

"And it's something that can't wait?" the journalist asked, sounding slightly exasperated. It wasn't that she was bailing on him that annoyed him; he was only after the story, not the killer, so it didn't matter if he was an hour behind the monster or a day, as long as he got to the truth before any other reporter. The gold was always in being the first. That was what got the book deals.

"Not sure," she said. "I'll see you at the border. Let me know if there's anything strange going on while you're waiting."

"Will do, but be honest with me, you're not cutting me out, are you? You're not off chasing a lead that will take you to the killer and leave me with nothing?"

"I promise," Annja said.

"I'm serious. I need to be the one who breaks the story. I've done all the groundwork. No one else was interested in what the people on the street were saying. This is my story, Annja. It could change my life, see me on the staff of one the nationals."

"If I turn anything up I'll let you know, but I promise you, I'm not trying to screw you. I don't even know what it is about this place. It just rings a bell so I need to check it out. I won't be more than an hour. Cover the border, and don't let the killer escape, Jan. This is bigger than just the story. Lives are at stake."

"I know that, Annja. I'm counting on you," the reporter said as he hung up. *Counting on her.* He wasn't the only one who was counting on her, was he? Every vagrant between here and the border was counting on her to stop the killer even if they didn't know it. Everyone sleeping on the street that night and every coming night was counting on her even if they never met Annja Creed. That was the burden of who and what she was, and only she could carry it.

She tripped the blinker and took the turn toward Benátky, hoping that the hunch would pay out.

As she drove, Annja half expected to see something to suggest she was on the right track, an omen, a portent, something, even if it was just a murder of crows lining the trees at the roadside. But there were no more blue flashing lights up ahead to indicate anything out of the ordinary. And that was what she was looking for, wasn't it? Something out of the ordinary.

She scanned the silhouettes of the buildings as she approached the town. The sky was full of stars, a reminder of just how far outside the city she'd traveled. A few of the houses still had lights on in their windows, but the streets were deserted.

She drove slowly through the streets, looking, but not sure what it was she was looking for.

This would be the perfect hunting ground for the killer if its prey could be found on these streets, she realized.

The needle on the speedometer barely touched fifteen kilometers an hour. No matter how much she looked, she couldn't see anything to suggest she was on anything but a wild-goose chase.

Annja pulled the car over to the side of the road, ignoring the parking restrictions painted on the asphalt. There wasn't anyone around to enforce them.

She needed to think.

She wanted to know where Roux was. More importantly, she wanted to know why he had left her in the hotel room.

He knew more than he was telling her, that much was painfully obvious. He felt some sort of personal guilt, too. So somewhere in between his secrets and his guilt was the difference between success and failure, whatever that might be. His tight lips frustrated her. They always did. So many times he had known things that he had chosen not to share until it put her at risk or dragged her deeper into trouble. He'd always protested it was for her own good, to keep her safe, but that was nonsense. It was to keep Roux in control. He was a control freak.

She killed the headlights, turned off the engine and listened to the silence of the street.

There was nothing.

The silence was absolute.

There were no background sounds of the city life Prague offered.

She settled back into her seat and waited.

So much for instincts. What was she supposed to do now that she was here? There was no point in sitting and waiting for something to happen. She had to be out there looking for the killer, who could be anywhere in the world—or if not the world, in the miles of countryside surrounding Prague—and almost certainly not here in this silent township in the middle of nowhere.

She looked down at her hands, wondering if she'd just made the mistake that would let the killer slip through her fingers again.

22

Garin slipped out of sight for a moment when he entered the town.

There was no other traffic around and following Garin too closely would only serve to arouse suspicion. There was nothing to be gained by giving the game away now, so close to the finish line. So much of the place remained recognizable despite the passage of time. There were changes, of course, subtle ones, little things like the overhead wires of the telephone network that would no doubt disappear again in a few years as 4G took hold and wiped out the need for landlines. But none of those subtle changes were enough to turn the town into an unfamiliar place.

Roux waited when Garin's sports car—as out of place as that fine craftsmanship could ever be—took a turn and disappeared out of sight.

He rolled down his window so he could listen for its engine as it negotiated the narrow streets.

He heard the sound of the engine change, grumbling throatily one last time before being silenced.

Garin had stopped not far around the corner, close enough for Roux to hear the echoing slam of the door as he closed it.

Roux left his own car where it was and climbed out, but unlike Garin, he closed the door as quietly as he could so as not to betray his presence. He hugged the wall as he made his way to the corner.

Hearing the sound of footsteps moving away from him, he chanced a look around the building's edge to see Garin disappear into an alleyway.

He knew that the winding passage would lead the way to the castle.

This was the place where it had all started.

It was also the place where he had thought it had all ended.

Roux had been wrong. He knew that now. Their presence here was all he needed to know just how wrong he had been.

But would the killer really return to this place?

Or was it worse than he had first suspected and it had never left? He couldn't bring himself to believe that, because that would mean someone else was mimicking its actions, and the only person capable of something like that—of having the knowledge, the skill and the sheer bloody ruthlessness—was Garin. And that was his deepest, darkest fear. Garin *was* capable of everything that killer had done. Had fighting monsters for so long, finally turned him into one? They had spent six centuries and more waging battles of one kind or another.

What had that cost them in terms of their souls and selves?

23

Prague. They had pursued the killer across Europe, through every valley and ridge, to finally find themselves in Prague, and yet they were still a decent morning's ride away from the site of the most recent death. They were always traveling in the killer's footsteps, gaining a little but never enough, and no matter how hard they'd ridden their horses, how many times they had changed their carriages and how little they had slept, the murderer was always ahead of them.

They had done everything humanly possible to keep up the punishing pace, taking it in turns to drive the coach they had bought, switching out the horses for fresh ones at inns along the way, but nothing helped. They still had to eat. They still grew tired. They still had to rest, pausing inevitably for longer than they needed to.

But always they gave chase again, dogging the killer's trail.

There had been stories of murders here—one of them recent, the other many years ago, but somehow a connection had been drawn between the two. In drinking houses in the back alleys of the town it was the only topic of conversation. The legend endured. "This has to be the end of it, surely?" Garin said. "We can't keep chasing this shadow forever. There has to be a place along the road where we say enough is enough."

"Admit defeat?" Roux asked, shielding his eyes from the early-morning sun. "Why would we want to give up? The killer *can't* keep going forever. It is impossible. We are closer today than we were yesterday. We have to catch up with him eventually."

"Can't it? How do you know that? Apart from optimism? Who says he can't keep going? I don't like the word *can't*, old man. After all, we seem to defy that word quite a lot ourselves, don't we?"

Roux fell silent.

There were things that he had no intention of sharing with his protégé, things that he would rather take to the grave. The idea of giving up, though, stuck in his craw.

Until that moment, until Garin voiced the possibility, it hadn't even crossed his mind.

"If you have all the time in the world, why would you give up on anything?" he asked. It was a philosophical question, but there was an element of truth to it. There was no finite "end" that said they had to give up the chase. There was no clock inside their bodies counting down to oblivion.

"There will always be another tomorrow," Roux continued, "and beyond that there will always be another day when we can think about doing something else. Today we catch a killer. It doesn't matter how many todays that takes, does it? When you have all the time in the world, why would you worry about wasting any of it?"

Garin only shrugged, but despite his grand words Roux knew exactly what he meant; he was growing bored of the chase. This had nothing to do with being concerned about wasting time or watching life pass him by. Garin knew that Roux was interested in finding the shards of Saint Joan's sword—he cried out in his sleep often enough, his guilt at the memory of watching her burn all but overpowering even after all this time. He even knew why he was so driven to find it: the belief that it might offer an end to their seeming endless time in this mortal coil. But unlike the old man, his apprentice had no hankering for death. He would quite happily live gloriously and eternally, sucking the marrow out of the bones of the world and all of the people he encountered along the way.

"So," Garin asked, letting that one word linger as he did his best to shift the conversation in a less contentious direction. "What do you think of all this gossip? Could we have been chasing a golem all this time? A man-made man?"

"Nonsense," Roux said. "There's no such thing. It's a fairy tale."

"How can you say that after everything we've seen?"

"Because it's all nonsense. No matter what else, we both know that it's impossible to make something out of nothing. You can't take a handful of dust and clay and turn it into a living thing. It cannot be done. It's wishful thinking. It's not magic or alchemy or any form of science. It is pure fairy tale."

"Or is it? Just because we haven't come across it on our wandering doesn't mean it's not possible, that there's not some underlying universal law beyond our understanding." Roux understood the point well enough.

"Yes, of course there is an element of truth to that," Roux agreed. "There is more to the world than any one of us knows. But do you really think there could ever be a science so powerful that it could fashion life not from the living?" The thing was, Garin was right; there was no way that he could be absolutely sure it wasn't possible. Living almost four centuries wasn't possible, and yet they had done it, hadn't they? And in those four hundred years Roux had seen a great many things that should not have been possible and yet they had happened.

But could that mean the killer they sought had emerged from myth? Surely not. It made no sense, no sense at all.

"It's the last great miracle, isn't it? Over the past century man has taken every power believed to be supernatural and found a way to harness it. All save the creation of life. So surely, that's the next step? That's the next great scientific leap? The mortality principle?"

Roux really didn't have the words to argue with the younger man. The world was changing. Fast. So many of those changes were happening faster than he could comfortably adapt to. This wasn't the world he had been born into. There would come a time when it had all advanced beyond him, he knew, and he did not look forward to that day.

"If you truly believe we are nearing the end of this journey, we need to find him before he moves on," Roux said. "End it here."

"You think the killer is still here? Surely he has already moved on. Kill and move. Kill and move. How else could he stay ahead of us?"

"I don't think he's left yet," Roux said. It had taken a while for a simple idea to percolate in his brain, becoming an itch that he couldn't quite scratch. It had nagged away at him for so long that there had been nights when he had lain awake trying to unravel a jumble of thoughts to find the irritant. But it was always there, and it always came back to the same question: *Why had no one seen a stranger traveling alone despite the distance that the killer had covered?*

It didn't make sense.

How could the brute make his way from town to town without ever being seen? Surely his simple presence on the road would raise suspicion. A lonely traveler leaving death in his wake? People should see him. People should be talking about him, fearful, suspicious…

Roux and Garin had raised enough eyebrows and they had been *following* the trail of death, always too late to be treated as suspects.

"Why?" Garin asked.

"I think he travels by night. And only by night." He said it almost before the thought had entered his mind, as if he had known the answer all along but no one had asked him the right question until that moment, not even himself. "That's why he hasn't been caught. He rests during daylight hours, moves on at night." He looked up at the sky. "Which means we have a few hours yet. He cannot be far away."

"So we rouse the neighborhood, have them out on a witch hunt beating down the doors to every place until we shake him out of the woodwork?"

"At the first shout of alarm the militia would have been out hammering on the doors. He's not in a house. He has to be somewhere no one would think of looking. Somewhere that would never fall under suspicion. Somewhere above reproach." His eyes drifted up the hill, toward the towering walls of the fortress overlooking the township.

"The castle," Garin said, following the direction of his gaze. "It makes sense. Who would think of looking there? It's impregnable, but more than that, it's symbolic. It represents safety, not threat. They look to the castle for protection."

"And behind its walls it's harboring a monster," Roux said, finishing his thought.

Garin fell silent.

Roux knew instinctively that they were right.

The castle was a bastion of safety. No one would ever imagine it could be sheltering a monster.

How many other similar havens had they passed along the way, châteaus and forts fallen into disrepair, the great family homes of the nobility? Hundreds all told. And it had never once crossed their mind the blue bloods could be harboring the creature. Never once. That was their first true mistake. He looked up at the castle now, the high walls casting thick shadow down over the forested slope and the towers that rose up like fingers clawing desperately at the sky. They had time to rectify their mistake.

At the very least they had nowhere else to look that they hadn't looked a thousand times before, so it was something.

But was it enough to give him hope that they might truly be at the end of the road?

24

Annja was alone out there.

The streets were deserted.

But why should it be any different? It was a small town, not a city. There was no expectation of night-life. It was the kind of town that closed as the sun went down and didn't open again until it rose. There was no reason for anyone to go out after dark in a place like this. None whatsoever. But still, the quiet gave her the creeps. It just felt unnatural.

The castle on the hill was lit up like a watchtower, but were there sirens on the rocks below? Her eyes were drawn to the bright lights. Were they calling to the killer? It didn't feel like a good place to hide or to find his next victim, but there was something about that place that sent a shiver right down into her core.

Annja was so intent on looking in the direction of the lights that she almost walked straight past the bundle of rags that betrayed a vagrant huddled in the doorway of the convenience store.

She paused, waiting to see if he responded to her presence.

The man didn't move.

For one sickening moment she thought he was already dead—if not at the hands of the monster, then at the mercy of the elements—but he grunted and shuffled inside the sleeping bag. The bag was pulled up around his head and the drawstring pulled tight so that the only part of him exposed to the night was his eyes, and even they lay in shadows.

Annja took another step toward the man, then hesitated, realizing that there was every chance that she was about to meet the killer. She had no reason to believe the thing she'd seen on the roof hunted like some lion on the Serengeti, maybe it was more like a fisherman dropping a lure into the water.

The thought pulled her up short, the cold stone of doubt settling in her gut.

But...

That word.

Always that word.

But what if she was ahead of the killer and the man in the bag was a victim in waiting? Did he even know he was in danger? Why should word of the killer have reached him? Didn't his very presence in this doorway mean he'd dropped out from the world in many—if not all—ways?

Annja didn't have a choice; she had to warn him even if he chose to do nothing about it.

She crouched beside the man, not sure how to catch his attention. Shaking him felt unnecessarily rude, aggressive. She placed a hand on the bag, not sure he'd even feel it through the downy padding, and said, "Don't be afraid," hoping he would understand.

The figure moved, shuffling about uncomfortably in the bag. Annja pulled back her hand, waiting for him to show that he was alert. The man pushed himself into a sitting position. Fingers emerged through the face-hole to draw down on the toggle and open the space wider, until the man's head emerged like some grotesque moth breaking out of its cocoon. The homeless man did not move any closer to the streetlight's yellow puddle of light.

"It's been a long time since a woman frightened me," the man said, amused. "But if anyone was going to, it would be you."

It took her a second to place the voice and words.

"Garin?"

She saw the grin through the dark.

"What are you doing out here? You do know the killer is heading this way."

He grinned again. "I'm banking on it. What am I doing out here? I'm bait. Better that than I find some unfortunate wretch to play the part and risk his life, don't you think? I've got no intention of trailing this monster halfway across Europe again."

Annja caught the last word, but made no reference to it.

Instead, she said, "You shouldn't be doing this on your own."

"I can handle myself."

"I know you can, but you don't know what you are going up against."

"Oh, believe me, I know *exactly* what I'm up against."

"And so do I," another voice said. She hadn't heard Roux approach behind her. The old man stood beneath the streetlight, bathed in its sickly yellow glow. "We've faced down this threat once before, haven't we, Garin?"

"Roux," the man in the bag said.

"But this is what I don't like. We killed it and placed

its body where it would never be discovered. So how can it be at large? Can you answer that, Garin?"

There was more than a trace of anger in his voice. There was barely contained rage. Annja glanced back at Garin just as he was shucking off the sleeping bag and clambering awkwardly to his feet.

She had assumed they were together, but that wasn't right. Garin hadn't known the old man was there.

Was that where Roux had disappeared to? Had he been stalking Garin all evening? She'd thought on some basic level he had ditched her to go after the killer. But she remembered his question: Did she trust Garin? She studied the old man's face. She knew he didn't trust him on a fundamental level, and with plenty good reason. Garin had broken his trust and betrayed him more times than could be counted, but as long as she'd known them they'd always been on the same side.

Not always, she thought, remembering the Mask of Torquemada.

But even then, Garin hadn't been a murderer.

This was wrong.

"It wasn't dead," Garin said.

Roux shook his head in denial of the only answer Garin offered. "Impossible. How could it *not* be dead?"

"I don't know."

"Let me try asking another way. How could it have survived for more than a hundred and fifty years when we left it for dead, dismembered, buried away in an impossible prison?" Roux waited but Garin had no answer for him.

"I really wish one of you would tell me what the hell is going on." Annja cut into their conversation. Even without hearing the end of Roux's story, it was obvious there were links between Mary Shelley's immortal tale and the creature at the window, but how did all of that possibly relate to this place, this time, these very real murders?

"It might make more sense if I just showed you," Roux said. "If Garin wants to wait here all night in the hope that the killer happens to stumble across him, let him. I've got better things to do with my time. But mark my words, Annja. This is all his fault."

Roux turned away and started walking.

Garin had extricated himself from the sleeping bag and stood half in, half out of the doorway.

"You coming?" Annja asked him.

"I'm not sure I'm invited."

Annja heard the grunt from Roux, who had clearly registered the comment. "That's as close as you're going to get to an invitation," she said.

Garin offered a wry smile. "Then I guess I'm coming."

25

Sunlight glinted from the windows of the houses.

People moved through the streets, giving them little more than a passing glance.

There was no sign of the fear that was expected.

Were they unaware of the danger they were in?

Ignorance was no shield to fend off death.

The main doors set into the castle wall stood closed to the outside world. They were thick timber, sturdy enough to repel an enemy horde if not impregnable. Bands of iron studded across the timbers, adding to their strength. A smaller door set into those huge doors was also locked and bolted, the hatches battened down for the night. It would demand more strength than either Roux or Garin possessed to break it down. Garin studied it, wondering if the great brute they'd pursued this long could have broken through, and realized it was possible, given its incredible strength, but there was no sign of forced entry. In his mind's eye he imagined the killer's version of subtlety was to wrench the doors off their hinges and hurl them aside, but even if not, there were no obvious signs of damage. The doors had not been cared for beyond being oiled for centuries to protect them against exposure to the sun.

"We could be wrong," Garin said.

"We could," Roux agreed. "But we are not. Just because nothing has gotten inside this way doesn't mean there aren't other ways into the fortress."

"A back door?" Annja supplied.

"An escape route?" Garin countered.

"Same difference," Roux replied. "Just not an actual door. Maybe a passageway from the dungeons that opens up in the forest, away from the threat. No one wants to trap themselves when the wolf turns up at the door."

Garin was doubtful. He thought the older man was clutching at straws, but there was no point in arguing with him. There either was a secret passage or there wasn't. They'd either find it, or they wouldn't. And if it was secret, the odds were that they wouldn't.

They patrolled the perimeter of the castle, looking up at the walls and down the slope for any sign of passage. There was nothing obvious to suggest the killer had found his way inside. Roux was convinced that the killer was still somewhere close by, but Garin had his doubts.

The younger man led the way, pausing every now and then to examine the ground, looking at the broken twigs blown from the trees as deadfall, and the stems of grass blown back in the wind, at anything that might prove someone had stood there in the past few hours. There was no sign of anything on the walls to hint that anyone had tried to scale them, no scrape of a muddy footprint on the stone, no deep imprint on the ground to announce that a ladder had recently stood there.

He was being more thorough than he needed to be, but he didn't want Roux claiming he'd screwed up.

If the killer had managed to get inside to hide, it was unlikely that it would have fashioned a ladder to climb onto the wall. Even the calmest of murderers would surely be concerned about the danger of being caught so quickly after killing his latest victim. So it would have chosen stealth over speed. Garin tried to put himself in the brute's place. If he could not put a distance between himself and his victim before the body had been discovered, he would have wanted to find a hiding place as quickly as possible. The question was, had it planned its hiding place before it committed the crime? That would make it ten times harder to find.

And was Roux's theory about the killer going to ground during daylight correct?

It was a simple answer to why no one reported seeing the brute, but if he was wrong that meant the hours spent searching only put more distance between them.

Roux seemed lost in thought. Garin pulled him back from his ruminations.

"Over here," the younger man called, his voice a mixture of excitement and urgency. Roux closed the distance quickly and crouched beside him to take a closer look at what Garin had discovered.

A metal grille had been set into the stone paving slabs close to the wall.

Garin tugged at it with one hand and it began to lift with little more resistance than a door that needed oiling.

"Not used every day," Annja noted as the metal grated back on rusted hinges. "And it's been locked until recently." She pointed out the different quality of the rust on the iron.

"Then we might just be on the right track, after all."

Roux smiled, but seemed reluctant to get his hopes up. He and Garin had been close before only to fall tantalizingly short.

The shadow of the wall revealed nothing of the blackness that lay beyond the grate. Garin reached inside and felt a metal handhold set into the foundation of the wall. A way down. Or, more importantly, a way out if the castle's occupants needed it.

"After you," Garin said.

"We need a light," Roux pointed out. "We can't face a killer in the dark. We need to be able to see what we are up against."

Garin slung the pack from his back and kneeled beside it. A moment later he had pulled out a small glass lantern with a stump of candle inside. They each caught the sudden smell of sulfur that wafted close by as Garin struck a match. He had the candle lit and the door of the lantern latched back into place a moment later.

"And Roux said let there be light," Annja quipped.

Garin slung the bag back onto his shoulders and strapped the lantern to it.

It wasn't the first time that the old man had led their way into darkness.

26

The lights of the castle caused its walls to cast dark shadows into the streets below.

Roux led the way unerringly to his intended destination. It was obvious he had walked this way before.

Annja hurried to keep up with him. Garin brought up the rear.

Roux ignored the great gates that were set into the high stone wall and the small door set into the doors, and continued past them, until he found what he was looking for: a grille set in the ground at the foot of the great wall.

"It's already been opened," was all he said.

"What has?" Annja asked.

Garin produced a flashlight and played it over the metal grille. The metal had rusted in place, but still looked as solid as the day it was cast. It gave little resistance as Roux swung it up on hinges that showed no signs of decay. A passage led down into the darkness beneath the wall.

This was clearly part of their joint history.

"It shouldn't go anywhere," Roux said. "At least not anymore. It used to lead beneath the wall and into a storage cellar. We sealed it a long time ago. But surprise, surprise, it looks as if Garin was prepared for a little trip underground."

Annja stared into the abyss. "You think the killer is down there?" It was a simple yes or no question, but the point of it wasn't to generate any great insight, merely to stop the simmering anger from spilling over into a full-blown fight.

"It would *still* be down there if someone hadn't released it," Roux said, chest rising and falling rapidly. She didn't like the flush of color in his cheeks.

Garin somehow resisted coming back with a petty rejoinder.

"But you're sure that he's down there now? Is there another way out?"

"Unless Garin has provided it with a five-star suite in the castle, I would say so."

"There's no other way out," Garin said.

Roux glanced up at him from where he crouched over the opening in the ground.

"There's nothing to say that it's down there. Yes, it hides in darkness by day, but there's nothing to say that it isn't prowling the streets in search of its next victim."

Something was niggling away at Annja—the constant use of the impersonal pronoun *it*. She'd seen the killer on the rooftop. Big, bulky, clumsy, but surely it was a man, even if a giant one?

"I saw a man running across that rooftop back in the city. We aren't hunting some wild animal."

At last Roux broke the silence. "This thing is no man. It may *look* like a man, but it's not human. If you've seen it, you know that it's considerably larger than the average man. It is also much stronger than a man. This thing will take some stopping even when we find it. That's why it should never have been let out of there. I've got no idea how it survives, but I know that it doesn't need to eat or sleep."

"It should have been left alone," Garin agreed, earning a withering look from the old man. "We should have razed this place to the ground and been done with it."

"So, then, what is it?"

"The…golem," Garin said.

Here it was, finally, Annja thought. Was she about to go head-to-head with the monster, proving its existence without Lars's camera and the inevitable massive-ratings footage that would save the show? This was everything the suits could have dreamed of for their live broadcast, and no one was ever going to know about it. The irony wasn't lost on her. She made a decision. She wasn't about to let that happen. It might not be the media spectacle the network wanted, but it wasn't going unrecorded.

"If it's down there, it's cornered." Annja pulled out her phone, its backlight illuminating her face as she swiped across the screen to waken it.

"Please don't tell me you're thinking about calling your favorite policeman, Annja," Garin said. "He won't believe you. This is our mess. We have to take care of this ourselves."

"He's right for once," Roux agreed. "This *is* our mess."

"I'm not calling the police, the militia, the army or anyone like that. I'm calling my cameraman. He can tape some of this."

"Are you out of your mind?" Roux protested. "Recording this is the *last* thing we want to do. Forget it."

"I wasn't aware that I needed your *permission*, Roux.

You two may have enough money for you to be able to go anywhere and do anything. We don't all have the same luxury. I have a job to do and I happen to enjoy it. My show is called *Chasing History's Monsters*, in case you'd forgotten, and that is exactly what we are doing right now. I am not about to let a bunch of micromanaging penny-pinchers take it away from me."

"There will be other jobs," Roux said. "Better jobs. And if it's a case of money…"

"I don't want your money, Roux. I've built this career on my own. This is mine. No one else's. Mine," she said, ignoring the slightly raised eyebrow. She knew that she owed a lot to him, but this was different. *Chasing History's Monsters* was her baby. She'd given the best part of a decade to it. She'd worked for every little glimmer of success she'd had. If there was a way that she could give the studio executives what they wanted without compromising the integrity of the show she believed in, she would do it. This was the chase coming alive. All she needed to do was get Lars out here with his camera.

"You really are joking, aren't you?" Garin added. "Please tell me this is just a deliberate attempt to screw with us."

Annja said nothing.

"Annja?"

Still she said nothing.

"The last thing we want to do is try to deal with this thing with one hand tied behind our backs. And risking someone else's life? It's madness."

"Then it's a good job we're all in this together, isn't it? All for one and one for all."

Garin shook his head. "Uh-uh. Not happening."

"Sorry," Roux said. "I'm not becoming a TV star to keep your boss happy. I'm not about to have my face plastered across the screen for tens of millions of people to gawk at."

"I think you seriously overestimate just how popular her show is." Garin chuckled.

Annja ignored the pair of them and called up her cameraman's number. Her finger paused for a moment before she tapped the screen to make the call. The cell phone at the other end rang five times before Lars Mortensen eventually answered it, his voice barely coherent.

"Annja?" he muttered.

"Who else calls you in the middle of the night?"

"What time *is* it?"

"The middle of the night," she repeated. "I need you to get your backside in gear. I need you and your camera out in Benátky."

"Benat-where-ey?"

"Less than an hour from where you are. Be at the castle before first light. I think we've got the story the suits back home are looking for."

She could hear doubt down the line. "But we can't set up a live feed just like that." He snapped his fingers. "Not if we want to have the kind of audience participation that they are after. That takes a media campaign, planning."

"Let me worry about that, you just focus on getting out here."

"But I don't have a car."

"Improvise. If we pull this off, Doug won't be worried about signing off on your expenses."

"What about Turek? Is he with you?"

"Not at the moment."

"But you are going to let him know what's going down? You promised he'd be a part of the story."

"Of course," she said, not actually knowing if she was lying or not.

After she had hung up, she held a phone in front of her, her thumb hovering over Turek's number.

She knew that she *should* call him. She'd given the journalist her word. She wasn't the kind of person who broke promises. But if they weren't going in until sunrise there was no rush, was there?

The iron grille was open; everything else was conjecture.

Were they standing at the entrance to the killer's lair?

She looked at Roux, then at Garin.

"I want the truth. Now spill."

Garin shrugged as if to say to Roux, *This is your show.* The old man's brow furrowed. He looked down at the hole in the ground, then out over the rooftops of the town below.

Finally he said, "All right. I surrender. I think my car is the closest. It's certainly the most comfortable. Let's wait there. We should be able to see the brute if it returns. Meanwhile, I'll tell you everything you need to know."

He lowered the grille back into place.

27

The daylight disappeared as Roux descended into the darkness.

Each handhold took him deeper into the grip of the abyss.

Only the wavering flicker of the lantern hooked onto Garin's pack offered any kind of illumination, casting monstrous shadows beneath him.

The floor took him by surprise, coming without warning as he put his right leg down feeling for the next foothold that wasn't there. Roux stumbled in a clumsy dismount. He counted down the remaining steps for Garin, steering him off the ladder so the noise didn't startle the brute, alerting it to their presence.

There was barely time to glance back up at the patch of blue above, and then they were moving, deeper into the pit, the sky left behind.

Garin released the lantern from his pack, and passed it forward to Roux. The old man raised it, walking forward with the lantern in one hand and his sword drawn in the other.

Garin had taken to using a flintlock pistol, an affectation Roux had never cared for. A pistol would be of little use in the confines of the subterranean warren. If he missed with his single shot, there wouldn't be time to reload before their quarry was on them. The sword was far more practical and deadly.

Roux was not sure what he had expected to discover at the bottom of the shaft—a beast's lair? A makeshift bed made from a bundle of rags? The fixings of a burned-out fire?—but it hadn't been the maze of tunnels that spread out into the black.

He thought grimly of the Minoan Minotaur's prison as he ventured deeper into the tunnel, going beneath the wall as it branched into two and then two more passageways. There was nothing to indicate which path the killer had chosen. They took the right-hand path, which only led into dead ends filled with empty bottles and debris. A metal gate lay at the far end of the second branch, but that was securely locked, and Roux could make out no obvious indications that the lock had been tampered with in a very long time. Without a key they weren't getting through it. Not that they intended to. The killer hadn't gone that way.

They retraced their steps and started again down the second fork; it bent farther to the left before branching again.

Roux felt a breeze against his face, meaning there was an opening to the elements somewhere else.

He tried to place their whereabouts beneath the wall and the main building of the castle, getting his bearings as he shuffled forward in the near-absolute dark. The shadows cast by the flickering light disguised their direction. Again the branch they chose led to another dead end, though this time the storage cellar held only half a dozen barrels.

"Brandy?" Garin suggested, already at the barrels

to examine them more closely. "No, not brandy. Gunpowder." He sounded disappointed.

It made sense.

The castle no longer needed to defend itself from invaders, but how did one go about disposing of so much black powder? Better to keep it close at hand, but also out of harm's way, in case need for it should arise again someday. It wouldn't spoil, after all.

"There's no telling how long it's been down here."

Roux hadn't noticed at first, but there was no other way out of this cellar, no direct route into the castle itself.

He led the way out of the room, back to the last branch they had encountered. There were more turns, more twists in the tunnels, each of them leading to another dead end. Of all the chambers and tunnels they had checked only the first offered any sort of access to the castle itself, and even that was secure against intrusion. That meant that the killer had to be here somewhere, down in the labyrinth, and all they had to do was keep on looking.

Sooner or later they would find it.

Roux held up his hand to stop Garin.

He listened to the silence, trying to make out any undercurrent or vibration that shouldn't be there. Nothing. Not even the shallow rise and fall of their own breathing. They continued on, deeper, utterly lost now.

As they walked the passageways, Roux felt the air around them grow colder. The stub of candle in the lantern flickered, threatening to fail and plunge them into darkness. At last Roux heard the sound of movement, a faint scuffing, but it was enough to send his heart racing. He fought the urge to run toward it, certain that his search was at an end. He had found the monster.

Roux led the way, edging forward carefully as he placed his feet down, so as not to betray their presence. Even so, the lightest of footsteps echoed around the walls. It was impossible that their quarry hadn't heard them.

Another sound: shifting and shuffling.

Garin urged Roux to go faster.

Roux touched his fingers to his cheek. The chill was noticeably worse.

"There's another way out," he said. "Feel the air."

"Then we take it before it can reach it."

They shouldn't have worried.

Even in the near-darkness as the candle stub burned down to nothing, Roux saw the shape in the corner the moment that the tunnel opened into a wider cellar.

He was a bear of a man, much bigger than either of them, but he barely moved as they approached.

Six steps.

That was all it would take.

Six steps and Roux could slide the cold steel of his sword between the killer's ribs.

Six steps and their quest would be over.

Six steps, then at last Roux would be able to sleep. Six steps and Garin wouldn't have a reason to moan about being dragged across Europe and could focus on what was important to him. Sex. Money. Money. Sex.

Six steps.

But he lingered too long to take the first one.

The brute was on his feet before Roux realized that he was even awake.

It might have been a colossus, but it was agile and it was shockingly fast.

The shadow moved in a blur, swinging an arm even as Roux raised his sword in readiness to deflect the blow. Steel made contact with the sleeve of the brute's heavy coat, the blade biting into the heavy material before being swatted aside harmlessly.

Roux took a stumbling step back, trying to dance out of the man's reach. He thrust the lantern toward Garin. The brute struck again before he could make the handoff, and the glass lantern went spinning to the floor. The window shattered and the candle snuffed out as the stub came loose.

For a long sliding second the world seemed to fall into absolute darkness, but a moment later there was light once more.

The flame had caught hold of straw strewed across the floor and now the ground beneath their feet was burning.

The big man swung again, oblivious to the danger that Roux's sword represented.

Roux grasped the hilt with both hands and swung as hard as he could.

This time the blade dug deep, slicing through the heavy layers of coat into the flesh of the brute's upper arm and striking bone. Roux's arms shuddered with the impact. There was a heartbeat when they were locked together before Roux yanked the blade free.

That moment proved costly.

The killer swung with his other clubbing hand, the blow slamming into Roux's temple, the sound of thunder detonating inside his skull.

Roux's grip on his sword relaxed, his reflexes reacting automatically to the skull-shattering impact. He staggered, dropped to one knee, but somehow managed to keep one hand firmly on the hilt as the tip of the blade struck the burning floor.

Roux lowered his head, willing the killing blow to fall.

He had no fight left in his old bones.

But the killing blow never landed.

Roux looked up as his senses were assailed by the smell of brimstone.

The brute fell backward.

He collapsed into the burning straw as the fire spread with alarming speed into old packing cases stacked unevenly against the wall.

Gunpowder.

"Up, old man. We've got to get out of here before the whole place blows," Garin barked, hauling Roux back to his feet. Garin's flintlock pistol still smoldered in his other hand.

The brute wasn't down for long—and most certainly not out. It struggled back to its feet, coat ablaze, smoke wreathing its giant frame and transforming it into a beast stepped straight out of his nightmares, as Roux caught a glimpse of its face for the first time.

Its features were out of proportion, too large for its face, unfinished. They shifted in the firelight and shadow, seeming to melt.

No matter what this creature was, it was less than human.

Around them the flames rose, the heat coming off them ferociously. Flame shot up the walls of the cellar. Stone and mortar groaned and wooden supports creaked and snapped as the moisture was leeched out of them by the blaze, adding to the conflagration.

"Now!" Garin demanded, dragging Roux back into the tunnel. "I'm not dying here, old man. I'm not ready!"

Fragments of stone crashed from the ceiling, sending a thick black cloud of smoke and choking devils of dust that poured back to fill the corridor. The flames turned the cramped tunnel hellish. They covered their mouths as they stumbled away from the heat, knowing they had seconds before the flames bit through the barrels and ignited the black powder.

Roux had no recollection of how they had come, which branches in the tunnel would lead them toward the shaft back up to daylight. The choking smoke made it impossible to tell where the walls began and ended. All they could do was chase the flicker of breeze, hoping it brought them to the light. They stumbled along in the darkness, fumbling their way along the walls, the heat in the stone scorching their hands as a deep grumble formed in the belly of the subterranean lair. The grumble deepened, resonating through the walls, filling the tainted air. Dust fell around them, clogging the air, making it harder to see and to breathe in the darkness.

The ghost of a breeze seemed to guide them to safety as it was sucked back toward the shaft they'd descended, billowing up into the daylight as they hauled themselves gratefully up the ladder set into the shaft's wall.

Roux closed his eyes as he emerged.

Alive.

Still.

"I guess it's all over," Garin said, climbing up behind him.

"Anything but," Roux said, choking back bitterness, dust and smoke.

He sank to his knees.

Bile rose in his throat. He leaned forward and spit on the ground.

He felt the explosion ripple through the soil beneath his hands, the dirt undulating like the skin of a storm-tossed lake.

A second explosion, more savage than the first, sent a rumble through the earth before the shaft gouted dust and flame through the vent in the ground.

Nothing could have survived that.

28

"And you are sure it was dead, whatever it was?" Annja asked, pressing home the point.

The three of them sat in the car waiting. She really hated waiting.

"Nothing could have gotten out of there, believe me. After the second explosion the tunnel began to collapse," Garin said. "Even if the fire hadn't killed it, or my gunshot and blood loss, it wasn't getting out of that hole in the ground."

"And yet it must have," Roux growled. "Somehow it survived down there until someone dug through the rubble to rescue it." He turned on Garin. "Tell me, be honest—how long did you wait before you excavated the ground? A week? A month? A year? We both know the thing didn't need food to sustain its unnatural life. So how long did you wait before you went back to dig it out?"

Garin met the old man's stare, and rather than defiance there was merely sadness in his expression as he shook his head in denial. "You really are convinced that I'm responsible for this, Roux? Even after everything we've been through, you think I'm capable of this?"

"I know you better than you know yourself, Garin."

"And because of that you're not even prepared to consider any other possibilities? Like maybe I've got nothing to do with this?"

"Don't waste your time pleading your innocence. Only the two of us knew it was down there. I didn't liberate it, and now you're here and it is on the loose again."

"Well, I hate to be the bearer of bad news, old man, but you're out of your mind. This isn't my fault. I saw the news, realized what it meant, but couldn't believe it was true, so I came here. I wasn't the one who cleared the rubble away. I didn't let it out of there. I came back to end it once and for all."

As Annja listened to the argument rage back and forth, one thing struck her: they were both working under the assumption that it was the same killer some two hundred years later, which really should have been impossible. She said as much. "Just for a moment, suppose it's not the same killer. I know you think that what you saw down there wasn't human, but that doesn't mean it's the only one, does it? Could there be more of them?"

"A second golem?"

"Even Frankenstein made a mate for his creation," Annja said. She wondered if the notion had even crossed their minds.

"I'm pretty sure that's only in the movies, Annja," Garin said. "And we all know how trustworthy Hollywood is when it comes to the treatment of the truth."

"Forget what you think you know about the Modern Prometheus," Roux countered. "Annja may be right, after all. In the Latinate version of the myth, Prometheus made a man from clay and water. A golem.

Just as the legend of the Maharal also goes. I have no idea if the author truly knew what she was writing about that summer, but the proximity is uncanny. Victor Frankenstein rebelled against the laws of nature and how life was naturally made, only to be punished by his creation. The monster turned on its maker. Mary Shelley's story is, of course, a tragedy. The monster is immortal. Death, you see, is a gift of the gods." There was a wistfulness to the old man's voice as he said this. "Mary called him Adam. Does this sound familiar?"

Annja thought about the ramifications of that name. "Where there is an Adam, surely there is an Eve?" she offered, using his arguments to support hers.

Roux had been so convinced that Garin was the root of all evil. That set him on a train of thought from which he couldn't break free. There were no certainties beyond the facts, and admittedly those facts were compelling—the entrance to the castle cellars had been cleared; there was a killer on the loose, preying on the most vulnerable members of Czech society; and from her own sighting, that killer was big, ungainly and unnaturally fast, with features like some child's drawing of a face—but that didn't mean they were tracking the same killer across two centuries.

Annja's head was suddenly full of doubts. Occam's razor came into her thinking: if in doubt, the most obvious answer is usually the right one. But what was the most obvious here? That a man-made creature had somehow woken after two hundred years of hibernation? That didn't seem obvious at all.

She checked her watch. Half an hour had passed since she'd called Lars. At the earliest he wouldn't be there for another half an hour or so. She thought about calling Turek again, to see if he'd come up with any-thing at the border, but before she could the shadow just beyond the reach of a streetlight seemed to change, becoming darker for a moment. It wasn't a trick of the light. She saw it move again and was sure.

"Over there," she whispered, indicating the thicker shadow with a slight nod. The shape burst from the shadows, running straight through the pool of light. She didn't get a good look at its face because a hood shrouded it.

"Time to put our differences aside. We both want the same thing here," Garin whispered. He leaned forward from the backseat so he could watch between them.

"Two hundred years," Roux said.

"Feels like yesterday, doesn't it?" Garin stated.

Annja watched as the figure strode across the road. She shrank in her seat in case it chanced to glance their way. The brutish figure was intent on moving toward the grille, and the entrance to the subterranean war-ren beneath the castle. The shape ran unevenly, drag-ging one leg with a strange limp, but whatever wound it carried didn't slow it at all. Despite favoring the leg, it didn't appear to be in pain.

"The golem doesn't feel pain," Roux said, as though privy to her thoughts. "Believe me. I caught it with more than one good blow with my sword, but it didn't cry out once."

"Nor when I shot it, or when its coat caught fire," Garin added.

"Maybe it's the voice that's lacking, not the pain re-ceptors," Annja said. "Because there's something wrong with one of its legs."

"Just because something is damaged doesn't mean

that it causes pain," Roux said. "Pain is a uniquely living quality. Something has to be alive to feel pain."

"That looks pretty alive to me."

"And again, just because something is mobile doesn't mean it is alive, or sentient, or any such notion. Mechanisms wear out."

"Speaking from experience there, old man?" Garin chuckled from the backseat.

Annja tried not to let the smile spread across her lips, but it wasn't easy.

The figure disappeared out of sight.

She felt her heart start to beat a little faster.

She wanted to get this over with, but the two men had a better idea of what was down there than she did.

"We should go straight in after it," Garin said. "Get this over with. I can't pretend I'm looking forward to it."

"We wait until Lars gets here," Annja insisted. "You both owe me that much."

Roux raised an eyebrow. "I wasn't aware that either of us owed you anything. This life isn't all quid pro quo."

She stared at him through the mirror. Did he really mean that or was he trying to rile her, push her away?

They were a team, weren't they?

She might be the junior partner, but she brought unique strengths to the table. They needed her. She'd always given as good as she'd got. Certainly she'd come a long way since she'd needed rescuing by the old man on that hillside in France or by Garin in the village below. No, that wasn't fair. They did owe her. They owed her plenty.

"Call him," Garin said. "Find out how far away he

is. Ten minutes here or there won't make much difference. Maybe he got lucky with the roads."

She knew it was a long shot. The worst case was
confirmed when he picked up.

"Where are you?"

"Stuck. There's some kind of holdup."

"Holdup?" Annja felt two pairs of eyes burning into
her.

"The traffic's at a standstill. Nothing is moving. The
lineup is half a mile long. All I can see in the road up
ahead are blue flashing lights. I'm not going anywhere
fast. Sorry, boss."

"Okay, there's nothing you can do about it," Annja
said. She could only stall Roux and Garin for so long,
and that wasn't going to be long enough. "Call me and
let me know when you're moving again."

She forced a smile and shrugged as she slipped the
phone back into her pocket. "Give him ten minutes,"
she said eventually.

"He won't be here in ten minutes," Roux said, as if
that ended the debate.

Annja had no choice but to admit defeat. Roux
opened his door without waiting for a response from
the others. Garin was out of the car a second behind
him, keen to get on with things. All hope of giving the
network what they wanted to save the show went out
of the door with them.

Without Lars there'd be no footage, and no footage
meant no salvation.

It was over. All that was left was facing up to that
fact.

Annja was the last out of the car.

She didn't lock it. She followed them up the hill to

the grille at the castle wall. Garin pulled a handgun from his waistband, checked the mechanism, then replaced it. Roux appeared to be unarmed save for the flashlight they had used to peer into the darkness before. In the distance the sky was beginning to glow, a stark reminder that dawn was not far away.

"You got a weapon, Roux?" Garin asked as he lowered himself onto the first rung.

Roux tapped his jacket, his free hand resting lightly on a bulge that Annja hadn't noticed before.

"No need to ask you, madam," he said to Annja. "Here goes nothing," Garin announced as he started to make his way into the darkness.

"You next," Roux said, playing the light over the iron rungs. "Don't do anything heroic down there. In and out, let's just get this over with."

"I'm not big on stupid," Annja told him.

"Then maybe it will all end here," Roux said. There was something fatalistic about the words that Annja didn't like.

29

Annja stumbled back into Garin's arms when she reached the bottom of the shaft.

"Thanks," she said, the sound of her voice echoing down the tunnel. Garin winced as the darkness multiplied the word a hundredfold. Annja glanced back up the deep shaft to see the dull light disappear as Roux made his way down.

Garin had his gun out, the muzzle pointing the way ahead into the darkness. The last time he'd been down there he had had a single shot from his flintlock. Now he could just about cut the brute in two with bullets before it could charge them. Times changed, and with them man's ability to kill.

Despite everything that the two men had told her, Annja realized that she had begun to think of the killer as human. Strange and deformed, yes, but still human. How else could it be alive? Even her memories of that childish sketch of a face couldn't change that. The rest, living for two hundred years or more? Well, her companions were proof that there were more things in heaven and earth than the mundane philosophies she'd believed for so long before she met them.

When the three of them stood together, Roux turned on the flashlight again.

He played the beam into the tunnel. The damage to the walls from the explosions and fire was still readily apparent, though it looked less like a raw wound now and more like ancient scar tissue.

"Left or right?" Annja asked.

"Right," Garin said. "Some things you remember like it was only yesterday when they happened."

"And sometimes it was yesterday when they happened," Roux said, still not prepared to believe Garin had nothing to do with the brute's resurrection.

"Draw your sword," Roux told her. It wasn't going to be comfortable to wield it in the confines of the tunnels. "And be alert. There are many twists and turns down here. It was a labyrinth then. There's no telling what it is like now, after the explosions. It was a warren with plenty of dark places to hide."

"And there's no guarantee the creature will have taken refuge in the same cellar," Garin said. "So, eyes and ears open. If we're lucky, we'll hear it coming."

That didn't sound very lucky to Annja, but she didn't need to be told twice.

She closed her eyes, summoning the familiar image of Joan's mystical blade to mind, and reached out for it as the two men moved ahead of her. As ever, she sensed the sword's presence in the mists of the otherwhere before she felt its familiar grip in her hand. Its weight there was reassuring, the thrill of elemental magic as she felt its pull, drawing it from the otherwhere in a smooth slow action. The move was part of a dance long since preordained.

As she had feared, there was precious little room to

swing the sword and to test her muscles after the fall, but simply holding the weapon was enough to make her feel whole again. It was as if she had found part of herself that she had almost forgotten had existed.

It didn't matter what lay ahead of them in the darkness, human or something else; she was ready for it.

The flashlight cast weird shadows as they walked through the tunnel in single file.

Garin led the way unerringly, not faltering even once as he kept them off the wrong track, which he promised dead-ended, through to where the tunnel had collapsed. The ground was still littered with rubble from the cave-in. The walls were charred black.

Annja stumbled more than once as she picked her way through, reaching out with her free hand to the wall to stay on her feet.

The air was foul.

As they made their way farther along the tunnel, Annja couldn't see any evidence that the killer had come this way. The rubble was undisturbed. She listened hard in the darkness, but heard nothing beyond the echo of their footsteps and the sliding stones as they dislodged them.

Before they reached the cellar where Roux and Garin had fought and thought they'd killed the brute all those years ago, their path was blocked.

There was no way through the cave-in.

Roux climbed on the debris, clawing at it in search of a gap to try to shine his light through. There was no point. Nothing had come that way. Either now or then.

"Anything?" Garin asked from the rear, but Roux just shook his head.

Annja said, "No," knowing that there was no way Garin could have seen the gesture.

"You could be right about a second killer," Roux admitted, staring at the stones.

"I'm not that worried about being right or wrong," Annja said bluntly. "I just want this to be over."

"We all do," Roux promised her.

Garin started to retrace his steps back along the passage to the last branch in the tunnel. Annja followed him a couple of paces behind.

"Did you feel that?" she asked as a chill breeze brushed against her cheek.

"Feel what?"

"Air, like there's another way out."

Garin shook his head. "This place is a maze. It wouldn't surprise me if we'd missed a secret entrance years ago. There are a million places to hide, why not a million and one?"

"I felt it back then, too," Roux said.

Annja held up a hand. Both men stopped, silent. She listened for any sounds in the dark, knowing that there was every chance the killer could move around behind them and escape while they were still down in the tunnels chasing it fruitlessly.

Roux pushed his way to the front with his flashlight, playing it over the ground as they picked their way back through the rubble. Garin, reluctantly, stepped aside to let him through.

The flashlight's beam picked over the rock dust and rubble, but the only signs of disturbance were their own.

As they walked she heard movement.

At first Annja thought that it was a groan from the

ceiling, their presence somehow disturbing the delicate balance that held what remained in place.

But it wasn't that.

Garin reacted first, moving like lightning between her and Roux.

She hadn't even realized there was a fork in the tunnel. By the time she did, he was gone.

"Garin," Roux whispered uselessly after his back.

Garin was already stumbling through the darkness, making far more noise than they had done since they'd descended into the network of tunnels. If the killer hadn't already known they were down there, it had to now.

Annja hurried after him, stumbling more than once before she was clear of the last of the rubble. She couldn't see Garin anywhere, but she equally couldn't see where he could have gone. She hurried on into the darkness, reaching a point where the tunnel branched into three separate passages.

"Garin!" she called out, giving up all pretense of stealth.

There was no reply.

"This way," Roux said, starting off down the right-hand tunnel.

"Are you sure?" she asked.

"No," he said, without turning. "But any decision is better than standing here doing nothing."

Annja resisted the urge to snap back at him that she wasn't doing nothing, and instead followed the old man into the tunnel. Roux played his flashlight in front of them, picking out a path.

Before they reached the end, the unmistakable sound of a gunshot echoed through the tunnel behind them.

Annja spun on her heel, ready to face down an invisible foe, but before she could move, a second shot and a third rang out, followed by an agonizing cry that filled every inch of the tunnels.

It was the sound of death.

"Garin!"

30

They ran.

The beam of the flashlight roved across the ground and walls as they raced back to the main tunnel. Over and over they called Garin's name, but there was no response. Annja knew that there was something wrong. Garin had the gun. That meant Garin had fired the shots. But that scream… That had been Garin's voice, and now he wasn't answering them.

Roux was thinking the same thing.

He had drawn his own gun, ready to take on the killer himself.

But if three shots hadn't been enough to bring the killer down, why should five, six or seven be enough to do the trick? Roux's insistence that the killer was inhuman haunted Annja. What if he was right? What if there was no way to stop it?

There was always one way.

Cold steel.

Annja gripped the hilt of the sword, the blade across her chest so that it was both at the ready should the brute go for them but safe from sliding between Roux's ribs if she should stumble.

The echo of the gunshots and the cry had long since

faded by the time they came to what had to have been their source. They moved quickly but carefully, checking the two cellar rooms into which the passageway opened. There was no sign of Garin or the killer. No sign that anyone had been down there at all.

"There must be more rooms, more branches we missed somehow," Annja said. "They can't have escaped the tunnels."

"Not without leaving a trail," Roux agreed. "One or both of them are hurt. Bleeding. Garin's strong, but there's no way he could lift the creature without help. So if he put it down, it'd still be down."

"But if it was Garin, who fell?" Annja asked, even though she knew the answer without needing to hear it.

"Then God help him. This way."

Roux followed another turn, almost missing an opening in the tunnel as something came barreling out of it.

The figure slammed the old man against the tunnel wall, driving the air out of his lungs and sending the flashlight flying from his grip. The light died as it hit the ground, plunging them into darkness.

Annja held out her sword, more in defense than attack.

It wasn't as if she could swing it, and risk slicing into Roux as much as their unseen assailant.

"Roux," she called, and heard his groan coming from the ground. That was enough.

"Stay down," she commanded, taking a step forward, feeling her way in the darkness with the tip of her weapon. A toe nudged Roux's body. She felt him shrink from the contact. She swung tentatively, the sword slicing through air until it made contact with stone and sent a shower of sparks to the ground.

She took another step forward and swung again.

Still nothing.

She heard Roux scrambling for his flashlight. It wouldn't help. Switching her grip to one hand, Annja slipped her left hand into her pocket and pulled out her cell phone. All it took was the touch of her thumb on the screen and it lit up.

There was nothing between her and the curve in the tunnel.

"You can get up now," she told Roux as she increased the intensity of the glow from the phone and switched it over to the flashlight function.

The battery needed charging, but it would last long enough to do what she had to do. "Come on," she said. "But this time, stay behind me."

Roux didn't argue with her.

She took a breath as they reached the bend, and pressed herself against the tunnel wall, listening to a strange sound coming from around the bend. She strained, expecting to hear breathing, or even the sound of gurgling as pain ripped through the man around the corner. But the sound was neither of those. It had an even rhythm, but it was not the sound of a living thing. All she could hear was a steady *click, click, click*.

She took another breath before stepping around the corner, knowing that the killer was almost certainly only a matter of feet away.

Annja pushed herself away from the wall and took the step.

She held out her sword in one hand, her phone in the other as if its glow was a shield.

The light was enough to startle the thing that was waiting for her on the other side.

Thing.

She stared at that strange, incomplete face, lit by the light from the phone as the killer raised its hands to shield its eyes from the bright glare.

At first she thought that it was going to turn and run, but then it staggered forward, striking out at Annja. Its great fists slashed at the light, the creature seemingly ignorant of the threat her sword presented. Annja pushed the blade as hard as she could, feeling it slide through its heavy coat and into the softness of the flesh beneath.

Strangely so much of the thing was in front of her that was far less than she had expected. She expected a blast of foul breath but none came, a waft of stale sweat, but there was nothing. She expected a heat against the coldness of the tunnel, but there wasn't any.

She noticed a faint smell, an aroma she could not quite place. And a vibration that ran the length of her blade all the way into her fingertips.

Most surprising of all was that there was no pain in its childlike sketch of a face, no change in the thing's expression despite her sword plunging into its body.

Annja pulled at the hilt to free the sword, but as she did, the thing swung a fist at her.

The impact of the blow sent her sprawling.

Roux, standing behind her, broke her fall.

Before she hit the ground the world turned black.

31

Somewhere in her dream she heard her name being called over and over again.

A hand slapped at her face, stinging her back to consciousness as if she were being interrogated, only she had no idea what the answer was to what they demanded.

"Annja! Annja!" She began to recognize the voice through the blinding pain inside her head. She opened her eyes to absolute darkness.

"Roux?"

"Welcome back. I was beginning to think it had broken you once and for all," he said, helping her into a sitting position. She opened her hand to reveal that she was still holding her phone, the screen still glowing. His face was haunted in the sickly light.

"You should know me by now," she said. "I'm tougher than that. What about Garin?" she asked.

"Gone."

"Gone? As in dead or as in run away?"

"Gone as in not here. There's no sign of either of them."

Annja struggled to her feet and felt around for her sword. There was no sign of it. She battled down the

urge to panic and reached out into the otherwhere to
retrieve it, knowing that it would have faded from this
plane of existence as her consciousness lapsed. As soon
as her fingers closed around the hilt again, the moment
of panic she'd felt melted away like frost.

"We need to find Garin," she said, drawing comfort
from the weight of the sword in the darkness.

"He's a big boy," Roux said, fiddling with his flashlight in an attempt to draw some sort of light from its
broken bulb. It was a fool's errand. "He can take care
of himself."

"Obviously he can't. You heard that scream as well
as I did. He's in trouble. We aren't walking out of here
without him."

"Remember—"

"Yeah, that he's one of us. So we are not abandoning
him. I wouldn't abandon you." It was as simple as that.
"Now, you've been here before. Is there another way
out of here? I felt that breeze on my face. That wasn't
blowing down through the shaft."

"One of the cellars has a door, an iron gate. *Had* an
iron gate. It was locked when we were down here before."

"They aren't here. They can't have gone out the way
we came in without getting past us. Could they have
gotten to the gate without passing us?"

"I don't know. I don't remember," Roux started
to say, blustering, but Annja was fed up with the old
man's stalling. Every second counted. She'd been on
the receiving end of a blow from that brute, and it had
damned near crushed her skull. She'd be hearing Garin's scream in her sleep for months.

"Just show me," she said.

As if on cue, the flashlight flickered for a moment, then burst into life. She had no idea how he'd fixed the broken bulb. It didn't matter. Roux started to lead the way back through the maze of tunnels. There were more offshoots than she'd noticed on the way in. A lot more. Some even looked fresh. Had the killer been carving out a new lair down here?

"He really will be fine, you know," Roux said, but it sounded like he was trying to reassure himself, not just her. A few minutes ago he'd been blaming Garin for all the woes in the world and had believed him capable of mounting a killing spree by proxy. "We've been through worse." Again, she didn't know who he was trying to convince, himself or her.

Annja kept pace with the old man as he moved quickly along the corridor. The flashlight played over the detritus of the castle, odds and ends that were no longer wanted but that no one could bear to throw away. They were signs of life that proved someone came down into this pit.

At the far end of the room she saw an iron gate set into the stone wall.

It hung open.

32

Stone steps worn smooth over centuries by the shuffling of tired feet spiraled upward on the other side of the gate.

Annja couldn't imagine the giant killer having come this way; the stairwell was incredibly cramped. It wouldn't have had the room to maneuver, surely? It would have been a tight squeeze for Garin.

Assuming Garin is on his feet and not being carried by the thing, Annja thought.

The door at the top of the stairs was closed. A faint glow of a light crept through the gap at the bottom. Roux paused when he reached it. He raised a single finger to his lips. Annja nodded, understanding.

The old man killed the flashlight and lifted the latch slowly, easing the heavy door open a crack as silently as he could.

Roux peered through for a moment before he opened it fully, allowing the light on the other side to flood into the stairwell.

Annja couldn't see beyond him.

She followed Roux into some kind of scullery—a living, breathing part of the castle's day-to-day life. There was no sign that anyone had been working there that morning, but the place was clean and well tended.

Annja wondered if it was a visitor attraction or a working kitchen.

It took a second for her to notice that someone stood in the room's other doorway.

"Can I help you?" the man asked as she met his eye, wondering how she could possibly explain the presence of the great sword in her hands.

She half turned sideways, shielding the sword with her body as she slipped it back into the otherwhere. The newcomer missed the minor miracle; he only had eyes for the 9 mm pistol Roux pointed squarely at his heart.

After the initial shock of discovery, Annja noted the man's uniform. He was a security guard. He looked too old to be a serious deterrent to anyone.

He wasn't the killer.

"Did they come this way?" Roux demanded.

The guard shook his head, not following. Roux repeated the question in Czech.

"I have seen no one. Only you. I heard a noise. I came to investigate. I hoped it was one of the girls making tea. There is nothing to steal here. Please. I don't know you. I will tell no one you were here. Just…" He raised his hand, palm out, to show he was harmless. "Don't make this worse than it is."

Roux slipped his gun back inside his jacket. The relief in the security guard's face was clear to see.

"Listen to me carefully," Roux said. "I do not mean to alarm you, but we have every reason to believe that there is a killer inside the building."

"But…how?"

"We pursued him down a shaft on the other side of the wall, which opened up into your cellar network. We lost him down there."

"Are you police?" the man asked, still staring at Roux's gun hand.

"Interpol," Roux lied smoothly, pulling what appeared to be an ID from his pocket. "Have you seen anyone come this way?"

"Nothing at all, sir," the guard said, suddenly eager to defer all responsibility to Roux.

"Do you mind if we take a look around?"

"Most of the castle will still be locked. I'm not sure I can open up anything until the manager arrives."

Manager? That was more than enough to convince Annja that this was a commercial enterprise rather than a family estate. There could be any number of places where the creature might try to hide in a place like this.

"I'm sure you can," Roux said. "This man is dangerous. We need to bring him in before he can hurt anyone else."

"The front door was open when I got here," the guard offered. "Maybe he already slipped out before I arrived." He thought about it. "The outer gates were locked, though. We could check the outbuildings while we wait for the manager?" He motioned them out through the doorway he stood in.

Annja noticed the key in the door, and for just a moment the idea of locking him inside—for his own safety as much as anything else—crossed her mind. It was tempting. But if they were wrong and the thing was still down in the maze, then they'd be locking him in with the creature. Not good.

"How many people work here?" Annja asked, walking alongside him, leaving Roux trailing behind them.

"Full-time? Six. The rest…give time free…more in summer. Students." He led them along a corridor and up a flight of stairs that brought them out near a pair of solid wooden doors. The heavy modern lock looked out of place on the dark oak.

"This way," he said, leading them into a courtyard. High walls enclosed the small space. The morning had already grown light if not bright and the sound of traffic, slow but steady, had begun to fill the air. It wouldn't be long before the world was full of the hustle and bustle of life, muted here in comparison to Prague, but vibrant just the same.

"Are any of these buildings unlocked?" Annja asked.

"Some. They have nothing valuable in them. Most will be locked. If you find any doors unlocked, look inside."

He tagged along behind them, curious.

"Just one thing, then you're good to go about your duties," Roux said. "The stairs that brought us up from the cellar. Is that the only way in and out of there?"

"From the cellars? No. There are a few, I think. One for sure brings you out to the rear of the castle, but no one could have come up that way."

"No?"

The guard shook his head. "There was a major collapse a long time ago. The entire roof came down. It's perfectly safe now, but there's never been the money to repair it, so it's just a dead zone. There's a vast section of the maze cut off because of it."

"Ah," Roux said. "You've been most helpful."

He waited until the guard had closed the heavy oak doors behind him, then he turned to Annja. "A vast section of the maze. We were wrong, weren't we? We left it to burn but it had another way out."

33

They were interrupted in their search by the arrival of the manager, who had Annja's cameraman, Lars, in tow.

"I take it this is who you are looking for?" the man asked Lars. "Now perhaps one of you would be kind enough to tell me what's going on here?"

"It's a long story," Annja started to say, but the man didn't look particularly interested in hearing it.

"I'm afraid I'm going to ask you to leave," he said. "If you would like to film inside the castle—" he paused to motion toward the camera case, which was now on the ground beside Lars "—you'll need to put your request in writing and I will make sure it is seen by the board of trustees, but it will take time to get it approved as they only meet once a month."

Annja was about to protest when Roux took a tight grip on her arm and started to propel her toward the gate. Annja had expected him to flash his fake ID and demand that they be allowed to search for Garin. He didn't.

"What the hell is going on, Annja?" Lars asked when the heavy gates were slammed behind them.

Annja wanted to tear the place apart stone by stone. And that was all she wanted to do. Garin was in there.

He had to be. He'd do the same for her if their roles were reversed. For all his bluster and selfishness, he'd put his life on the line for her every single time she'd asked, without question.

"Nothing for you to worry about," she said.

"Nothing to worry about? Seriously? You dragged me out of bed, only for me to sit in a traffic jam for a couple of hours and leave me to hang around out here like a bad smell and it's all good?"

All she could do was act as if there was nothing wrong.

Thinking on her feet, she said, "I needed some shots of the castle at night. We managed to get access to some tunnels beneath the cellars. It's a maze down there, but it was a one-shot deal. We won't get the chance to go down there again."

"That's a shame," the cameraman said. "We could have used some nice wobbly infrared footage, heat-sensor stuff like those ghost hunters use. That would have cranked the tension right up."

"I managed to take a few minutes' worth of stuff with this." She fished her phone out of her pocket. "It's not great quality. Really shaky-cam stuff. What do you think?" She called up the video file to show a few frames of the footage she'd recorded while they had been down there, using its light to guide their way. The screen showed the tunnel in a grainy color, the passage shifting and going out of focus for a moment before sharpening up again with every step she took.

"It might work. It's got a real found-footage feel to it, " he said. "I can try to get it cleaned up. Use a few editorial tricks to loop it to make it feel longer. No one will notice. Dub in some heavy breathing and you can do a voice-over. It's certainly different to the usual stuff we shoot, and that's what the suits want, right?"

Annja nodded.

He continued to watch the shaky footage.

Annja realized what was about to come next.

It was too late to snatch it back from him.

The screen captured the moment as she rounded the corner to be confronted by the creature.

"What the holy fu—" Lars said, almost dropping the phone in surprise. "Okay, how the hell did you do that? That makeup job is brilliant. Who was it? Garin? Roux? Love it. You guys are insane."

"It's not us," Annja said, deciding that the truth was better than any lie she could come up with. "We think it's the killer."

"You mean the guy killing the homeless? Turek's golem? That's crazy. You came *this* close to a murderer and called a cameraman, not the law?"

"Because we need to get this shoot done. Without it, the show's over."

"But we're talking about someone who has killed a bunch of people!"

"Yes, we are, more than you can possibly imagine, Mr. Mortensen," Roux said.

"Hang on, you think he's still in there, don't you?"

Lars hadn't taken his eyes from the screen. He'd frozen the image of the golem's face with its blurred features on the screen and couldn't look away.

"Unless it came out through those gates, it's in there."

Lars finally raised his eyes from the screen to look back at the castle. "It didn't get past me. So what now? Call in the law? You should at least tip off Turek. I mean, look at that thing. He's right, isn't he? So he deserves to be in on the takedown."

He was right. The journalist did deserve to be told that they had the killer cornered. Like it or not, they wouldn't have gotten this far without him. Everyone else had seen a serial killer where he had seen a monster. And he'd been right.

This was it, the end of his story, and instead of being in the thick of it, he was wasting his time hanging around at the border.

She made the call. He didn't pick up. She was connected to his voice mail.

"Jan," she said, "it's Annja Creed. Sorry to bail on you, but on the bright side, my hunch paid off. If you want to be in on the action, get yourself to the castle at Benátky." She waited a moment, giving the next two words significant space to sink in. "He's here."

She hung up and stared at the phone for a moment, then sent the footage to Lars's email before slipping it back into her pocket.

"This is turning into quite a party," Roux said. "All save the guest of honor."

Lars looked at Roux, confused.

"Not your drinking partner," the old man said.

"Grab some footage of the castle," Annja interrupted. "Make sure that you get a decent shot of that metal grille in the ground over there by the wall."

"So what do we do now?" Roux asked once the other man was engrossed in his task. "Assuming the thing is holed up safe and sound, it won't move again until dark."

"Garin's still in there. Dead or alive."

"He's still alive," Roux said without a trace of doubt in his voice.

"How can you be so sure?"

"Because I would know if he was dead."

He didn't say any more than that. He didn't need to.

34

"We need to get back in," Annja said. "We can't just leave him there because you know he's not dead yet."

Roux wouldn't be drawn into explaining how he could possibly know Garin was alive. There was no point in pushing him; if he didn't want to talk he wouldn't. She could only assume it was due to the unique bond the cursed pair shared, some kind of sixth sense that came along with it, maybe.

A coffee shop across the road was opening its doors. There wasn't a morning rush. There was no one in the street. They decided to leave Lars to his work while they grabbed something to warm up.

It had been a long night.

"And we will get back in there…soon," Roux said. "We'll just walk in with the paying public, buy a couple of tickets, take the tour. As long we're not trying to take a video, no one is going to complain."

"Not *we*, Mr. Interpol. There's no way that guard is going to forget his brush with a serial killer. Me. I'll get the ticket and stay with the crowd. It would have been better if they hadn't seen me, though. It's harder to get into the interesting places the public isn't allowed to go when they know what you look like."

"Then I'll just have to make sure they are distracted."

"And the distraction? You're not planning to blow anything up or start a fire, are you?"

"Do I look like Garin?"

She didn't answer that.

Roux took a mouthful of coffee while he thought.

"It's a long shot," he said, licking his lips, "but I've got an idea. It might just be big enough to keep them busy while you do what you need to do."

Annja kept her eyes on him, but he wasn't about to offer anything more concrete. She sighed. She was in his hands. More importantly, so was Garin, and the longer they left him alone in there, the greater the chance that he wouldn't come out alive.

"Is there anything you need me to do?" she asked.

"Just keep your cameraman out of the way."

He remained enigmatic, still giving nothing away.

"Do you get a kick out of keeping things from me?" Annja asked. "I just need your help. I don't want to waste time playing guessing games."

"Sorry," Roux said, putting his cup down and raising his hands in surrender. "You're right. I should trust you. You deserve that much. I saw some things down in the maze that, with a little luck, I might be able to use to cause a distraction. I don't know if it will work. I won't know until I give it a try. But believe me, I'll find a way to buy you time. Trust me."

"Okay." She glanced at her watch. "They'll be opening up soon."

Through the window she could see a group of school-age children piling out of a coach to gather around the gates while a handful of adults tried to marshal them into some semblance of order.

"Think you can blend in with them?"

"What, I don't look like a yummy mummy?" Annja laughed, and drained her coffee cup.

"I need to pick up a couple of things from my car," Roux told her. "Give me a few minutes, then bring your man out to the front. Maybe he can get a few shots of young children running out of there with their mothers following after them as if they were afraid for their lives."

"What?"

Roux grinned, scratching at his beard. "Don't worry. They won't be in any real danger. But there will be plenty of real panic."

Annja didn't know what to say to that.

He stood and slipped a bill underneath his cup. It was more than enough to cover the cost of their coffee. It was more than enough to cover the day's earnings for a small place like this. The old man believed in tipping generously. Sometimes Annja wondered if he had any concept of the value of money.

She poured the last of the coffee into her cup and sipped it while she watched Roux open the trunk of the black four-by-four parked across the street from the café. A stream of traffic crawled past, blocking her view. By the time it had cleared, the trunk had been closed and Roux was nowhere to be seen.

She drained the coffee cup and headed outside.

She spotted Lars sitting on his flight case on the far side of the gaggle of children.

"Did you manage to get some good stuff?" she asked as she approached.

The big Swede nodded. "Plenty," he said. "What's the plan?"

"I'm going to head in with the kids. Why don't you take a few minutes to grab yourself a coffee, then set up to take some externals of the gate and meet Turek when he arrives. There's going to be a bit of excitement in a little while, and you won't want to miss it," she said, every bit as enigmatic as Roux.

Lars treated her to the same withering look she'd shot the old man a dozen times since he met her in the hospital.

"I'm beginning to feel like a third wheel," he said, getting to his feet.

He lugged his case across the street to the café.

Before he disappeared inside, the castle gates swung open and the level of excitement amplified from pandemonium to the next circle of hell. The children jumped up and down, eager to be inside.

The old security guard was going to have his hands full.

That was not a bad thing.

35

Roux used a length of rope to lower the gas can down the shaft ahead of him. He gritted his teeth, refusing to panic when it started swinging. The can clanged against one of the metal rungs in the darkness below, ringing like a clarion bell. He looked around nervously, but there was no one nearby to hear the chime. It shouldn't have seeped into the castle itself, barring some freak of the acoustics. No one had secured the grille, so perhaps the old security guard hadn't yet explained to the officious little twerp of a manager how they happened into the scullery. Maybe they'd get lucky and memory loss would strike before he could. If it didn't, he'd improvise. After the life he'd lived, thinking on his feet was second nature.

Roux reached the bottom rung and stepped off the ladder. He glanced back up the shaft at the patch of blue and wondered for the first time in a long time if this might actually be the last time he would see it. It wasn't mawkish nostalgia so much as fatalist curiosity. If Annja knew what he had in mind, she'd have tried to stop him. It was dangerous, and she was overprotective. She'd have insisted he come up with another plan, arguing that there had to be another way, all the while wasting precious time. Garin didn't have long, assuming he wasn't actually dead. He'd lied to Annja, claiming to know his protégé was alive, knowing she'd believe there was some kind of mystical link between them. That was easier than just saying he had no idea if Garin was dead or not, but that he feared the worst. She needed to believe there was a chance of saving him.

And she was counting on him for a pretty explosive distraction. She hadn't told him not to blow up anything; she'd only asked if he was planning to. It was a technicality, but murderers had gotten away with far flimsier excuses.

He slung the rope over his shoulder and picked up the gas can, setting off into the darkness before he turned on the flashlight. The beam speared ahead, lighting his way. The noise that filtered down from the street was soon lost in the echo of his own footsteps and the slosh of gasoline in the can as he moved deeper into the maze of tunnels. It was incredible to think this elaborate network of passages has survived centuries of neglect, but he didn't recall them being this elaborate the first time he had been here.

With every bend in the tunnel he half expected to come face-to-face with either the monster or Garin's lifeless corpse. And the deeper he went into the maze, the more convinced he became that that was exactly what awaited him around the next corner.

At last he reached the fork in the tunnels he was looking for.

This wasn't the one that would lead eventually to the flight of stairs up to the scullery, but nearly two hundred years ago it had harbored barrels of black powder. The kegs, even if they remained, would be useless. But he wasn't looking to create an explosion that would bring the castle down on its foundations. All he wanted to do was create a distraction. Something dramatic, yes, but not life-threatening.

He wasn't sure what he was thinking; even if the barrels he thought he'd seen weren't the same barrels, maybe some of the gunpowder residue had trickled down between the cracks in the floor and still remained there even after all this time. It wasn't like cleaners would ever have been down here washing the stone floors. Splash the gasoline around, ignite it, step back and hope something went bang?

He left the rope and the gasoline can at the junction in the tunnel, said a silent prayer and hurried to the cellar, hoping against hope God was on his side.

The small barrels were still staked exactly where they had been all those years ago, and playing his flashlight over them, he read the same markings branded onto the ancient wood. It was hard to believe they hadn't succumbed to damp and decay—or flame during the first explosions that brought the ceiling down—but there was so little moisture in the musty air…that had to have held back the rot.

Even so, in places, rotten wood had split and started to crumble, allowing the black powder to spill out. It formed solid lumps on the floor.

Roux knew that would be of no use.

His best hope was that the small barrel at the top of the stack had been kept clear of the damp.

It was all about noise, not damage. He just wanted to make a loud enough bang for people to hear it, stir up some panic to turn eyes away from Annja.

He tested its weight with one hand, rocking the barrel

slightly where it perched on top of the others. He wasn't sure how heavy he'd expected it to be, but there was clearly something pretty weighty inside it. Roux examined the wood and iron bands, both sound and showing no sign of giving way, so he moved it as best he could.

The barrel was too cumbersome to carry, but he manhandled it to the ground and started to roll it into position. Negotiating the tunnel wasn't as easy as he had hoped. More than once the natural lay of the ground meant the barrel picked up speed of its own accord, threatening to get away from him. The barrel was old. Any sort of impact could undo the little integrity the wood still had.

He angled the barrel back toward the iron gate that barred the way to the stairs up to the scullery, and rested it against the iron. Roux pried the bung out with the tip of his Swiss Army knife. The dry cork crumbled in his hands. The piece of wax paper that had provided the seal fell to the ground.

He lowered his nose to the opening and took a deep breath.

He knew the smell well enough.

Without a working fuse, he was going to have to improvise. That was where the rope and the gasoline came in. He knew that he could run a trail of powder and gamble that it would buy him enough time to get clear, but given the state of the powder there was no guarantee that it wouldn't fizzle out long before it reached the barrel.

The rope was a good old-fashioned three-strand twisted natural rope, not the kind of nylon climbing rope that was more modern and stronger. It did not have the same feel about it. In this, as in many other things, Roux was old-fashioned.

He had always known that his path would lead him back to this place at some point in time. He'd brought the rope in case the iron rungs had been either removed, or damaged beyond use by the fire.

The gasoline, well, that was just a case of making it up as he went along.

But it would work.

It had to.

36

Annja could feel more than one pair of eyes staring at her.

She obviously wasn't part of the school trip.

The old security guard lurked by one of the doorways, whispering conspiratorially to the manager, who after a bit of huddled conversation called over an equally officious-looking man. The man was dressed in a tailored jacket with some sort of logo emblazoned on the left breast. He was obviously a guide. The man said something, to which the manager nodded in Annja's direction. The guide followed his gaze, meeting Annja's. No doubt he was being warned about Annja.

She was going to need Roux to come through with a pretty impressive distraction if she was going to give the security team the slip and get to properly poke around.

Annja was only half listening to the guide's talk, glad that she had stumbled on a tour that was being held in English. The history of the castle held no real interest to her, until she heard the guide mention the name Kepler. Then some things started to fall into place. She remembered where she'd first heard about Benátky— at the Kepler Museum in Prague. This was one of the places that the astronomer had first worked when he'd arrived here.

"Sorry, is it possible to see the observatory?" she asked, interrupting the woman while she was in full flow.

"I'm afraid that's closed to the public at the moment," she said, barely pausing for breath before resuming her well-rehearsed routine, not paying Annja any further attention.

"May I ask why?" Annja asked, interrupting again, much to the woman's consternation.

The guide gave a very audible and very exaggerated sigh that seemed to fill the room with its discontent before saying, "Refurbishment. Buildings like this require regular attention to maintain them."

Annja hadn't seen a great deal of work going on outside the castle, certainly no signs of construction or leftover debris. Something was rotten in the state of Benátky, she thought.

A map on the wall showed the layout of the castle, including the observatory.

She studied it, committing the twists and turns to memory. The observatory was going to be her first port of call after Roux did his thing. She couldn't help but think there was something there someone didn't want people to see, which meant she very much wanted to see it.

Annja trailed along with the rest of the tour group while the security guard followed them from room to room. The old man paid more attention to her than he did to the gaggle of children. The kids themselves seemed intent on making as much noise as they could and ignoring anything remotely cultural in the process.

She caught his eye a couple of times and smiled, but he didn't respond. She was obviously losing her charm. The old guy seemed determined not to let her out of his sight, which was a problem.

She checked her watch, wondering what was keeping Roux, and beginning to think his distraction wasn't going to happen.

As soon as the thought crossed her mind, it was greeted by a sound that could have been a car backfiring or even a gunshot, but somehow it seemed to grow and continued to grow.

She heard someone whisper what sounded like "Bomb" and that changed the atmosphere of the tour. A couple of the children screamed. She saw a younger girl cling to the arm of one of her teachers, while the teachers themselves were pale faced and panic-stricken. Pieces of porcelain began to rattle against the glass shelves in a display cabinet. The world moved in slow motion. Flakes of paint and plaster drifted down from the ceiling like whispers of snow.

The children's faces filled with something akin to wonder, but far more shrank into themselves, terrified because they didn't understand what was happening. The teachers tried to restore some semblance of calm, huddling their charges together and ushering them toward the door.

Before they reached it a huge mirror slipped from its mounting and slid down the wall. It hit the ground and toppled forward, the glass shattering into a thousand pieces. The shards stung the legs of the children closest to it, the pain met with more shrieks of terror.

In less than five seconds the air filled with dust shaken from every crevice in the place. Everyone in the room coughed and choked against the thick dust as they struggled to draw breath.

"This way," said the guard, the only person in the room aside from Annja who appeared to be calm in the apparent crisis.

Roux had done well, better than she could possibly have hoped.

This was her chance.

But there was one very obvious problem.

The old guard wasn't flapping about like a headless chicken with the rest of them. He was acting on instinct, putting the safety of the visitors above the security of the building and its contents. In other circumstances she might have been impressed, but right now she was annoyed. He even put the safety of others ahead of his own safety. That was a rare quality. His primary concern was getting everyone out of there. She could only hope that his focus was on the kids, not her.

"Everyone stay calm," he said, his voice cutting above the aftermath of the explosion. "Everything's okay. Follow me. We will go outside to the courtyard. Stay with your teachers."

The alarm was doing nothing to quell the sense of panic.

The teachers did their best to echo his calm, issuing their own instructions, telling the kids to hold hands and walk in single file, following the guard outside.

Annja hung back. She needed to go in the opposite direction. She guessed she had maybe two or three minutes before anyone realized she was missing. She needed to make the most of them.

Starting now…

Annja slipped out of the room.

37

Roux pulled a book of matches from his pocket and tore one free.

He remembered having picked them up in a café overlooking the Seine a couple of months ago, but he could not remember the name of the woman who had shared his table. It had been a chance encounter, a couple of hours with a stranger who could have been anyone, but for an hour or two their lives interconnected. How many other little connections had he made during his six centuries? More than six lives' worth, he was sure of that. His unnaturally long life seemed to have been dotted with encounters that meant nothing in isolation but as a whole represented a hollowness that the veneer of loneliness had taken shape around.

Sometimes it felt that those times were nothing more than dots in a puzzle that might one day be connected to produce a picture that actually made sense. More often than not, it was more like the kind of Rorschach inkblot that kept some psychiatrists in gainful employment for years.

Roux struck the match.

The sudden flare was outside the beam of the flashlight he held between his teeth. He touched the match to the end of the gasoline-soaked rope, then started to run. He had no way of knowing how long it would take the voracious flame to snake along the three-strand rope or if the makeshift bomb would actually explode without a proper detonator. But at best he had seconds.

So he ran.

Roux might be immortal, or as near as it made no difference. The idea of eternity buried beneath several tons of rubble wasn't particularly appealing.

He raced through the narrow passageways, feeling the weight of the world above pressing down around him, as if the hounds of hell were on his tail. The flashlight's beam roved over the walls of the tunnels, pointing everywhere but straight ahead and conjuring all manner of shadow demons in the process.

He had barely covered half the distance back to the shaft when he felt the sudden punch of air from the explosion an instant before he heard it.

The substance of the world around him thrummed to the vibration of the explosion. He couldn't keep his focus or his balance. A heartbeat later the tunnel was full of rage. It began with a sudden deep thunderclap before becoming a deeper grumble that began to build and kept on building, chasing him. No matter how desperately he ran, he knew he had no prayer of outrunning it. But he kept on, charging through the tunnels, head down, as the shockwave overtook him in a rush of air that pushed and bullied him from behind. The shock of it caught Roux off balance and sent him stumbling to the ground.

Rock started to rumble and tear with the agony of fracturing bone. Behind him, chunks of the tunnel's ceiling came tumbling down.

He had seconds, if that, before the weight of the earth above him ruptured and brought the whole tunnel crashing in on itself, and then there would be no getting out.

Daggers of broken stone dug into his hands as he scrambled back to his feet, trying to run before he could walk.

The smoke of the explosion roiled around him, swelling to fill every inch and cavity of the tunnel.

The flashlight was useless. Even with it he couldn't see the detritus strewed in his path as he stumbled through it, blinking back the tears stung from his eyes.

He reached out for the wall with his free hand, pushing himself along it, breathing hard, head pounding with the intense swell of pressure the blast had brought on.

He had to keep going.

There was no alternative.

At last a shaft of light appeared ahead of him. He stumbled, coughing and gagging, toward it.

He could only hope that he had done enough.

Now it was up to Annja.

He reached for the first iron rung that would take him up to safety, looking up, and in that moment something struck him on the back of the head and his vision clouded, the world around him swimming out of focus. His legs buckled beneath him, the strength fleeing his body.

And then he let go.

38

Annja placed her hand on the large brass knob and turned it slowly, pressing one ear to the wooden door in case she could hear anything on the other side. Not that she could have heard anything above the pandemonium that had now spread out into the courtyard, and the wailing alarm.

The door handle offered little resistance. The lock was old and substantial. She felt, rather than heard, the deep *click* when the mechanism caught. The door opened slowly. If there had been builders working inside, she reasoned, they would have evacuated with the alarm.

It was both a relief and disappointment to find that the room was empty. She realized she'd expected to find Garin in the observatory, but there was no sign of him. Neither was there any sign of any restoration work. The room hadn't been touched in a long time. So, whatever the reason for its closure, it certainly wasn't to allow workmen access.

Annja stepped into the room.

There was a telescope in place, the viewing aperture open and turned to the sky, but a worktable was covered with much more practical tools including screwdrivers and tweezers, wrenches and soldering irons. They were all distinctly modern, so they couldn't be connected with Kepler or his efforts. So if it wasn't a display, what was it all about?

She scanned the area, searching for some kind of clue.

From the distance Annja heard the distant wail of sirens approaching. They were another forceful reminder that she only had a short amount of time up here alone. She hurried around the workbench, running her fingers across the old pitted wood. Unlike the tools it could easily have been in place when Kepler and his contemporaries spent time in this room. It offered a real link to the past, but there was no way to draw out the memories of things it had to have seen.

There was nothing to suggest that Garin had ever been there. She did see a heavy-looking coat thrown over the back of a chair. The dark material was damp to the touch. When she picked it up, it felt as though it was about to disintegrate between her fingers.

It looked familiar.

Or was her mind simply finding connections that she wanted to find?

The more she looked at it, the more convinced she was that it was the same coat the killer had been wearing when she'd chased him across the rooftops.

She knew she was right.

And being right, that meant there really was a connection between this place and the killer.

Through the window she saw a fire engine making its way in through the castle gates. Several men in flame-retardant clothing tumbled out of the cab, moving with practiced precision as they set about releasing the hose and preparing to fight a fire she couldn't see. A moment later a police car joined them.

One minute, two at most, then the firefighters would be inside the building.

The observatory wouldn't be the first or even the second place they checked—the explosion had come from down in the cellar tunnels—but given everything, being found wandering around inside wouldn't go down too well, especially if they put two and two together and tied her into Roux's sabotage. She had no idea what kind of charges causing criminal damage carried over here and she had no burning desire to find out.

Things could become very messy.

She draped the coat back onto the chair and made her way down the stairs.

The air was a little clearer when she reached the ground-floor corridor, although everything was now coated in a fine film of dust.

Roux had almost certainly done more damage than he'd anticipated—hopefully it was enough to keep the emergency services busy for a while so she could get out of there.

That hope was short-lived.

She heard someone start to open the main doors.

Annja headed in the opposite direction, ducking around the corner before the newcomers could see her.

She rushed down the passageway, looking for a fire exit or other way out of the building. She took another turn and then another before she spotted the sign for the fire exit. The siren was still blaring, so she didn't worry about tripping any alarms as she hit the bar across the center of the door and slipped out. The door opened onto the rear of the castle, away from the hubbub of the courtyard. Now all she had to do was slip back into the crowd and it'd be like she'd never been away.

Annja made her way around the side of the castle to join the others.

As she came around the corner, she walked straight into a ferocious stare from the manager, who was just wrapping up his business with the fire chief. He was obviously running through the morning's events in his head, trying to find a way to hold her personally responsible, which of course she was.

The fire crew was already inside.

"Did you get lost?" the manager asked.

"Just wanted some fresh air," she said. "What happened?"

The man didn't answer her. Instead, he went across to talk to the old guard, who was comforting a crying child.

Annja had to find Roux. They needed a new strategy. As useful as it had been to find the coat, it didn't help with the immediate problem of Garin's disappearance. She scanned the faces in the crowd for Lars, who had to be somewhere. Some of the children were still nearly hysterical while others were absolutely fascinated by the fire truck and had completely forgotten what had happened inside the castle.

No one paid Annja any attention as she slipped through the gates and out into the street. A small crowd of locals had gathered, drawn by the chaos of the evacuation.

"Annja!" a voice called through the throng. "Over here."

She raised herself on her toes and craned her neck to see between the people who were standing in her way. Eventually she caught sight of Lars waving at her. She pushed through the press of people, none of whom seemed to want to give an inch for fear of losing their view.

"You okay?" he asked when she finally reached him.

"Yeah," she said. "Any sign of Turek?"

"Not yet. The police have thrown up a roadblock about a couple of kilometers back, stopping people getting in and out of town. The joys of the modern world. Whenever anything happens, the first assumption is always that it's some kind of terrorist attack. Anyone hurt?"

She shook her head. There was an ambulance parked in the street, but it couldn't get any closer because of the crowd that had massed around the gates. A single police officer stood in the center of the gates, doing his best to usher them away. It was a fruitless battle.

"Have you seen Roux?"

"Nope, but then it has been a little crazy out here. I take it the explosion was our old friend's doing?"

There was no point denying it. "Come with me," Annja said as Lars packed his camera back into its case.

They had to skirt around the crowd, working a path that took them around the back of the ambulance before they could pick up the dirt path that ran along the side of the castle wall.

Annja looked back over her shoulder more than once to be sure that no one was watching them.

The grille was still open, but there was no sign of Roux.

If he'd come out this way, surely he would have closed it behind him, wouldn't he?

She peered into the darkness, but there was nothing to see.

No. She was wrong. There was smoke.

"He's still down there," she said, sure that she'd just lost her second friend to the maze.

39

Annja saw the glow of the flashlight in the darkness.

Her heart sank when she realized it wasn't moving.

"Roux," she called.

There was no response.

She took a step toward the light and called his name again.

Nothing.

Another step, another cry of "Roux?" without response.

Something was wrong.

Annja hurried toward the flashlight.

There were shapes on the ground. Shadows. The tunnel had collapsed.

Roux was trapped beneath the rubble.

He wasn't moving.

Annja knelt beside him, and reached out to feel for a pulse, dreading what she might not feel beneath his skin.

His neck was still warm, his pulse weak and thready. He didn't flinch or stir when she squeezed his hand.

She needed to get him out of there and quickly.

His heart was beating now, but would it stop eventually? She knew his body had prodigious recuperative powers, beyond hers even, but was there a limit to what it could withstand? Could the cave-in literally crush the life out of him? She'd always thought of him as immortal, but in the back of her mind she'd known that something surely could happen to end that.

Annja started pulling lumps of stone and rubble away as fast as she could, heaving one after the other and hurling them aside, moving faster and faster until she was clawing at the rubble like a madwoman trying to tear him free.

And all through it he remained absolutely silent, absolutely and eerily still.

Her fingers bled as she tore at the debris.

Some of the rubble was little more than egg-size, some like a football, but there were huge slabs of masonry that had come down, and one such piece pinned him across the legs. She couldn't get the leverage with her bare hands to shift it. Try as she might, it just wouldn't budge. She needed something to give her more leverage. Annja cast about the inside of the tunnel, but aside from a few spars of rotted wood there was nothing that would work. Without thinking, Annja reached instinctively into the otherwhere for the sword, knowing that she could work it beneath the huge boulder and pry it up far enough for Roux to wriggle out from under—if he would just wake up.

She heard him let out a groan.

For one heart-stopping second she thought it was a death rattle.

Then he stirred again, a deeper, more broken sound. The sound was no louder than a whisper, but oh-so-welcome.

"Roux!" Annja said, pausing for no more than a heartbeat as she reassured herself that he was still breathing, that he was still alive. She worked harder, faster, putting every ounce of strength she had into the herculean task of getting him out from under the collapsed ceiling. She didn't even want to contemplate the mess his bones could be in, or the damage to his internal organs. Right now it was enough that he was alive. The rest could wait.

"Come on, old man," she shouted at him, urging the life back into him. "I could use a little help here."

Roux groaned. The groan became a grunt became a cough.

He tried to drag himself out from under the huge slab of masonry as the weight was gradually being lifted from him, but it was desperately slow-going.

"Come on," she urged, the tension thrumming through her arms, every muscle corded and burning from the strain. She gritted her teeth against the pain, determined to hold the stone clear of the old man for however long it took for Roux to crawl free.

He clawed at the ground in front of him. The pain was evident on his face.

"Come on, Roux."

He pulled himself forward an inch at a time. The longer it took to get him out of there, the greater the risk that the killer might return or disappear altogether, taking Garin with him.

At last he was free to kick away the remaining rubble, though his legs weren't working properly. His trousers were covered in blood, and she saw a spur of bone from his shin poking out through a tear in the fabric. She cursed, knowing she couldn't leave him there and go hunting for the beast.

"I'm going to lift you," she said. "It's going to hurt, but we've got to get you out of here." Annja put the flashlight in his hands. "Show me the way." She walked into the light, each faltering step leading back toward the shaft of light that led to the surface. He weighed nothing in her arms.

"Talk to me," she said. "Anything, just stay with me. We'll get you out of here, then we'll have to regroup and think. This changes everything."

"No," he said. "Just…give me a few…"

"Your leg's a mess. It's broken. Badly. It'll need splinting. Setting. It's going to be a while before you're fit for the fight."

Roux shook his head. He looked ghastly in the pale light, groggy, but he was hanging in there. "Just get me to the air. Then…set the bone. I'm walking out of here…under my own…steam."

"Don't be ridiculous."

"Don't argue with me, girl."

It took a minute to work her way back to the shaft. She gently set Roux down, leaning his back against the wall, then tore the strips of cloth away from the bloody mess where the bone had pierced the skin. "I'm going to need something to splint it."

"No. Just pull the bone. Get it back into place."

It was going to be agony. And she had nothing he could bite down on. "But—"

"Just do as I say."

Annja crouched in front of Roux, placing her hands on either side of the jagged end of the bone. It was a bad break. It would almost certainly need pinning, and he'd be walking with a limp for a long time—if not the rest of his life.

She nodded. "Ready? On three. One…" Then she pulled down hard, twisting the bone until the edges locked back into place. Roux's screams were unbearable. Raw. Broken. He gasped, panting hard, sweating, when she was done.

"Now…we…wait."

"I can't. Garin's still out there."

"Then help me stand."

"Are you insane? Your leg is broken. It'll never hold your weight."

"Then we wait. That is the choice."

"I can't," she said helplessly.

Roux reached up, his hand closing around the pitted iron of the bottom rung on the ladder, and with colossal effort and willpower, he began to draw himself upward, careful to put no weight on his damaged leg. Annja stared at him like he was out of his mind. Roux twisted, then reached up with his other hand for the rung above, and began to climb without using his feet, lifting himself toward the light one rung at a time.

Annja kept herself a few rungs behind him, ready to catch him if he fell.

As he approached the top, a hand reached over the edge and helped haul him out.

A few moments later the same hand reached down toward Annja, and she was glad to accept it.

Lars stepped back to give her space to climb from the shaft. From the low angle she saw Roux's leg. The skin had already healed around the wound, and the blood had dried into rusty brown flakes. The scar tissue was raw and pink. She looked up at the old man standing there, trying to understand how he could possibly be on his own two feet after what had just happened to him.

His trousers were in a worse state than his leg.

Annja shook her head. She knew her own metabolism was capable of crazy things when it came to recovery, but she'd never seen anything like this. The bone and tissue had meshed, essentially healing itself, if not as good as new, then more than adequately, in just a few minutes.

"Can you walk?" she asked, feeling stupid as she posed the question.

"The bone will be weak for a while."

"Okay, then lean on me. We need to get you somewhere you can sit. We need to take stock."

The old man nodded.

"Hell of a show you put on," the cameraman said, grinning approvingly.

Annja kicked the grille back into place and dusted herself down. It was going to take a lot more than that to make her feel clean.

"You didn't find Garin?"

"No. But I found something in the observatory— the killer's coat. It was draped over the back of a chair. There was nothing else in the room except for a bunch of tools spread out over a bench."

"Then where has he gone?" Roux asked, leaning on her as they walked back down the bank to the main road.

"He's got to be in there," Annja said. "He didn't go out past you, did he, Lars?"

"No," the cameraman confirmed. "No one came out through the main gates when I was watching."

"So that means he's got to still be inside the castle," Annja said, as if the absence of one thing proved the presence of the other.

"No," Roux said categorically. "He's not in there."

"How can you be so sure?"

"Because cars don't drive themselves."

He was right. There was an empty space in the row of parked cars where Garin's sports car had been.

40

Had it been there when she'd gone underground after Roux?

She didn't know and couldn't believe she hadn't noticed before, but now that she had, it stood out like a raw wound in the heart of the street.

"I guess I missed him," Lars admitted, shrugging. "But I could have sworn he didn't come out this way. It was chaos out here, though, and I wasn't checking the cars. I didn't even know which one was his."

"But you were recording?" Roux asked.

"Absolutely. Primed to get some footage of the panic. Most of the shots covered the castle, the crowd, the emergency vehicles as they arrived. That sort of stuff."

"And the street?" Annja interrupted. "You must have got some shots that would have included the car, or lack of. We might get lucky."

It took them only a matter of minutes to make their way to Annja's car, even with Roux leaning heavily on Annja every step of the way. Lars hooked the camera up to a portable monitor and spooled through the footage, slowing only when the street was in the frame.

"There it is," Annja said when they caught the first sight of Garin's car still parked a short walk away from the café. She checked the time stamp. It was only a few minutes before the explosion-driven exodus. "Keep going."

They watched as people moved at double speed and triple speed.

A crowd began to form as if in stop-motion animation.

The camera panned across the street, following the fire truck now as it moved quickly toward the cameraman's position, coming to a shuddering halt at the gates, then disappearing through the gates after they opened with almost comic timing.

An instant later a blur of red pulled away from the curb, barely caught in the motion of the camera.

"Stop," Annja said. Lars froze the frame, then spooled back so that they could take a closer look at it. Slowly he moved the image forward a couple of frames at a time until the Ferrari was in the center of the screen. He froze it again.

Like it or not, that was Garin in the driver's seat.

"I'm going to finish him this time," Roux said, shaking his head.

She thought he meant Garin, but looking at the face of the passenger he could just as easily have meant him. She didn't want to ask.

"That's..." Lars said. "That face... That's the thing from your phone, isn't it?"

He was right.

Two people in the car. Garin and the killer.

There was nothing to suggest Garin was a prisoner or victim in all of this.

"I'm through with him, Annja. This is it. It ends here. No forgiveness. No wheedling his way back pretending to be friends. I'm done."

Had Roux been right all along? The thought made

her feel sick. She'd believed in him. Even against all the evidence, she'd been absolutely sure Garin wouldn't betray them again.

"Fool me once, shame on you. Fool me twice, shame on me," she said, and she meant it.

"We find one, we find the other," Roux said flatly.

"Where, though? All we know is they went that way." She pointed the way that the Ferrari had gone. From the end of the street the road connected with every possible destination in the world. Garin had a head start on them and a faster car. She checked the time stamp. He had the best part of an hour's head start. The top speed on the Ferrari was a little over two hundred miles per hour, but there was no way he could hit that kind of speed on tight country roads. But when they got to the freeways, he could be out of the country before they'd even started chasing him.

"We'll take a leaf out of that duplicitous bastard's book," Roux said.

He fished his cell phone from his pocket and made a call, wincing at the stab of pain the movement drew. "Owen?" He nodded as though expecting the man on the other end of the line to see the gesture, then said, "I need you to track a car for me… Yes, it's a sports car. I don't know the model or the license plate… Yes, I understand there are a lot of sports cars in the world, and yes, I understand that I'm not giving you a lot to work with. I'm aware that a VIN would be helpful, but it's not my job to be helpful. I'm paying you so that I don't need to be. The car is either registered to Garin Braden, or one of the shell companies he has a holding in, or hired by him from one of the international brokers around Prague and the surrounds… Yes, I am aware that it's like looking for the proverbial needle, but you're an industrious guy, and I'm sure you can do it. I believe Ferrari uses onboard trackers to help with finding vehicles after they have been stolen… GPS and GMS tracking? CobraTrak? I'm sure you are right, but it doesn't mean anything to me. Get back to me when you have found it."

Roux killed the call and slipped the phone back into his pocket. "He moaned a lot, said it would take as long as it takes, but that he'd find it if it was there to be found, so now we wait."

"I'm impressed," Annja said. "He'd expect us to track his phone, not the Ferrari's security. That was smart."

"I've lived a long time, Annja. You learn some tricks when you get to be a gray beard. What do you say we hit this road and see where it leads?"

Annja didn't need to be asked twice.

In her rearview mirror she could see the castle's manager standing in the street, gesticulating animatedly as he talked with a police officer. She could guess what he was complaining about. Time to get out of there. Turek wouldn't be happy, turning up to find them already gone, but there was nothing she could do about that. He was a big boy. Annja keyed the ignition, then gunned the engine into life. She pulled away without using the blinker, throwing a backward glance at the castle as she peeled away from the curb.

She might never learn the rest of the Benátky castle's secrets, but they had a killer to catch, and that took precedence.

It took a thief to catch a thief—that was the old saying. Did that mean it took a killer to catch a killer? Was that what Garin was doing? Putting himself in harm's way in order to bring down the killer? It was better than the alternative, but that wasn't as comforting as it might have been.

41

The call came through as she was driving.

Roux put his phone on speaker so she could hear what Owen had to say.

"It wasn't easy," the hacker said, his voice a tinny crackle. "But because I'm a genius and specialize in making the impossible possible, I've got him." Annja knew the voice. She couldn't say for sure who it belonged to, but she got the distinct impression she'd talked to the guy before—almost certainly on Garin's behalf. Roux had used one of Garin's hackers to track Garin. Not only was Roux using his own tricks against Garin, he was using his own people. This was a more devious Roux than she was used to. "I'll send you a package. All you need to do is click on it. It'll self-install and execute, giving you access to the Cobra system. You can follow him to your heart's content, and if you really want to mess with him, you can isolate his engine."

"As in disable it?"

"As in exactly that. Did you know a few years ago there was even talk about putting thin metal threads in the seat fabric so you could theoretically send an electric pulse through the seat if someone stole the car?"

"You mean electrocute the car thief?"

"Yep, and get this, the doors would be on autolock so they'd keep getting shocked until the cops turned up."

"That's twisted," Annja said.

"I thought it was quite clever," the hacker replied.

"We keep this between ourselves," Roux stated.

"Absolutely, business is business. He who pays the piper calls the tune. Isn't that what they say?"

"That depends if you have rats that need getting rid of," Roux said, and ended the call.

Annja had no idea if the other man had heard, or if Roux had intended for him to hear. Roux had called Garin a lot worse than a rat, but mention of getting rid of him reinforced the bad feeling she'd had earlier when he'd promised to finish him. She couldn't believe Roux really meant it. She knew they'd had their issues—issues that had lasted centuries and had culminated in duels and assassination attempts and a personal war that had raged all across the Theater of Europe, but neither man had actually gone through with it all the way to delivering the killing blow.

Would Roux do it now?

She didn't want to believe that he was capable of it.

The problem was that she knew he was.

The notion frightened her.

Annja kept her eyes on the road while Roux fiddled with his phone. There was a soft ping when the package came through. A minute later, Roux said, "Got him."

"Where?"

"A long way from here. He's driving like the devil's on his heels. He's already out on the other side of Prague."

"Where the hell is he going?" Annja asked, earning a smile from Lars.

"Hell sounds pretty appropriate if it's the devil chasing him." Roux grunted. "But it looks like Turek was on the money."

"How? He went to the Polish border? That's the opposite direction."

"He went to the border," Lars said. "He just went to the wrong one." He was looking at the red dot on Roux's phone. "If he stays on that road, it'll take him out of the country."

"Germany? Or does it go south into Austria?" Her sudden grasp of European geography was due to the fact that she'd taken a glance at a map back at the hotel.

"Germany," Lars said. "He'll cross the border at Waidhaus, and judging by the speed he's clocking, he'll be there inside the hour. The way Granny Annie here is driving, we'll be there in about three."

That earned the Swede a withering look, but Annja took the point and pushed her foot flat to the floor.

"We have a problem, though. I don't have my passport with me," the cameraman said. "We'll need to stop by the hotel so I can grab it."

"No time," Roux told him. "Whatever he's up to, he's got an hour on us and is making more time with every passing mile. Once he hits the autobahn, he can go twice as fast as us. We can't afford to give him any more of an advantage, sorry."

"We can't just throw him out of the car," Annja protested.

"Of course not," Roux said. "I'm not suggesting that. We'll drop him where he can hitch a ride back to the city. He doesn't look like a serial killer. He should be just fine."

"I am here, you know," the cameraman said. "Don't I get a say in this?"

"Call Turek," Annja told Lars. "Let him know what's happening. Get him to pick you up on the way. Stop off at your hotel and stay in touch. I'll text you directions."

Lars sulked. "That's better than being tossed in the gutter. Marginally."

"Don't be a drama queen," Roux said. "You're not helpless. And this isn't a DMZ. You'll be fine."

Annja eyed Lars in the rearview mirror. He didn't seem thrilled with Roux's idea, but there was no logical alternative. He was unhappy that he hadn't had the presence of mind to bring his passport to Benátky. That was amateurish. He'd worked with Annja enough to know exactly what the job entailed. The watchwords were *Go with the flow.*

"I used to like you, you know," he said, shaking his head as he slumped back in his seat. He rested one hand on the camera case that sat beside him.

Annja gave him a warm smile, and then concentrated on the road.

A signpost indicated an upcoming tram stop.

It was as good a place as any to drop him.

Annja pulled over. Lars didn't try particularly hard to hide the sulk when he got out of the car. He hauled the camera case out after him.

"You'll miss me when I'm gone," he said. "Keep me in the loop. We need everything we can get for the show. Remember that when you're off saving the world or whatever it is you do when I'm not looking."

He patted the case before he closed the car door and waved her off.

Lars was right. She needed him if this segment was going to save the show, but short of someone dying live on air she couldn't see anything saving the show. It was defeatist, she knew, but that was just how she felt right now. Maybe she should have listened to Doug and put on the bikini once in a while.

She barked out a short sharp laugh, earning a frown from Roux. "Let's go catch us a killer."

She pulled away from the curbside and worked her way back to the road she had come off, putting her foot down as soon as they merged with the faster moving traffic.

"We've lost time," Roux said bluntly.

Everyone in her life had suddenly become so wise.

"We couldn't have left him at the border when he couldn't produce his passport."

"The Czech Republic is part of the European Union. Germany's part of the union. I doubt there's even a border patrol."

"Then why make the fuss about dropping him off at the border?"

"I wanted him out of the car. This is about us. You, me and Garin. I don't want to be worrying about strangers getting in the way. This isn't going to end well, Annja. You know that, don't you?"

"What if you're wrong? What if Garin's not in on this whole thing?"

"You're too sentimental," Roux said. "But then that's always been your problem. It's why you've never reached your full potential."

"And what the hell is *that* supposed to mean?" she demanded, but Roux fell silent yet again. He was really starting to grate on her nerves.

"Just drive. I'm tired. My leg is killing me. And before the night is out I am going to have to kill—or try to kill—my oldest friend. I don't feel like talking to you right now."

"Come on, Roux, you can't lay something like that on me and just clam up. How have I failed you? Ever? How have I disappointed you? When have I never given my all for you? Done everything you've ever asked of me? Name one time. Just one. Tell me the truth."

"The truth?" The old man shook his head. "What's the truth? What if we have different truths? What if there's nothing absolute about it. What if what is true to me is false to you? Whatever the truth is, you have to learn it for yourself, make your own decisions about who you are going to be, because your television show isn't going to last forever. This thing we've got going on between us isn't going to last forever. So, think about it, be the best *you* you can be. Don't let someone else force their version of the truth upon you."

It made little sense.

"Fine. You don't want to talk about it, I get it. What about Garin? Why are you so sure he's in it up to his neck? You've got to have a reason."

"I wish I knew," the old man said. "A life of disappointment, maybe?"

Annja shook her head. "That's not it, and you know it. You're lying to me."

"Truth and lies again. It's all subjective, Annja. Let that be today's lesson. It's all subjective. But perhaps we will get lucky this time. Perhaps Garin will deign to confess before I execute him. Or maybe winged bacon will be spotted over Paris."

Despite herself, she half smiled at that.

"Every word that comes out of that man's mouth weaves part of an elaborate web of lies. He has been weaving that web so tightly and for so long that he's absolutely forgotten what the truth ever was. All what remains is *his* truth. I doubt we'll ever understand why he does anything he does."

"But we forgive him every time, don't we? It doesn't matter what he does. Sooner or later we let him back in."

"Because he's like us. Because he's the only other one like us. All three of us may be different, but we have more in common than we would care to admit."

He was right.

Annja knew that he was right.

And she hated that he was right.

There was loneliness in his truth. She didn't want to live in a world where the only two people like her were constantly at each other's throats, trying to kill each other. Where did that leave her? Alone.

She had no idea of how long her life would be, but she'd felt her body changing in so many subtle ways since that first time Saint Joan's sword fused under her grasp, whole again. Hers wasn't going to be a mortal span. It may not be as long as Roux's, but her old age wasn't going to be passed in a nursing home playing shuffleboard. The sword would make absolutely sure of that. She would be fit and strong as long as it needed her to wield it; that was the pact she'd made with the holy artifact. That was her legacy, the gift she'd inherited from Joan herself.

"Where are they now?" she asked when she caught sight of him looking at the screen of his cell phone again.

"They are still on this road, but we've closed the distance between us, which doesn't make sense. He should be moving considerably faster than us. Our top speed is almost one hundred miles an hour slower than his. He should be leaving us trailing in his dust."

"Don't complain," Annja said, accelerating again as they hit an open stretch of road, leaving the city lights behind them. "Maybe his passenger gets travel sick. Garin isn't exactly a Sunday driver, even if he isn't in a hurry to get anywhere."

"Or perhaps he knows we're tracking him," Roux suggested, looking down at the little red dot in the center of his screen. It moved imperceptibly while he stared.

"That," she said. "Or he figures we're still clawing through the rubble back there looking for his beautiful corpse."

"Which is always possible," Roux agreed.

Somehow, though, she didn't really think that was likely. Not after everything they'd been through.

"This isn't right," Roux said after another fifteen minutes. "Garin doesn't do anything without researching every angle. He's a stickler when it comes to thinking through every implication and possibility of any given course of action."

"Well, you could always hit the kill switch on the sports car, right? Stop him dead in his tracks. That'd throw a monkey wrench in the works."

Roux shook his head. "That won't help. Right now we know exactly where he is, and we can follow him to wherever he's going. Disable the car and we give him an hour to lose us without us being able to call in more favors to track him. No, we'll just see where he leads us."

"Actually, I think I know where he's going," Annja said, and it was true. It had been nagging away at the back of her mind since Lars first mentioned Germany.

There was a link, tenuous, but a link nonetheless, between Benátky and Germany. "Okay, bear with me on this. It might sound crazy, and I'm almost certainly clutching at straws, but there's a link between where we were and where I think we're going."

"Spit it out," Roux said.

"What do you know about Kepler?"

"Johannes Kepler? He was a decent man," he said. "Fiercely intelligent, ahead of his time, dedicated to his work. His first marriage was not a particularly happy one, I don't think, but I understand that his second was much better."

It wasn't quite the response she'd expected, but of course this was Roux. Why wouldn't he have met one of the greatest minds of the age? Any age? She'd known the old man long enough to take that kind of familiarity in her stride.

"Ours paths crossed on several occasions, most notably the year we lived together at the royal court in Prague, but there were several other meetings down the years. Why?"

"Where? Specifically."

"Like I said, there was the court of Emperor Rudolph II, and Linz. That's just across the border into Austria."

"But Garin is *definitely* heading for Germany?"

"Without question," Roux said, taking another reading from the GPS tracker on his screen. "He would have taken the last junction if Austria was his intended destination. I assume that supports your theory?"

"I don't know. I told you, I found the killer's coat in the observatory…"

"Which, as you know, was where Kepler worked when he first came to Prague." Roux nodded. "He was still a young man then, of course, but already stretching the limits of understanding in terms of astronomy, though like many of the day he was compelled as much by astrology and the irrationality that the stars somehow controlled our destinies. But even then he was expressing ideas that would change the way we think about the universe, even if Brahe and his cronies took credit for some of the works they did together as master and apprentice. It's funny how you forget some of this stuff after so much time, things that seemed so important then, like the ownership of ideas." Roux shook his head. "No doubt you are aware a lot of our understanding about planetary orbits and motion come from his studies in that room?"

"Absolutely. We owe him and many others a huge debt."

"Indeed, and Kepler was one of the very first and most important of those," Roux said. "So tell me how finding the killer's coat in his observatory is important beyond simply knowing we were within touching distance?"

She wasn't sure. It made sense in her head, but saying it aloud would only demonstrate how thin the theory actually was. But if this was connected to Kepler somehow, it would make a kind of sense; it would provide a pattern that she could follow. Random events had no pattern. That was how serial killers hid or gave themselves away, patterns of behavior. That and the fact that Garin *had* to know that he was driving a killer across the country.

"Are you sure about border control here?" she asked suddenly.

"No. The last time I traveled by train between the

countries, the army ran checks on the train as we entered the country," Roux said. "But I think that was before the Czech Republic officially became part of the union."

"If Garin is taking the killer across the border, and there is border control, the killer would need a passport, wouldn't he? If Garin wanted to move the killer without documentation he'd fly, surely? Grease the right palms at the airport, disappear through customs without ever officially coming or going. That's who he is. That's how he works. Whatever else he is, he's not an idiot. Why risk being detained at the border?"

"Doesn't seem like him, unless he knows there is no risk," Roux agreed, not entirely sure he was following her line of reason.

"So just because we know that Garin had the killer with him when he left Benátky, we're assuming the killer is still with him? That's a big assumption."

Roux fell silent.

"Here's what I'm betting," Annja offered. "It's important in how we judge culpability here. If Garin takes the killer over the border, it will only be because Garin has provided him with forged papers, wouldn't it? He wouldn't risk being caught without the proper documentation. If he has done that, it means that the two of them are in cahoots. What happened back there wasn't just a random meeting."

Roux picked up the thread. "But if he doesn't take the killer over the border, then maybe he's still our boy. Is that what you are thinking?"

She nodded.

It was hard to argue with the logic, and somehow it seemed to fit with the way that Roux had felt right at the start. He had been convinced that Garin had been involved with this killer somehow. Providing the means of the killer's escape from the Czech Republic would cement those suspicions beyond any shadow of doubt.

She watched the road ahead as the car ate up the miles.

Roux stared at the screen in his hands, without answering.

The gap was closing slowly, which it shouldn't have been. The Ferrari should have been outpacing them by at least fifty miles every hour, maybe more if Garin was driving recklessly. But it wasn't. And the little GPS tag's stuttered journey across his screen didn't give any indication the car had stopped, not even long enough to let his passenger out. Annja couldn't tell if Roux hoped the killer was still inside the sports car or not. There was something disturbing about the old man's expression. He appeared resigned to whatever fate had to throw at him.

"Okay, one last question," Annja said after a while. "Is there anywhere you can think of in Germany with a connection to Kepler? I keep thinking he's the alpha and the omega in all of this."

42

The sound of her cell phone ringing caught Annja by surprise. The car's Bluetooth system picked up the signal, allowing her to answer without having to take her hands from the wheel.

"Annja!" The familiar voice of Doug Morrell, her producer, filled the car.

"Doug. Dare I ask?"

"Things are hot here, hot and sticky, and not in the good way."

"Sounds delightful."

"I could live without it, if I'm being honest. Corporate is breathing down my neck all hours. So, speaking of the Evil Overlords, how are things going with the segment you're working on? Tell me you've got something awesome planned to save my bacon here."

"It's all coming together," she half lied. She doubted she sounded all that convincing, but he was five thousand miles away, so maybe her self-doubt wouldn't carry.

"To be honest, I'd rather hoped we might have had some ideas from you by now."

"I need to get permissions to film in a couple of places. Creepy tunnels, that kind of thing."

"Excellent. And the million-dollar question…this is going to be workable live? The suits are hot on this whole social-media event angle."

"It'll take some planning, but yeah, we should be able to pull it off."

"I'm serious, Annja. All the usual crap aside, I'm on your side here. If this doesn't work, it's not just you out of a job."

"I get that," she said.

"So you're thinking *big*, right? Really big. Edge of your seat big. This needs to be the water-cooler event. We need everyone going into the office or on the street saying, 'Holy crap, did you see *CHM* last night? Oh, my God!'"

"I get it. Big. I've got Lars getting some footage we can loop in between the live stuff so we can have a bit of control to the chaos."

"Good thinking," Doug agreed. "Look, we all know how boring these live events can be. So we're going to need to fake some spice if needs be. Give 'em what they want upstairs, and it's all good. We have a lot of loyal fans, Annja. People who tune in every week. We've got to find a way to interact with them."

Meaning they had to find a way for Corporate to monetize them. The bean counters wanted cash. Advertisers kept the show afloat. Why would they possibly want to bite the hand that feeds? They wanted ratings. Ratings drove advertising, and like it or not, *Chasing History's Monsters* wasn't big enough to deliver the kind of numbers the network wanted.

They expected her to fail.

That was the unspoken reality of the situation.

She was absolutely sure they were already mapping

out contingencies, developing some sort of reality show monstrosity of fake celebrities and their car-crash lives. "I'm on it, Doug, promise," she said. "I won't let you down."

"I know you won't, Annja. If I was going to put my life in anyone's hands, it would be yours. But keep me in the loop. Silence spooks me, okay?"

"Of course," she said.

She killed the call and adjusted her grip on the steering wheel. She hadn't realized how tightly she had been squeezing it while she was on the phone.

Sensationalizing the story of the golem and the serial killer currently stalking Prague was ugly. It wasn't her. But recalling those childish ink-sketch features of the killer, she wondered if the truth might actually be too much for viewers to believe. Or didn't that matter anymore? Had they reached the point where excitement outweighed veracity? Was it their job to be the arbiters of truth? Or was it all just grist to the entertainment mill now as long as they gave the thrill seekers monsters to chase?

43

"They've stopped," Roux said suddenly.

"Are you sure?"

"Absolutely."

"Where are they?"

"The border."

"This is going to be some episode of the show, isn't it? We chase a killer across the country only for border patrol to arrest him before Garin can smuggle him out of the country. I can see the suits loving that. I can also imagine the Twitter hashtags."

"Sometimes it sounds as though we are speaking different languages, girl. Whatever happened to English?"

"It's not compulsive viewing, is it? It's not that pursuit where we have a helicopter tailing the killer as he attempts to flee justice. We've got a red dot on a cell phone. It's a bit pathetic, really. What am I going to tell Doug?"

"There will be other stories if this doesn't pan out, Annja. Europe is filled with monsters old and new. We will find you another one if it comes to that. Catching the monster must be our only concern here. And given what we know about the beast, the last thing we really want is for the killer to fall into the hands of the police. They would never understand what they were up against. It would be a massacre."

She hadn't thought of it that way.

When she did, it sent a cold shiver of dread down her spine.

But what was the alternative? Letting the killer escape? That wasn't an option. That wasn't part of the soul pact she'd made with the sword. She had to be there at the end. The sword had to be there when the showdown came. If anything could end the unnatural life of the golem, it was Saint Joan's mystical blade. What better weapon to fight an ancient evil?

"So what do we do?"

"We forget the show, for now. This is bigger than you or me, or your network. This is about the lives of innocent people, and nothing is more sacred than that. The sanctity of life is paramount. That is why we are here, not some evil curse that kept us from death. We are here because life is sacred and the Lord has chosen us as His warriors."

She didn't say anything; it wasn't like Roux to speak like this, but sometimes she forgot how it had all started for him—a warrior of Joan of Arc, following a saint into battle. How could he not be deeply religious at the core? Did he believe his longevity was God's blessing or the devil's curse?

"He's moving again," Roux said. "He's crossing the border into Germany."

"Do we follow him? I mean…did Garin ditch the killer before leaving the country, or did he just smuggle him out?" There was no way of knowing, of course, not without understanding the significance of Germany in all of this. And that came back to the unanswered question: *Was there anywhere in Germany with a connection to Kepler?*

"We have no means of following the creature if it has parted company with Garin, so our only option is to hope they are still together."

"We could always just call him," Annja suggested with a wry smile.

"I think not."

And that was the end of the discussion. Or, at least, that discussion. Roux steered it back toward Annja's questions about Kepler.

"There is a university in Linz named after Kepler," Roux said, picking up the conversation thread as if it had never been dropped. "Though it wasn't built until a long time after his death. And a space station or a satellite. I rather think he would have appreciated the idea that something bearing his name would float out there for eternity, a man-made star. I'm not sure I remember much more that's worth telling. I can't recall any patronage from Germany, though of course there was no such nation at the time. Many of the wealthiest families in Europe were keen to be very visible supporters of the arts and the sciences. I'm sure some of the Prussian families were more than familiar with his work. He certainly benefited from patronage. He went where the money took him, I suppose, but aside from the obvious, that he was a German national by birth, you may be clutching at straws."

She shook her head. "Murders took place twice in the vicinity of his work. Not once, twice. Maybe more times than that for all we know. Don't say that's a coincidence. It can't be. So look at that map, zoom out to

view possible destinations and try to recall any connections Kepler might have had with the region."

Roux fiddled with his phone, eventually working out
how to pinch-and-zoom the tracking program to widen
its area of search.

He fell silent.

She knew he'd remember something.

"Out with it," she said.

"Regensburg. That's where he died."

"Kepler?"

"Yes. The Thirty Years War was at its height and he
was being forced to move from place to place, never
getting any peace to devote to his study. Regensburg
was the end of his journey. He fell ill and died there
soon after arriving."

"Okay, so where's Regensburg?" she asked, even
though she knew the answer already.

"Dead ahead," Roux said.

Her theory wasn't looking so thin, after all.

44

They tracked Garin's car all the way from the border, losing the signal within minutes of him entering Regensburg's city limits.

"He's playing us," Roux said. "He must have known we'd track him, and decided to let it happen, right up until this point. Right here, right now. I should never have expected anything less. It's too late to disable the car." Roux slammed his open palms against the dashboard in front of him. "This has to be Owen. Garin's outbid me. He's used the hacker to mess with me. That's why he drove slowly. He wanted me to get close enough to determine where he's heading, and now he's killed our only means of surveillance. We're blind. He could do absolutely anything and there's nothing we can do about it."

"But why would he hurt us like that?" Annja asked.

"Because he could. Because he likes playing games. Because he's Garin Braden."

"Or because he *needs* us."

Roux barked out a short bitter laugh. "Why would he need us? Give me one good reason. And while you are feeling creative, explain away the fact he didn't just *ask* for our help?"

"Oh, I don't know, maybe he figured we'd be so convinced he was guilty we wouldn't give it? Whatever he needs us to be here for is something that we would probably have just walked away from if he had come out and asked us?"

"So, what, suddenly he's the *victim* here?"

This was an argument that she was not going to win.

Whatever response she offered, Roux was going to be ready to slap it down.

She wanted to prove him wrong. More than anything she wanted to wipe that smug look right off his face and prove once and for all he was capable of getting things wrong when it came to Garin.

"Fine. Where to now?" Annja asked.

"If you are right and there genuinely is a Kepler connection in all of this, then that has to be where we make our start, with Kepler."

"His grave? His workshop? Wherever he actually died?"

"The churchyard was destroyed in the war. He had only been interred for a couple of years, if that. I believe there is a grave marker somewhere, but that is not where he was buried."

Annja tried to think.

The answer had to be here.

Garin had drawn them into a puzzle; he wouldn't just leave the last piece out so they couldn't possibly solve it.

"You got any ideas?" she asked.

"Beyond the usual sources—library, any museum, the tourist office? Someone somewhere must know, but my guess—this is the kind of stuff that's been lost through the years. I don't expect anyone to be able to point to a door and say, 'Here, this is what you're looking for. *X* marks the spot.'"

It was hard to argue with that.

It was also the kind of thing that Garin would expect them to do. Like Roux said, it was a short list of all the usual suspects.

Annja found a space to park the car.

A little way down the street she saw a familiar word on the facade of one of the buildings. It was the same in both German and English: *museum*.

"Okay, you go in there and see what you can find out. I'm going to check in with Lars." She didn't wait for him to argue. She fished her phone out of her pocket and made the call.

Roux clambered out of the car and slammed the door as Lars answered.

"Where are you?" She checked the time on the dashboard clock.

"Almost at the border. I'm assuming that we're still heading the right way?" he asked.

"Yeah, sorry. There didn't seem like a lot of point just calling to say keep on going," she said. "Once you're over the border, stay on the main road until you reach Regensburg. We're at the museum there right now. Call me when you get here."

"Any sign of the thing yet?"

"No. Not yet. We've been in town all of ten seconds." She glanced from the windshield to every window, checking.

"Do me a favor. Don't do anything stupid before we get there, okay?"

"I'll save up all of my stupid for when you catch up, promise."

"That's not what I meant," Lars protested.

"I know, but it's the best I can offer. Like it or not, we're going to need some decent shots of him if we're going to make this show work." And by saying that out loud she realized that it didn't matter what Roux said. She couldn't just forget about the show. The show was her life, her ordinary life. Without it she wouldn't be Annja Creed anymore. She'd be cut adrift of the only anchor that kept her feet in a world that wasn't filled with the impossible and the miraculous, never mind the deadly. It wasn't just the mysteries she chased on the show, she realized, or the monsters scattered up and down time. It was a normal life. And that was the most elusive prey.

She needed to buy Lars time to get there with his camera without putting anyone else's life at risk.

"I'll call you when we get there."

Annja said her goodbyes, then hung up. She pocketed the keys and hopped out of the car. Roux had already disappeared inside in the museum in search of answers. She wasn't sure it would harbor any he was interested in, certainly not the most pressing ones. Annja decided against going in after him—they wouldn't learn more simply because the two of them were asking the same questions.

She scanned the signs up and down the street, seeing a smoke shop, a fast-food joint, what looked like a more exclusive sit-down restaurant and a beer cellar promising a variety of imported cask ales. On the other side of the street she saw a café. The siren song of coffee called to her, but for once she ignored it to track down a street map of the town center from the smoke shop.

She emerged just as Roux was leaving the museum.

She jerked a thumb toward the café and he nodded, waiting for a gap in the traffic to cross. Annja reached the door as a young mom was wrestling with her stroller, trying to unfold it and juggle bulging bags of groceries without dropping her baby. Annja helped her with the mechanism, then with juggling the bags. By the time she was done Roux had reached the door.

Annja's plan was no more complicated than spinning the coffee out long enough for Lars and Turek to reach the town.

She moved toward the counter, but a blond-haired blue-eyed waitress gestured for them to take a seat, promising that she would be with them in a moment.

"So, what did you find out? Anything?" Annja asked when they were settled down, coffees in hand. She held the cup to her lips, feeling the steam against her skin.

"They don't have a great deal in there that was of interest," Roux said. "But I took a leaf out of our quarry's book and was charm personified. There was a young gentleman who was only too happy to point me in the right direction for a price, which I happily paid."

"Come on, enough with the suspense. What's the right direction?"

"Unsurprisingly, perhaps, there is a castle here," he began, offering a slight smile. Despite everything, he was enjoying himself. He might rage and rail against his erstwhile apprentice, but they were more alike than he'd ever admit. Six centuries in each other's company would do that to you, she figured. "This one is now the home of the prince of Thurn und Taxis, though they've only lived there since 1748. And guess what?"

"Oh, don't tell me—Johannes Kepler stayed there during his last days?"

Roux inclined his head slightly. "And you say that I am the one who enjoys taking all the fun out of life? At the time it wasn't a castle, it was a monastery. One of Kepler's deepest fascinations was an attempt to calculate the true date of the birth of Christ based on planetary movements and the passage of comets. That will have brought him close to the church."

"Okay, that's a place to start at least."

"More than that. My young friend suggested that we might find some journals in the castle that were left behind when the monks moved out. Abbots liked to keep a record of comings and goings. It was a compulsion with them."

"It would be good to get a look at them."

"It would. But it would also be very unlikely. He had been doing some research on Kepler's time there himself some years ago. It took a *lot* of negotiating before he was even allowed to look at them, but—and this was the interesting part—the abbot made several references to the astronomer's strange traveling companion whose features—and I quote—would have been better placed on a cathedral wall than on a man's head."

Annja was sure the monk hadn't been suggesting that he was angelic looking. She had seen the strange and twisted features of enough gargoyles to know what those words meant. And there was no getting around the fact that it was proof that the killer they were hunting had been around as long as Roux and Garin.

"Anything else?"

"Not enough for you?"

She held up her hands. "Look, if this really is all part of Garin's game like you think, do you really believe he would just offer up the connection quite so easily?

Like you said, this is just the start of the end, not the end itself."

Roux paused and took a sip of his coffee.

She knew the look.

He was holding something back from her, deliberately waiting, choosing his moment to reveal it.

"I wasn't the first person he spoke to about that little detail in the abbot's writings," he said at last.

"Let me guess…Garin?"

"The very same."

"I showed him a photo of Garin. He confirmed it was him."

"You carry a picture of Garin around with you? The old gentleman definitely doth protest *way* too much," Annja joked.

Roux shrugged. "Hardly. He's the one person in this world I know will either get into trouble or get me into trouble. It's handy to have it for identification purposes. You never know when you're going to need to utter the immortal words *Have you seen this man?* Of course, I don't mention the fact that the photograph is over thirty years old and all that has changed is the haircut."

He showed her the shot, teasing it out of his wallet. It looked like it was taken last week. Of course, it could have been taken fifty years ago and it would have been the same. A century earlier and it would have been sepia-tinged, but the subject's raffish charms wouldn't have dimmed. "He's leading us around by the nose, Annja, and no doubt enjoying every damned second of it. We'll see who's laughing at the end, though."

She spread the tourist map on the table in front of her and quickly picked out the castle of Saint Emmeran, placing a finger over it while she located the museum that Roux had visited. "So everything leads us to this castle, which just happens to be within walking distance. Fancy some exercise?"

"We'll take the car."

"Right. Your leg. Jeez, I didn't even think about it. I can't believe we're talking three or four hours since you broke it, and it's like nothing happened."

"Oh, something very much happened," he said. "I'm just trying not to think about it. The healing process isn't exactly painless. Imagine being able to feel the bone knit, fusing together."

"I'd rather not, if that's okay. Are you sure you're up to this?"

"I will live," Roux offered. It was about the only thing she was sure about, no matter how things went over the next hour or so. The old man would live. It was what he did. "But the car would be good in case we need to beat a hasty retreat."

Roux saw her take a glance at her watch even though she'd tried to be surreptitious about it. "They are not going to make it in time, and I'm through with waiting. This needs to be over. Sorry, but we aren't waiting for them."

"If Garin's so desperate to get us here, I'm sure he'll hold off with the fireworks for a few minutes."

"I have no intention of playing by his rules. From here on in, we make up our own rules. We say where, when and how high we jump, not him. I'm hoping that you want the same thing."

She knew what she wanted—to unmask the killer on film, and record the whole thing.

"So what's the plan, Stan? We just drive up there,

knock on the front door and ask if Garin is coming out to play?" Annja asked.

"I don't believe that anyone is even aware Garin has taken up residence there."

"Why not? He's a charmer. His silver tongue can open any door…"

"It can open more than just doors," Roux said with a trace of distaste. The inference was obvious.

"Right. So if we're not just banging on the front door, what are we doing?"

"We are going to use our heads. Do what we do best. Ask questions, gather answers and make an informed decision about what happens next. We are meeting the librarian at the castle in forty-five minutes."

"But surely we know all we need to know, don't we?"

Roux nodded slowly. "I suspect we do, but rather importantly, this meeting gets us *inside* the castle gates. There are benefits to old-fashioned legwork. Anything we actually learn there will be a bonus."

There was more to this than he was saying, she was sure of it. There was the beginnings of a plan somewhere deep in the old man's brain. He'd get them inside the castle gates. What happened when they were there was anyone's guess. She was banking on it falling into place when the time came.

Roux pushed back his chair, removing a few notes out of his wallet and laying them on the table, again overpaying ridiculously for two black coffees, no matter how good they were. "Time to go," he said, and he made his way over to the door.

There was no sign of the cavalry.

Annja pulled out her phone and sent a one-word text: Castle

45

She had been expecting someone considerably older. She always did when someone used the word *librarian*, as if the title came with pince-nez spectacles and a blue rinse.

The man welcomed them with a broad smile, offering his hand. He couldn't have been more than thirty. Late twenties, with soft hands that had never done a hard day's work. They did, however, give a warm shake. Annja noticed that his nails were immaculately manicured and varnished. She wasn't sure quite what she thought about the affectation, only that it lent a peculiarly sexless quality to his hands. The librarian was dressed in a charcoal suit, white shirt and a gray-and-red tie that added a splash of color to his otherwise drab appearance.

"I am led to understand that you are interested in Johannes Kepler?" he said, flashing a smile of perfect teeth. Not only was he younger than she had expected, he was considerably more attractive and obviously aware of the fact.

It took her a second to place who the man reminded her of.

It was Garin, of course.

"We are indeed," Roux said, effortlessly taking control of the situation.

On the short drive to the castle, he had assured Annja that he did have a few ideas about what they should do, but didn't deign to mention what any of them might have entailed.

"Hopefully the assistant curator—the gentleman you spoke to at the museum—explained that our library here is a private collection. Obviously if you wish to apply for a reader's card, I will do my utmost to expedite your application with all the necessary pace."

"But that won't be today, I assume? We're only in town for the afternoon."

"Ah, yes, I'm terribly sorry, but I am sure you understand. There are processes and procedures in place, checks and balances, and despite your companion's obvious popularity, unfortunately none of these measures either move very quickly or can be circumvented. These things are bound up in rules and rituals that were set in stone long before either you or I were put on this Earth."

Roux gave no visible reaction, though Annja could imagine what he was thinking.

"Surely Kepler scholars visit the area regularly," Roux suggested, making it sound more like a statement than a question, where obviously it was leading.

The younger man shook his head. "Actually, no. Despite the fact that this is his final resting place, there's precious little that remains to be seen here. He was only with us for a very short time." He spoke as though he himself had held the door open for the astronomer's visit and laid him to rest at the end of his days. It was as though he considered the building part of his own personal fiefdom. Pure arrogance. It was another reason why he reminded her of Garin.

"Was he working on any particular theories while he was here?" Roux asked.

The man's expression changed.

It seemed like an obvious question, but clearly it wasn't one he was used to coming up against, so he didn't have any carefully prepared answer tripping off his tongue.

"Actually, I don't know," he was forced to admit. "As I said, very little survives from the time. Ravages of war. But I can tell you he fell ill very soon after he arrived here. He may indeed have already been in the slow process of dying before he arrived. We have nothing in our library to suggest he worked on anything during his days here."

"He was always working on something," Roux said. "Always. The man was an obsessive. He couldn't rest. He seldom slept because his mind would not slow down. There was always something going on. Could he have kept his studies secret while here? Is that possible?" Before the librarian could offer an opinion, Roux continued. "Of course it is. Of course it is. How would you know? He lived in constant fear that someone from the scientific community might either steal his ideas or, worse, laugh outright at them."

"Hasn't that always been the way with so many geniuses? Jealous and secretive? Keeping themselves to themselves, the knowledge lost forever when they are gone?"

"Indeed," Roux agreed.

"So, if I were to read between the lines, I take it that you suspect that he was working on something while he was here, and now you're hoping to find out what it was."

Roux held his hands up in surrender. "Guilty," he confessed. "As I am sure you're aware, none of the journals Johannes kept during those last few years of his life have ever come to light. Sadly if they are not here, I suspect the truth is that they never will."

The hook was baited. Now all he needed to do was reel the big fish in.

"I know it's almost crass to ask, but do you think these lost journals would be valuable?" the librarian asked, biting.

There were two lies Roux could sell him now. It just came down to which one was more likely to appeal to the man before him—money or knowledge? He picked the latter. Had the man been interested in material gain, he would have been a stockbroker, not the loving curator of a private library in the farthest reaches of the country.

"In themselves? To be honest, probably not, but the ideas he was working on? Well, you know his mind. Anything on that front could prove invaluable."

The librarian nodded sagely, drawing in a slow, musing breath. "If there was anything in the library, I'm sure I would be aware of it," the younger man said finally.

"Of course, of course, as no doubt would many others. After all, neither of us are the first to wonder about the fate of those ideas, are we? Not over the course of centuries. It is inconceivable to think that greater men than us haven't come looking for the same knowledge."

"Indeed," the librarian agreed. "I'm sorry I can't be of more help to you. It is such a shame, given you have come all this way."

"Actually, there is something you might be able to help us with," Annja said. "Would you happen to know where in the castle Kepler stayed when he lived here?"

"Ah, indeed, yes, I do," the man said, the smile on his face reappearing as he found himself back on comfortable ground. "Obviously, given the prevailing fears of the day, there was some concern that his illness may be contagious. Both he and his servant were given quarters in one of the outbuildings rather than here in the main building. Their meals were taken to them so they did not need to enter the ecclesiastical buildings."

"Would it be possible to take a look at them?" Annja asked.

"There's not very much to see, I'm afraid, and sadly I have another appointment in ten minutes so I can't really give you the grand tour. There are no written materials, or tools of the trade, but if I point you in the right direction, do you think I could leave you to your own devices? Feel free to have a wander around the grounds. It is quite beautiful here at sunset."

"Certainly," Annja said. "And thank you. You've really been most helpful."

"Well, we try to be accommodating when we can be," the librarian said. Annja got the distinct impression this was his version of flirtation.

She rested a hand on the man's arm as he guided them toward the door. "Checks and balances," Annja said. "Processes and procedures."

"You must think we're terribly set in our ways."

"Not at all," Annja lied. "It's rather nice to see somewhere that upholds the nobility and traditions of a better, vanished time."

"My thoughts precisely," the librarian said. "It is a

pity you are leaving this evening… I don't suppose I could interest you in a drink at the beer cellar later? Who knows, perhaps I could find some papers that might be of interest." This was definitely his version of the mating ritual.

Annja smiled sweetly at him. "Anything is possible."

"I will be done here in an hour."

46

"You're worse than Garin, you know that? Batting your eyelashes at the poor boy."

"If you've got it, flaunt it," Annja said as they walked in the direction of the building that the librarian had pointed them toward before he had disappeared inside again. "I guess our luck's turned."

"Luck?" Roux shook his head sadly as he opened the door. He felt around inside the small room for a light switch. A bulb burst into life. "It had very little to do with that, capricious little madam. It was a gray-haired old man who thought things through."

"What are you talking about?"

"What I said. It's not luck that meant that our charming friend couldn't show us around the building because he had another appointment so soon after ours."

"Roux, that's bad," she said, smiling as a similar grin spread across the old man's face.

"I made the call before I left the museum. He had to apologize that he had a couple of time-wasters already on their way to see him, but he was sure that he would make time for a visiting dignitary."

"Visiting dignitary? Dare I ask?"

"Comte de Saint-Germain," Roux said, with that wicked grin of his. "Son of Francis II Rákóczi."

"Who just happens to have been dead for two hundred years?"

"Or has he?" Roux tapped the side of his nose and smiled. Sometimes she couldn't help but admire him. It was moments like this that made her grateful these two incredible men had stumbled into her life. "These Germans don't know their famous French alchemists from their reality-TV stars."

"How many lives have you actually lived, you old rascal?"

"Sometimes I think too many, other times not enough."

"Good answer. How long do you think we've got before he starts to wonder why his ancient dignitary hasn't turned up?"

"Oh, we should have a good twenty minutes, I would think. Maybe longer, if he allows for the fashionably late quirks of the rich and famous. I warned him that I was visiting a school before our meeting, and there was every chance it might overrun by a few minutes given the unruly nature of children. He was quite understanding."

"You're a disturbingly convincing liar, Roux. Have I ever told you that?"

"I'm not sure you have. But I'll take a compliment when it's on offer, assuming that was a compliment. It makes life that little bit more interesting if you can spin a good story."

Annja followed him inside the first room. There was nothing at all remarkable about it. The room's walls were whitewashed, the floor bare stone. A collection of broken furniture was stacked against the far wall: a couple of straight-backed wooden chairs that had broken stakes, a cabinet that had a slit up one side. All of the pieces looked as if they might be repairable, and almost certainly antique, which would explain the reluctance to discard them.

The next room had a workbench in the middle and was dominated by the smell of fresh sawdust and varnish.

"Some kind of workshop?" Annja suggested.

"Or at least a storage room for while the salvageable stuff waits for repair," Roux replied. He walked over to the bench and picked up a small disk. He turned it over in his hand, holding it up to the light before putting it down again.

"Do you think Kepler worked in here? Or did he just sleep and eat while he was ill, knowing that the end was growing nearer every time he closed his eyes?"

"It's possible," Roux said. "He wasn't just an astronomer. He was an astrologer, a mathematician. He was many things."

He scuffed his foot through some of the sawdust on the ground.

The old man seemed to be lost in his thoughts.

Annja could tell from his furrowed brow that something was nagging at him.

Finally he said, "Do you suppose that whoever has been working in here has finished for the day?"

She looked around at the debris. It was impossible to be sure it was from that day or three months ago: the tools that were scattered across the bench, the piece of wood still gripped in the vice and the sawdust that seemed to cover everything.

"Have you ever been in a workshop like this before?"

"Can't say that I have."

"Well, in every one that I've ever been in the mess has *always* been cleared up at the end of the day so the craftsman has a clean start the next morning."

"You think he's coming back?"

"No," Roux said. "I think he's still here."

He crouched and ushered her over to take a look as he brushed away more of the sawdust.

"What am I looking for?" she asked, then saw what was wrong with the picture. The detritus didn't move as he brushed his fingers over it.

"I don't…"

Roux held a finger to his lips, and with his other hand felt around until he eventually found the edge of what appeared to be a piece of carpet.

As he lifted the edge, the sawdust didn't move. There was a thin polyurethane glaze across the surface, gluing it in place. As he drew the carpet aside, he revealed an iron rung set into the stone floor. There was a square outline where the hatch of the trapdoor had been recessed. It looked incredibly heavy. Heavier than would have been comfortable for an average guy like the librarian to lift. But not heavy for a brute like the killer. She noticed a thin filament thread attached to the carpet and looped through the iron rung and realized that whoever was down there could easily have drawn the rug back across the stone door from the inside to hide it after they sealed themselves in down there. Unless someone was looking for it, he or she would never notice it. And who came into a place like this looking for a secret door? She looked around again, seeing the thin patina of dust on the tools and the disarray of the jumbled furniture, and realized it was very unlikely a carpenter ever worked in the room at all. There was something about it that smacked of abandonment. She was used to abandoned places; they had a certain air about them. This room had that quality.

Roux touched a finger to his lips again and shuffled back so that he could tug at the ring. He winced as he knelt, favoring his broken leg. Again she was amazed at his ungodly powers of recovery. That bone should have kept him off his feet for months, not hours. She'd seen it sticking out through his skin. Ordinary people didn't just get up and walk away from that kind of damage; but then Roux wasn't an ordinary person, was he?

Annja didn't need to be told what she needed to do.

She braced herself, closing her eyes to focus on the outline of the sword in her mind's eye as she flexed her fingers and concentrated. The sword was ready for her, as eager to feel her touch as she was to close her fingers around the hilt.

Annja drew the blade gently from the otherwhere.

The metal felt alive in her hand.

It was so much more than a length of cold steel. It was so much more than a weapon designed for dealing out death. It was part of her soul, that immortal timeless thing that existed inside her and bonded Annja to this universe. It was fire to her ice. It was steel to her silk. It was faith to her doubt.

"Ready?" Roux whispered, the word barely above a breath.

She nodded.

He grasped the iron rung and, with two hands, heaved, gritting his teeth against the stab of pain as he drew the heavy stone out of its setting. It came away easier than he expected, because it was on some kind of elaborate hinge mechanism that took most of the weight. The device lifted it clear of the hole and dropped it smoothly on the other side, making a doorway wide enough to allow Annja to pass through. Roux shuffled his feet, stepping back from the aperture. Sweat beaded his brow. His skin looked pale, waxen. She wasn't used to seeing him like this; he looked lessened. Weak.

Annja nodded. "You okay?"

"Don't worry about me." He was breathing heavily. "I won't be far behind you."

47

A flight of stone steps led down into the darkness. The middle of each was worn smooth and dipped more than an inch below the sides. A rope had been strung down the wall to act as a handrail.

She could have used Roux's flashlight, but even without it she could make out just enough to see where to place her feet. Before she reached the last step, Annja could see the faint glow of a light along the passageway leading away from the stairs. She paused on the bottom step and listened for an unseen threat.

The darkness was alive with creaks and groans.

The light from above disappeared as Roux lowered the trapdoor in place above him. Suddenly cut off from the world above, the darkness took on another quality; it felt like a grave.

Roux felt his way down in the darkness.

Annja stepped off the last step and moved to the side to allow him down.

Once he was beside her Annja took a step toward the light.

She held Saint Joan's sword in front of her, a two-handed grip on the hilt. The dim light flickered along the length of the blade, adding to its ethereal otherworldly quality. Her breath came in slow, calm, deep breaths. She had no idea what was going to happen in the next few minutes, but knew that everything she knew and accepted was on a knife's edge and could fall either way. Garin could be proved to be the friend she knew in her heart he was, or the foe Roux seemed determined to prove he had always been.

And then there was the killer.

Annja scoped out the narrow passage, which was much like the warren beneath the castle at Benátky, she realized.

Unlike the state of the workshop above them, the tunnel was free of clutter once they were away from the worn steps.

Despite the fact there was no debris underfoot and the ground was flat and smooth, Annja moved carefully.

They weren't creaks and groans, she realized as she moved closer to the source. They were clicks. *Click, click, click.*

She'd heard that sound before.

Her eyes adjusted gradually to the meager light spilling into the tunnel from up ahead. It drew her on like a moth. Annja lengthened her stride, covering the ground quickly, but still placing her feet down lightly, careful to make as little noise as possible.

She had to bite back a startled gasp as Roux placed a hand on her shoulder.

She stopped in her tracks and turned to look at him.

"Let me," he said. "This is my fight, not yours. Don't argue."

But she *wanted* to argue with him. He was in no fit state to fight, but before she could open her mouth to object, Roux took a step past her and was between Annja and the light.

She wanted to say, "Stop being a fool. I'm the one with a weapon. Let the thing come for me. I can handle myself," but someone else beat her to it.

"Finally. I was beginning to think I'd die of old age before you got here," a voice from beyond the light said. "You're only just in time."

"In time for what?" the old man asked the light.

"Don't be shy. Come in and take a look for yourself. You've come all this way. A few more steps won't make any difference."

Roux waited, then took a single step inside.

Annja edged a little closer—close enough to make out a few more details in the room and what lay closer to the source of the light.

"You, too, Annja. Join the party," Garin called.

She didn't move a muscle.

"She's not here," Roux said. "She's flirting with the librarian."

"Ah, dear old Frederick. He likes to think that he's God's gift when we all know that's me. He's just a glorified cleaner. As far as I can tell, all he does is dust the books. I'm amazed he managed to see you at such short notice given all the dusting he has to do."

"Let's stop this silliness, Garin. You've got about thirty seconds to convince me not to kill you, and a good twenty-nine of them are already gone."

"Why is it always a fight with you, old man?"

"There are two types of people in this world—mice and snakes. And you are no mouse."

"There's a compliment hidden in there somewhere, I think."

"I wouldn't bank on it. Okay, Garin, time's up. This ends now."

"Here's the thing. I don't see a gun or a sword. Now me, I've got a gun. I mean, who would go to a gunfight empty-handed?"

"I don't need a gun to kill you, Garin. Not when I've got these." Annja saw the shadow shapes on the ground move as Roux lifted his hands. "Now, where's your murderous friend?"

"Friend? Oh, right, you mean *Joe*."

"Joe?"

"It seemed as good a name as any. The poor fellow is mute, can't read or write, and has absolutely no way of contradicting me when I call him that."

"Good for you. Where is it?"

"*He* is resting," Garin said, stressing the personal pronoun to emphasize the difference in how he considered the brute compared to how the old man did. "He's rarely up and about during daylight hours, you recall? Give it half an hour or so, and he'll make an appearance."

"You've got one chance to explain this, Garin. You've had us chasing you across Europe…"

"That's a slight exaggeration, Roux. You only had to cross *one* border. I'd forgive the poor grasp of geography if you were from another continent, but from a European, and no less, a Frenchman? I expect better." Garin let out an exaggerated sigh.

"No need to be so damned pedantic," Roux snapped. "I really don't care what you have to say. I'm just offering you the chance to explain yourself, to make your peace with God, before you finally meet Him."

"No one's going to die here today, Roux. At least, neither of us."

"I wouldn't be so sure about that."

"You really are a drama queen, aren't you? If you must know, I needed you here because of *who* you are, Roux, or rather *what* you are, even if I don't understand what that is."

"And Annja?"

"Irrelevant. This is just between you and me, like the old days. She doesn't belong with us, not here. This goes back to when we were much younger. Days, dare I suggest, when you were like a father to me."

Annja bit her tongue. It might bruise her ego to be discounted so easily, but with six centuries between them the men were connected in ways she couldn't even begin to imagine. There was no point getting bent out of shape over it.

"Then why go to the sham of making us think that we were chasing you, when you were leading us here all the time?"

"Ah, you're getting better at this, Roux." She could hear the smile in Garin's voice. "You have no idea how much it cost me to outbid you with Owen. Well, I suppose you do. He certainly made a killing. I needed him to sell you on the idea you were being clever. Tracking the car rather than the phone, though, I'll admit I hadn't expected you to think of that. I rather imagined you'd turn my own cell phone tracker trick back on me, so I had to make sure the old GPS was beaming my location out just on the off chance you decided to double down. You have no idea how hard it is to appear to be cautious and yet deliberately drop as many bread crumbs as possible. So what gave me away?"

"You were driving too slowly. I know you. No way you'd stick within the speed limits in an expensive, top-of-the-line sports car unless the cops were on your tail. But when you hit the autobahn and didn't open her up? That set off all sorts of alarm bells. Don't just look for the extraordinary, look for the out of the ordinary, anything that deviates from normal behavior. I don't think you've driven so slowly in your life. That must have *hurt*."

"Ha! Believe me, you have no idea," Garin said.

The voices fell still. Annja watched the shadows. She could imagine Roux standing there in a silence that he was not prepared to fill. He would want Garin to do the talking. There was no point in wasting breath in asking questions. Garin would still only tell him what he wanted him to hear. Like the old man said, he kept his truths close to his chest.

"I worked out what Joe was," Garin said, breaking the silence eventually.

"Apart from being the sadistic killer we tracked across the Old World, you mean?"

Garin grunted. "Being a killer has *nothing* to do with what he is, or what he was."

"Just stop talking in riddles, will you? I really don't have the patience to deal with you today. What do you *think* you've discovered and why do you think it has anything to do with me?"

"Oh, it has everything to do with you, my old friend. Everything."

"We buried that killing machine years ago. It was over. Dead. Gone. And then Annja's life was in danger. I couldn't walk away then. Not knowing everything I know about the golem."

"You know nothing, Roux. Less than nothing. Everything you think you know is wrong. Annja wouldn't have been in any danger if she had only left it alone."

"You could have told her that yourself."

"I did," Garin said. "In my own special way. I tried to distract her, but you know that damned woman. She wasn't interested. She had the bit between her teeth. She wanted the story. It's always the story with her."

"That's what it always comes down to with you, isn't it? Distractions? Lies. Anything to take you away from being responsible."

"Really, Roux, if that's what you think of me after all this time, I'm not even going to try to change your mind. You're so stubborn, but even you couldn't have done differently in my place, not once I knew the truth."

"So now you're claiming a moral compass? Will wonders never cease?"

"I wasn't going to leave that poor creature to the dangers that a modern world presents. I couldn't do it. Joe's a work of genius, Roux. Unadulterated genius."

Annja heard a sound from somewhere along the tunnel—the *click, click, click.* Louder now. The acoustics of the tunnels made it impossible to judge how close it was, but the two men had to have heard it, too. They fell quiet.

Roux stumbled out of the room, his face locked in a grimace. Annja saw his hand go to his thigh. The knitting bone was causing him pain.

He winced, eyes going instinctively toward Annja a second before Garin followed him out of the room. She didn't have time to fade into the shadows.

"Ah, looks like we've got the band back together then, after all," Garin said as he pushed past Roux. He found a switch, suddenly flooding the tunnel with light. This was not the rough-hewn stone of the tunnels beneath the castle at Benátky, but a whitewashed brick that had been cared for over generations. These were passageways that had been used by the monks back in the days when the old castle had served as a monastery. She saw scratches on the walls where ancient scores had been settled, counting out whatever the monks had stored down there. The electricity was a more recent addition obviously. The gray cable was roughly tacked in place, looping from one bulkhead lamp to the next.

Garin didn't slow his pace. He moved through the tunnels with the familiarity of a man who had spent some considerable time in them.

"Come on," he called back, but it was obvious to Annja that Roux was having difficulty keeping up with him. Roux bent over suddenly, reaching down to massage the knitting bone.

"Go," he said, looking up. "I'll catch up in a minute. Healing comes in fits and starts. It doesn't happen all at once. Some parts of the process are more painful than others."

Annja nodded, understanding.

This wasn't the Roux she knew and loved. That irascible old man was always ready for action, fitter and stronger than she was herself. She wasn't used to seeing him humbled so. Annja patted him once with her free hand, meaning it as a comforting gesture, an acknowledgment of his strength between friends, and started to run.

Click, click, click.

She knew what the sound was, even if she didn't understand what it meant.

The golem was waking from its slumber.

Garin had some means of controlling it. She didn't know the hows or whys or what drove him to want to control it though.

Every permutation that had gone through her mind didn't come close to the reality that awaited her as she entered the room behind Garin.

The brute was strapped to a table, straining fiercely against leather restraints that bound him. The creature's mouth was open, but the only sound that emerged from deep within was the steady *click, click, click* that haunted the tunnels.

"Hold him," Garin said with a hypodermic in his hand. "Quickly."

Annja didn't move.

"Listen, I need you over here. Don't be squeamish. He's mostly harmless. But he won't be if we don't get him sedated. Hold his head still for me."

Annja made a decision to trust Garin. She relaxed her grip on the sword and it faded into nothing, returning to the otherwhere.

Garin barely gave it a second glance, his attention fixed solely on the creature on the table. Annja couldn't decide if he was a captive or a patient.

She held its head still and looked deep into its eye sockets. There were no eyes inside the cavities, which explained part of the peculiar features. The mouth was a ragged wound, like the slash of a knife, and the nose two puncture holes. It was easy to imagine a child creating this stylized doll out of clay.

Turek was right in so many ways he could never have understood; it really was the golem, or any other number of names that might have belonged to it over the centuries, but it was more than all of them, too.

Garin pressed the tip of the syringe to the back of his head and slid it in smoothly. The needle met no resistance. The golem continued to thrash against the leather straps before it calmed. When it finally did, the only sound in the room was the steady whir of machinery.

Roux stood in the doorway.

"What exactly are you doing to that thing?" Roux appeared pale in the stark light. He breathed heavily. There was something wrong, more than just the broken bone, but he would never admit it in front of them.

"This *thing* could very well be the greatest invention that the world has never seen," Garin began. "And before you start…yes, I am well aware he has killed, many times, but he is so much more than just a killer. There is beauty in his mechanisms. Believe me, such incredible beauty. And genius. But right now he needs our help."

Roux said nothing.

"Or rather," Garin continued, now getting to the point, "yours."

"Help? I don't think so."

"Roux—"

"It is a wild beast, Garin. It needs to be destroyed. You should have left it trapped in those tunnels, don't you see? This is a mistake. It can't end well."

Garin still had the syringe in his hand.

"This," he said, holding up the syringe for the old man to see, "contains a measure of my blood, Roux. It keeps him alive, but it does not last long. When he was created, he was able to sustain himself with no more than the changes between light and dark, warmth and cold. His physical heart is still operating, but he needs more and more blood to keep his brain active. My blood is not enough. He needs something more. He needs some of your blood. Maybe whatever keeps you here will transfer to him. Mine worked for a long time, but he's become resistant to its healing properties. You're his only hope now."

"Are you insane? Obviously you are. That *thing* is getting nothing from me."

At that moment the creature gave an extra surge of effort, straining against the straps until first one leather strap snapped, then another, the incredible strength of the golem tearing the buckles from their mounts.

"Help me!" Garin yelled, but as he tried to restrain the golem again, one of the creature's great arms swung out, a fist slamming into his chest.

The impact sent Garin staggering back, reeling as he went crashing to the ground.

As he landed, his head hit the wall with a sickening crack and he slumped, unconscious, broken.

Before Annja could visualize the sword and reach out, Roux had stepped between them.

The golem tore at its remaining bonds, ripping them straight out of the harness, and rose from the slab, an unstoppable force.

Roux met it head-on.

An immovable object.

The two came together, and for a single heartbeat it looked as if Roux was going to be able to hold the golem in check with his bare hands.

The golem swung its great fist, striking at the old man, but where Garin had gone sprawling across the floor, Roux barely grunted, taking the full force of the blow without flinching. A second blow snapped his head back, but still he refused to give ground.

A third blow shattered something inside.

Roux's leg buckled and he went down, betrayed by the still-healing bone.

The creature brushed him aside, going for Annja.

Huge clubbing fists swung wildly, whistling just inches away from her face as she danced back two, three, four steps at a time, always just out of the golem's reach. Roux charged the beast from the back, wrestling with it. Beads of sweat formed on his face in a matter of seconds as the strain of trying to hold the golem back took its toll.

The thing showed absolutely no change in its hollowed-out expression. It was remorseless in its will to move forward. From within its gaping slash of a mouth, Annja heard the relentless *click, click, click* of its mechanisms grinding on.

Eye to eye, inches from it, there was nothing remotely human about its parody of features. Its skin was deathly gray.

It pushed again, and this time Roux could not hold it.

There was a sudden sickening *crack* followed by the most ungodly scream from Roux as his leg gave way beneath him, the bone wrenching apart, undoing all of the miraculous healing in one twig-like snap.

Roux struggled desperately to maintain his grip on the golem, but couldn't.

The pain would be excruciating. Blinding.

And the golem was relentless. It turned on the old man, closing its great arms around him, intent on crushing the life out of him.

"No!" Annja yelled defiantly, knowing that it was

pointless but not caring. The sword trembled in her hand. She knew the golem couldn't hear her; Garin had said it was deaf. There would be no peaceful resolution to this.

She threw herself into the fight, drawing its wrath.

It was the only thing she could think of to save Roux.

The golem cast the old man aside like a rag doll, turning to face the new threat.

Annja grinned wickedly, alive, ready to slice and dice the thing, ending the threat it posed and avenging all of those poor helpless souls who couldn't fight for themselves.

It attacked her.

Annja danced to one side, fluid, light on her feet. The sword flashed out, an extension of her arm, slicing along the length of the golem's swinging arm and opening its pale flesh.

She took a step out of reach, keeping the sword between her and the brute.

It swung again, coming up short.

For all of its strength it was ungainly, unfocused.

It might be stronger, but she was faster, and she was fighting for her friend's life. She had no idea what drove the creature.

She took a step and swung her sword, changing the trajectory of the blow at the last possible second, rolling her wrists to sweep the blade in an upward arc. The sword stuck the creature on the side of its head; the impact shuddered along the flat of the blade and all the way up her arms.

It shook the golem but did not incapacitate it.

The great brute lumbered forward, swinging, each wild blow coming with more force behind it than the last.

Annja felt the breeze of each swing across her face, like slaps from an invisible hand.

She whipped back her head, rolling with the last of the blows as the massive fist whistled only inches from her cheek.

Annja swung again, this time slicing the tip on the sword through the rags draped over the golem's huge form. The blade bit deep, cutting through its side.

And still its visage didn't change from that expressionless, openmouthed, dead stare.

The blow had cut deep, opening a gaping tear in its flesh.

The air filled with the relentless *click, click, click* of its mechanisms.

Annja slipped under the next swing and launched herself around the golem, vaulting onto the table that had been its prison only moments before. As the killer lumbered and flailed blindly, she continued on, crossing the table in three short steps before launching herself again, this time at the wall. Annja ran along the vertical brickwork, circling the golem, then exploding in a blistering attack, the silver sword weaving a web of death.

Side-on, trapped in the tunnel, there was no way the golem could protect itself. It raised its enormous hands, trying to ward off the attack, and stumbled as Annja delivered blow after devastating blow, slicing into the golem's pallid flesh again and again.

The final cut tore deep into its neck.

The golem turned, the sword still buried deep in its flesh, yanking the weapon out of Annja's grasp.

She fell back, gasping and unarmed as the golem reached up, trying to take hold of the sword. But as its hands closed around the weapon, the blade seemed to shimmer and dissolve. The golem's meaty fists closed around nothing at all.

Saint Joan's sword re-formed in Annja's grip. Quickly she planted her feet and with both hands wrapped around the hilt, she launched another devastating assault, pummeling the beast with a vicious series of cuts, hacking into its body.

But still it didn't fall.

It stood there, head lolling at an odd angle.

She'd delivered twenty devastating blows, each one tearing into the rags, shredding through the material as it opened deep cuts in the golem's flesh.

But there was no blood.

Not a single drop.

It was impossible to tell if any one of the blows had caused it pain—or if it was even capable of feeling anything as mortal as pain.

It tried to move, to face Annja, swinging wildly, arms gouging in the space before it. *Click, click, click.* There was no coordination. Beneath the rags its flesh was dull, caked like clay, and webbed with a hundred scars, each one bearing testimony to the tale Roux had told. This creature really was as old as he claimed, but it wasn't immortal.

It had never before faced a foe like Annja Creed.

She crouched, and then as it stumbled toward her, she sprang up, planting the blade in its gut and dragging it up through the broken flesh as she climbed its body, revealing what lay underneath.

Instead of spilling blood and organs, what in any other fight would have been the killing blow revealed only metal and machinery.

No matter what Garin had believed, this was no living thing.

Any sense of restraint, of trying to find another resolution here, melted away.

Click, click, click.

Annja swung at its throat again, the tip of the blade whistling just short of the thing that was doing its best to kill her.

"Stop!" Garin shouted. "Wait!" Annja didn't waste her breath answering. She knew exactly what she was doing. She was putting the golem down. She had eyes only for the enemy; moving in a blur, she focused on disorientating the damaged machine. It tried to turn, swinging blindly over and over as it struggled to stay on its feet, but Annja was too fast. She swung a final time, putting every ounce of strength she had into the blow. The blade sliced through the golem's neck, severing its head cleanly from its shoulders.

The whirring of the machinery continued on for an eerie moment—*click, click, click*—before it toppled.

The gears in the guts of the thing continued to click and tick for a few minutes before she was sure it no longer posed a threat.

Annja stood over the fallen golem's torso. She had stopped it.

She wasn't sorry.

It was a monster.

She turned to see Garin cradling the golem's head in his hands as though mourning the passing of a friend.

48

Roux was in pain.

There had not been enough time for his leg to heal. No matter how stubborn he was, mind couldn't always triumph over matter. There were limits to human flesh. He was, at the end of the day, only human.

It was a long time before he was able to stand, even with her help, but there was no immediate hurry to get out of there. It was done. The golem was dead, the guts of its gears strewed across the stone floor.

"You owe us the truth, Garin." That was all he said.

"I don't owe you anything," Garin shot back, but despite the bitterness and anger in his voice, he told them.

Listening to his confession, Annja remembered what Roux had said about each of them having their own truths and knew that Garin's tale was colored by his own experiences. Garin rose unsteadily, carrying the golem's head. Its features looked anything but innocent as he carried it to the desk on the other side of the room and set it down.

"I found these notebooks," he said, pulling them out of the drawer. He leafed through the pages, shaking his head. "It took me a long time to work out what they were, or rather what they meant. These are the last thoughts of our friend, Roux. These are the very final thoughts of Johannes Kepler."

"Go on," the old man said.

Garin nodded. "In his final days he was working on something new, something he hadn't even shared with anyone other than his surgeon. It was perhaps his greatest—certainly his most audacious—idea. It was centuries ahead of its time, but flawed. He intended to build a mechanical man that would keep him alive even as his traitorous body failed him."

"You're kidding me," Annja said.

"No. Cankers were consuming him. He grew weaker and weaker by the day, but he was determined to complete his work, and to do that, he had to find a fresh vessel to carry his mind."

"So that thing? That…monster? His surgeon actually went along with this insane idea and, what, tried to graft his brain into that machine?"

Garin lifted the golem's head again, offering it to Annja.

"See for yourself," Garin said. "There is certainly a brain inside this head. Kepler left specific instructions with his surgeon about the kind of nutrient that would be needed to maintain the golem's life. They were complicit in one of the most amazing creations of man, a literal creation."

"But it didn't work. It couldn't communicate. Look at it. Whatever lingered was trapped in there, mute, filled with rage it couldn't vent. That's horrific," Roux said.

"Tragic," Garin said. "That's different. It drove the creature out of his stolen mind. Immortality is a curse if you are trapped like that, voiceless, for eternity. Able to move, think, function, but not in any way remotely human, not even close to what you had been before."

"What happened to the surgeon?" Annja asked.

"There has to be a first victim," Garin said. "He was found murdered barely a week after Kepler was supposed to have died."

There was a moment of silence as each of them took in what they had been through, absorbing the facts to create their own truths.

Annja had no idea what Garin had thought he could achieve by protecting the golem. Even if Roux's blood had somehow given the half man/half machine a further lease on life, what was that existence worth? Wasn't it just adding to the tortures of several hundred years? The old man's blood couldn't have cured it, could it? Death, this time, had been a blessing. It had redeemed what little remained of the scientist. Perhaps he could find peace now.

She looked up to see Lars in the doorway, camera in hand, Turek beside him.

She didn't bother trying to explain it. Lars had caught the entire thing on film.

Beside him, Turek looked like he'd won the lottery only to realize he'd lost the ticket in the wash.

49

Annja ran.

She glanced back every now and then but she looked as if she was running hard, the cameraman struggling to keep up with her. The suits around the conference table watched the big screen, engrossed with the story of a chase to catch a monster straight out of history.

It was everything they had hoped it would be with one important difference—it wasn't live. There was no social media event here.

Lars had worked for a week splicing the footage, making loops out of the scenes he'd filmed to give them depth and heighten the tension. They'd stayed in Prague for three more days getting more material to show how a myth could be superimposed on a real monster and how even today that myth could endure.

It was part drama, part adventure, part history lesson, part social commentary, and it had them on the edge of their seats. Annja could see it in their faces.

No one moved.

She looked across the table at Doug Morrell.

She couldn't read his expression.

The image on the screen shifted. Now it was a composite of the material she'd shot on her cell phone, the video where they first saw the golem. So grainy were the shots that it was impossible to really focus on it. The first sighting of the childish ink-sketch face had one of the suits fidget nervously in his seat. Annja could hear the murmurs as they talked among themselves, unable to take their eyes from the screen. She had them in the palm of her hand. Lars had used all of the tricks that horror movies and those tacky ghost-hunting shows employed, but they worked. He knew exactly what he was doing.

And the best was yet to come, the final reveal of the slain killer, the Golem of Prague.

At the end of the screening, the shot returned to that same image, the first freeze frame that Lars had captured of the golem, and Annja hit Pause on the remote, leaving it up on the big screen as the lights went on again.

She waited.

No one moved.

No one made a sound.

She looked at Doug, who seemed absolutely horrified by what he had just seen.

She waited some more, giving one of the suits the chance to say something. Anything.

Silence.

Then the woman, the one who had talked about them having a duty to the shareholders, began to clap somewhat uncomfortably. Annja wasn't sure how to react to it. No one else moved.

"It still needs a little more work in the editing room— it's too long—and we haven't got the whole social media angle sorted yet, but you said we weren't here to educate the world. If I remember correctly, you said our purpose here was to entertain it. And what I've given you is an hour of heart-thumping entertainment." Annja grinned and pointed to the unsettling image.

One of the men leaned back in his chair, shaking his head. "I don't think anyone here can deny that you've given us exactly what we asked for, Miss Creed. In fact, if anything, you've given us too much of it." He clasped his hands together as though in prayer. "Unfortunately, we can't possibly use it as part of *Chasing History's Monsters*. It just won't happen. I'm sorry."

"I don't understand. You said yourself it is exactly what you asked for. Why can't you use it?"

"Because," the man said, "and it pains me to say this, no one will ever believe that it's true."

"So, is that it? Are you telling me it's over? That everything we've done was for nothing?"

"I'm sorry, Annja," the man said, using her name for the first time in any of their meetings. "Our hands are tied. We explained how it was. We aren't a charity. The show is hemorrhaging money. The network can't afford to keep it on the air. It's just not viable. Besides, we did say we needed a live presentation, hence our problem with people not believing this."

"No," Annja said. "It can't end like this. It's not fair. Doug? Say something. Please. You've got to give us another chance."

One of the other suits leaned forward and planted his elbows on the table in front of him. He raised his index finger. "All right, Miss Creed. You have one chance. As it stands, we still have a problem, we haven't got a final show. What we've got is an empty time slot. I suggest you do everything in your power to fill it with sixty minutes of incredible television."

EpilOgUE

Two weeks later

Annja waited in near darkness.

Could you do us a little favor, Garin had said. *It won't take long*, Garin had said. *Piece of cake for someone with your particular talents*, Garin had said. *Think of it as a nice couple of days in the sun*, Garin had said. *A holiday on us.* What he hadn't mentioned was the bit about risking life and limb, or the fact that these particular folks were not having a quiet night in—as they were no longer dead!

The sky was clear and the moon full, like a silvery bullet hole up in the blackness. The canopy of branches high above held the night at bay. She'd been out there for the best part of an hour, moving along the tree line, but keeping well clear of the path. Every rational part of her mind wanted out, anywhere but here. She shouldn't be there on her own. The irrational side of her that made up a huge part of who Annja Creed was argued tooth-and-nail that she should have brought a camera with her. And yet here she was, in Haiti, alone, no camera, letting down both sides of her personality at the same time.

All she wanted to do was watch. Having to do it

through the filter of a lens would only serve to make that so much more difficult. And frankly, she still wasn't one hundred percent sure Garin wasn't having a laugh at her expense. If he was, well, that wasn't the sort of thing she wanted recorded for posterity. So, she waited and tried to ignore the sounds of nature, keeping low, and still and silent now. She heard feet trampling through the undergrowth some distance away. The sudden flurry of noise sent a tropical rainbow of birds flying up through the trees.

Annja took a breath and pressed herself tighter to the trunk of the vast tree, feeling the wet stickiness of the bark pressing against her cheek.

This was a Bad Idea.

Haiti. Middle of the night. Full moon in the sky. A voodoo moon. What the hell was she doing out here?

Right… Garin.

She could have happily killed him, if she thought there was the slightest chance he could die. He hadn't said exactly what he needed from her, only that he thought there was something here, a relic of some ancient voodoo cult that was capable of raising the dead. She'd mocked him. He'd challenged her to come and prove him wrong.

And here she was, proving him wrong.

There were people up ahead. A dozen, maybe more. Each one carried a flaming torch to light their way, filling the space beyond the line of trees she was hiding in. Their silk ebony skin glistened with sweat in the flickering light as they moved without speaking. Annja saw daubs and swirls of white paint on their faces and chests, conjuring elaborate and arcane patterns. They planted the torches in the ground, the flames form-

ing a circle. Annja had tried to ask some of the locals
what happened out here in the dark woods, but only
one man would talk to her and all he would say was
"Go away." Nothing else. There was no mistaking the
fear in his eyes.

All she had been given to go on was that enigmatic
message from Garin.

When she had first read the email she'd been convinced that it had to be a hoax, but Garin swore it was
on the up-and-up.

The problem, as far as she was concerned, was that
outside a few scary movies, there were no such things
as zombies. When someone was dead, they *stayed* dead.
That was pretty much the one definitive fact of life.
Sure, Garin and Roux might be able to cheat it, but
once you shuffled off this mortal coil there was no way
back onto it. And yes, she'd seen plenty of stuff that
seemed impossible, but almost always had rational ex-
planations, so, was that what this was? A seeming impossibility that was actually quite rational? It certainly
didn't look like it.

The silence was broken by the sound of a single
drumbeat as the one remaining torch was carried to the
center of the circle and the bare chested Haitian knelt,
touching it to the treated woodpile, igniting the blaze.

Annja watched, waiting to be sure that all of the people who were supposed to have gathered in the clearing had taken their places around the fire, then risked
taking a couple of steps closer, banking on the fact that
everyone's attention was held by the spectacle before
them. The drum struck up a steady rhythm, one note
over and over, *boom, boom, boom.* Annja paced herself,

making her steps in time with the beats, trusting the sound to cover any that her feet might make.

Flames licked up from the bonfire, high above the heads of the throng gathered around it. Arms outstretched, fingertips touching those of their neighbor, the bodies formed a ring around the fire and began to circle slowly around the fire, moving to the rhythm of the drummer. It was hypnotic. The sweltering heat had her shirt clinging to her back, soaked through. Annja's hair clung to her brow. *Why am I doing this again?* She thought, shaking her head as voices began to chant in time with the mystical beat of the drum. It matched the pulse pounding through her veins, she realized.

The words meant nothing to Annja, but the men and women in the clearing were caught up in the chant, giving themselves over to the rite.

Faster and faster they moved, the symbols inked onto their skin seeming to glow in the firelight.

She needed to get closer if she was going to be able to see *exactly* what was going on.

There was no escaping the rapture that seemed to have swept the participants up. They were blind to her presence, heads thrown back, chanting and wailing, always moving. One of the men in the ring started to beat at his chest, hammering his fists off two sigils swirled around his nipples. He cried out, his voice a powerful counterpoint to the chant, filling in the spaces between the other voices.

Annja risked taking another step, and then another, until she was on the fringe of their circle.

Still, no one seemed to even notice her.

The bodies moved past her, sweat glistened on the map of their flesh, the contours catching the refection of the firelight until the symbols on their skin seemed to have a life of their own.

Annja had seen things like this before, a sort of mass hysteria brought on by belief—obsessive belief—and superstition. Rituals and rites were the same all over the world as far as she could tell. The faithful believed body and soul. That made them dangerous. But contrary to Garin's claim, there was nothing here she hadn't witnessed in some form or other before. Certainly nothing worthy of a show, and not a show exciting enough to save *Chasing History's Monsters* which of course was what it was all about. The suits might have offered a stay of execution, but the reality of the situation was without something big they were sunk... Zombies would have been big. That was why she'd taken up Garin's ridiculous plea for help and ended up in the middle of nowhere, sweating to death, watching seminaked fanatics dance around a fire. The one thing missing was the one thing that would have made it interesting. The dead.

The drumming stopped as suddenly as it started.

Two men approached the fire.

They were twenty feet apart.

There was something between them.

At first Annja didn't recognize the body for what it was, because of the way writhing shadows masked it on the bier.

They set it down beside the fire.

The circle fell silent, motionless, then one by one the dancers fell to the ground.

They lay there, eyes on the flames, ready, anticipating whatever was to come next.

Annja watched the man on the other side of the fire smear his glistening black skin with daubs of white—

great slashes across his pectorals and stomach, like wounds.

The air filled with his laughter.

The circle of followers prostrated themselves on the ground, pressing their faces into the dirt. Annja caught sight of the man on the bier's face for the first time. Her mind raced. There were two possibilities here, one, he was a corpse they were trying to resurrect, the other that he was a sacrifice.

She couldn't just stand there and let them murder him—but that assumed he was alive to be murdered, which was far from guaranteed.

She tried to make out any signs of life, knowing that even if he was alive they'd almost certainly drugged him to keep him calm as they ended his life. Unless he was another fanatic eager to go into the flames or whatever else was about to happen. She was outnumbered twelve to one. She'd fought against much worse odds than that and come out on top.

The painted man brandished a silver knife for his congregation to see.

Annja could *feel* the collective intake of breath at the sight of it.

He raised the knife, holding it high above his head, breathing fast and hard, nostrils flared as he prepared to plunge it into the body's heart—

When the silence was broken by the blaring wail of an American pop song. Damn. She'd meant to change her ring tone for months, but had never gotten around to it.

Annja tapped the earbud Garin had given her so she could operate hands free.

She was quick, but not quick enough to stop the young singer from doing her thing, loudly.

"This isn't a good time," she whispered, not taking her eyes off the man on the bier.

It was too much to hope that no one had heard the song, or that they were so out of it under the influence of whatever they were feeling that they just assumed it was part of the ritual. But one by one heads began to turn in her direction.

"Annja," the voice said, filling up the inside of her head. She'd never get used to how weird it felt having someone's voice piped directly into her ear. "Got a second? I've got news."

It was Doug.

"Not really," she answered, this time a little louder than a whisper. She wasn't sure if her voice would carry all the way back to New York. Telepathy would have been better, but sans some amazing psychic breakthrough in the next few seconds, whispering was the best shot she'd got at remaining hidden.

The ringleader grunted and howled, leveling the knife dead between the center of Annja's eyes.

The whole get-involved-or-don't decision had just been taken out of her hands.

She could charge in amongst them or turn and run.

It didn't matter which; what she couldn't do was stay where she was. Her cover was blown. This wasn't about a story. Right now it was about getting out of there alive.

"Can you hear me?" Doug said again. "Annja? It's great news. They've had a change of heart upstairs. At least for now. I've argued and fought for us, and you're going to love me."

Annja shook her head, trying to focus on the mass of bodies rushing towards her. Only one had a weapon that she could see, but the madness in the eyes of the horde was more than a match of any brain-hungry frenzy. With one hand she reached into the otherwhere, feeling the familiar grip of her sword begin to solidify in her hand as her fingers closed around it. She savored the adrenaline rush as her blood pumped hard through her veins. This was what she lived for. Not the show. The show was her identity out in the real world, but this was who she really was.

In a single fluid movement she drew Saint Joan's blade into existence and held it at the ready to fend off the charge of blood-crazy fanatics racing toward her.

It wasn't Joan's blade, she thought to herself, not anymore. It was hers. All hers.

"They picked up the back six, so we've had a reprieve, Annja. Now we've just got to come up with six shows that knock their socks off. Think you can come up with a killer concept or six?"

Annja barely took the news in.

She had more important things to deal with, like getting out of this mess without harming twelve people.

She gripped the sword with both hands.

There was an undeniable madness in the eyes of the people running at her, but there was something else beyond that, something more powerful: fear.

Beyond them the painted man still stood over the victim or sacrifice.

The body lay motionless on the bier.

"What's going on, Annja? I thought you'd be happy?"

"I am happy," Annja said as she swung at the first of the men to reach her. "I'm delirious with joy." The flat of the blade slammed into his upper arm hard enough to have him crying out and spinning away in pain as he clutched at the numb and useless limb. "This is what I sound like when I'm happy, Doug." The next attacker fared no better. She was laughing as she drove the third to his knees with a hammering blow from the sword's pommel crunching against the side of his head.

"Are you at the gym? It sounds like you're working out."

"Something like that," Annja said as a third man crumpled to the ground like a marionette whose strings had been cut. She had no wish to kill any of these unarmed people, just neutralize them, and as long as they only had their fists to fight with she was happy to put them out of action as opposed to out of their misery.

"Oh, okay, well, look, when you're done doing whatever it is you're doing, swing by the office, would you? I think this calls for a celebration."

"I can do that," she said, "but it might be a while. I'm not exactly in the neighborhood."

"Where are you?"

"Haiti."

There was a pause at the other end of the line. "Chasing a story?"

"Something like that," Annja said, deciding against elaborating. The less Doug knew, the better when it came to her other life. "It's not as glamorous as it sounds, believe me."

The man with the knife gave a cry of ecstasy.

"Oh, it sounds…pretty interesting whatever it is," Doug said, having obviously heard the cry.

The man raised the blade again, gritting his teeth, poised to plunge it downwards.

The crowd of bodies stopped surging around her, the seven still on their feet turned back toward him, seemingly no longer interested in their uninvited guest.

For the first time Annja got a good look at the man lying on the bier.

He turned his face toward her and offered Annja a rueful smile.

"Garin!"

The painted man's knife moved inexorably downwards.

"What's going on?" Doug asked. "Annja? What's happening?"

There was no way Annja was going to get to Garin in time, even if the crowd parted like the Red Sea to let her through.

Instead of fighting against them, Annja launched herself into the air, planting herself on the back of the man in front of her before she kicked off, higher, her sword sweeping through the air in a silver arc of moonlight as she hurled it at the chanting man.

Her aim was true.

The blade turned through the air in slow motion.

For a heartbeat the world stood still.

Annja felt herself falling back to the ground. She held out her hand for the sword, not trying to break her fall. She landed on one knee, looking up in time to see the point of the blade pierce the chanting man's throat and open a second bloody mouth for him in the instant before he would have plunged his own blade between Garin's ribs.

A moment later the sword was back in her hand, slick with the dead fanatic's blood.

The silence in the clearing was eerier than the chanting before it had been.

"Okay, look, I can tell you're not paying attention, so I'll let you get on with it."

"It is good news, Doug. I appreciate everything you've done for me down the years, you do know that, don't you?"

"Careful, it almost sounds like you like me."

"You know that of all the men I know called Doug you're my favorite one," Annja said, pushing her way through the last of the confused onlookers. Now that the head priest or whatever he was had been silenced, none of them seemed to know what was going on around them.

"Sarcasm. That's more like it. If you kept being nice to me it'd only go to my head."

Somehow, impossibly, the painted man reared up in front of her. He'd been dead, she was absolutely sure of it, but even as she slashed out instinctively with her sword and took his head clean from his shoulders, she knew that there was absolutely *nothing* behind his eyes. The painted man's head hit the grass and rolled toward the flames.

"Wouldn't want you losing your head or anything," Annja said, bleakly.

She reached Garin.

The knife lay on his chest. There was a pool of blood around it, but no sign of any wound. But there was so much blood. So much.

One eye opened and looked up at her before a smile crept across his lips.

"You know, I'd begun to think for a minute you weren't going to turn up," Garin said.

"And miss out on all this fun in the sun? Never."

* * * * *

COMING SOON FROM

GOLD EAGLE

Available October 6, 2015

GOLD EAGLE EXECUTIONER®
UNCUT TERROR – *Don Pendleton*

Mack Bolan sets out to even the score when a legendary Kremlin assassin slaughters an American defector before he can be repatriated. His first target leads him to discover a Russian scheme to crash the Western economy and kill hundreds of innocent people. Only one man can stop it—the Executioner.

GOLD EAGLE STONY MAN®
DEATH MINUS ZERO – *Don Pendleton*

Washington goes on full alert when Chinese operatives kidnap the creator of a vital US defense system. While Phoenix Force tracks the missing scientist, Able Team uncovers a plot to take over the system's mission control. Now both teams must stop America's enemies from holding the country hostage.

GOLD EAGLE SUPERBOLAN™
DEAD RECKONING – *Don Pendleton*

A US consulate is bombed, its staff mercilessly killed. The terrorists scatter to hideouts around the globe, but Mack Bolan hunts them down three by three. When the last one vanishes, the world's leaders are caught in the crosshairs and the Executioner must stop the terrorists' global deathblow.

CNMGE0915R2

COMING SOON FROM

GOLD EAGLE

Available November 3, 2015

GOLD EAGLE EXECUTIONER®
DARK SAVIOR – *Don Pendleton*
Cornered at a mountain monastery in the middle of an epic winter storm, Mack Bolan will need both his combat and survival skills to protect a key witness in a money-laundering case from cartel killers.

GOLD EAGLE DEATHLANDS®
DEVIL'S VORTEX – *James Axler*
When a group of outcasts kidnaps an orphan with a deadly mutation for their own agenda, Ryan and the companions must protect her without perishing in her violent wake.

GOLD EAGLE OUTLANDERS®
APOCALYPSE UNSEEN – *James Axler*
The Cerberus rebels face a depraved Mesopotamian god bent on harnessing the power of light to lock humanity in the blackness of eternal damnation.

GOLD EAGLE ROGUE ANGEL™
Mystic Warrior – *Alex Archer*
Archaeologist Annja Creed must face down a malevolent group of mystic warriors when she discovers an ancient document that could lead to lost treasure.

CNMGE1015

SPECIAL EXCERPT FROM

Check out this sneak preview of
MYSTIC WARRIOR,
by Alex Archer!

"Grab the crystal. Let's go!"

Annja was happy to see that Orta was already picking up the manuscript sheets and replacing them in their protective case. Annja quickly shoved the gear into her backpack and pulled it on.

Orta looked at her. "There are more of these men?"

"Yes." Annja pulled the ear-throat mic into place and clipped the walkie-talkie to the ammo belt. A deep, controlled voice spoke at the other end, demanding that Fox Six reply. She ignored the command and nodded to Orta. "You know the campus layout. Which is the quickest way out?"

"Follow me." Orta headed to the back door.

Krauzer had the crystal wrapped in one arm like an oversize football and was reaching for the other machine pistol lying on the floor.

Taking a quick step, Annja kicked the weapon out of Krauzer's reach.

He whirled on her, his features taut with rage and fear. "What are you doing?"

"Trying to keep Orta and me alive," Annja said. "You're a movie director, not a commando."

"And you think you're some kind of action hero?"

Annja glanced at the two unconscious attackers. "I've got experience with this sort of thing."

"I can shoot! Two guns are better than one!"

"Are you coming?" Annja asked as she jogged toward Orta at the back door.

Krauzer started to go around the table, but another gunman slid into place out in the hallway.

The radio came to life in Annja's ear. "Fox Leader, Fox Six is down. The woman has a weapon."

"Kill them," the deep voice ordered. "Do not harm the crystal."

Annja lifted the machine pistol and fired off three short bursts. Bullets hammered the door frame, throwing splinters out into the hallway, and they struck the gunman, knocking him down. Annja didn't know where the man was hit and didn't have time to check.

After fumbling with the back door, Orta opened it and shoved his head outside, then yelped and pulled his head back in just ahead of a salvo of bullets.

Annja pulled Orta back from the door, squatted, and snaked around the door frame. Two men held the hallway, machine pistols at the ready. As Annja leaned out, one of the gunmen rushed toward her.

Annja brought up the machine pistol and fired.

Don't miss
MYSTIC WARRIOR by Alex Archer,
available November 2015 wherever
Gold Eagle® books and ebooks are sold.

Copyright © 2015 by Worldwide Library

GERAEXP57

JAMES AXLER
DEATHLANDS®

The saga that asks "What if a global nuclear war comes to pass?" and delivers gripping adventure and suspense in the grim postapocalyptic USA.

Set in the ruins of America one hundred years after a nuclear war devastated the world, a group of warrior survivalists, led by the intrepid Ryan Cawdor, search for a better future. In their struggle, the group is driven to persevere — even resorting to the secret devices created by the mistrusted "whitecoats" of prewar science.

Since the nukecaust, the American dream has been reduced to a daily fight for survival. In the hellish landscape of Deathlands, few dare to dream of a better tomorrow. But Ryan Cawdor and his companions press on, driven by the need for a future less treacherous than the present.

**Available wherever Gold Eagle®
books and ebooks are sold.**

**GOLD
EAGLE**®

GEDL2015